EXPIRED

EXPIRED

EVIE RHODES

Dafina
Books

KENSINGTON PUBLISHING CORP.
http://www.kensingtonbooks.com

DAFINA BOOKS are published by

Kensington Publishing Corp.
850 Third Avenue
New York, NY 10022

All Kensington titles, imprints and distributed lines are available at special quantity discounts for bulk purchases for sales promotion, premiums, fund-raising, educational or institutional use.

Special book excerpts or customized printings can also be created to fit specific needs. For details, write or phone the office of the Kensington Special Sales Manager: Kensington Publishing Corp., 850 Third Avenue, New York, NY 10022. Attn. Special Sales Department. Phone: 1-800-221-2647.

Dafina Books and the Dafina logo Reg. U.S. Pat. & TM Off.

ISBN 0-7582-0871-5

First Printing: January 2006
10 9 8 7 6 5 4 3 2 1

Printed in the United States of America

Expired is dedicated to my husband, James Rhodes,
who is a shining, brilliant light of
faith and inspiration!
This is for you, Jimmy.
I love you truly. Be Blessed!

Acknowledgments

First of all I'd like to thank **The Lord Jesus Christ!** All of my blessings have come through him, and I have to give him the glory! Thank you for such a wonderful gift and the great inspirations, Lord! In the name of your son, the Lord Jesus Christ, my profound thanks to you, Holy Father and to the spirit of the Holy Ghost; truly I am humbled by your presence in my life. Thank you for giving your Son.

For my husband, James Rhodes, even though I am a writer I cannot find the words to express my love, appreciation, and joy at your unswerving, undying belief in my talents. I thank you from the bottom of my heart for your faith and support. You have paid the price for me to shine.

James Rhodes Jr. and Jamie Lynne Rhodes, you are my sunshine. Thank you both for your sacrifices. Much love to you, my babies.

Next, I'd like to thank the Booksellers who work harder and give more than people know to bring important and needed stories to the readers. I don't have enough words to express my gratitude. You are to be commended. Many of you have contributed so much. Thank you for all your support of EXPIRED as well as for helping me to bring this story to the forefront. May the Lord in his infinite wisdom bless you.

Most grateful thanks to the sales reps, distributors, and wholesalers as well for all of your support and hard work.

Many thanks and blessings to my agent Robert G.

(Bob) Diforio of D4EO Literary Agency who from the day he entered my writing arena has been by my side helping me to build my career steadfastly. You're a gem, Bob! I've always said that!

Many thanks and blessings to my editor, Karen R. Thomas, who believed in the vision I structured on paper, who nurtured that vision, and who put her own years of hard work and experience behind my writing to back it.

May the Lord bless you for that, Karen!

Thanks to the entire Kensington Publishing family for your excellence in the publishing of EXPIRED. There are many unsung heroes behind the scenes and I thank each and every one of you from the bottom of my heart. Laurie Parkin, thank you for your support. I'd also like to personally thank Kensington Publishing for creating vast opportunities for African-American writers. Walter Zacharius and Steven Zacharius be blessed.

Dr. Kenneth Terry of The Gospel Magazine Inc., thank you for your support of my writing, for providing an arena for my work, and most of all for believing in the spirit of it. May the Lord Bless you abundantly!

There are many of you who are in my mind, heart, and soul. Jesus knows who you are. Thank you for giving.

And last, but not least, I'd like to thank Rozzie Lee Jackson, my mother. Although you've passed on and are not here with us anymore, your gift of poetic writing, your love, your sacrifices are living on. I wish you were here to see this. Much love to you Roz in the Spirit. May you rest in peace in the arms of the Lord Jesus Christ!

To all who know me I remain *STANDING IN THE SPIRIT.* May the Lord Bless You All!

1

She was what she was, and to that end she would be. "Go! Go from this place. Nothing good can come of this for you," said Anita, the bourgeois psychic phenomenon of Harlem's teeming streets.

Anita stood on the sweltering sidewalk brimming with people. It was one of the hottest summers Harlem had ever seen. It was so hot, the sidewalk was buckling.

However, the heat and the world around her faded away as she stared at Tracie Burlingame, who had stopped at her table for a reading from her crystal ball.

Anita had not even touched her, but the instant Tracie stopped in front of her table, she had transformed into a spiritual quilting right before Anita's very eyes.

Tracie Burlingame was a patchwork quilt, a live patchwork quilt. Just like the ones Grandma used to make to throw on the bed, from every piece of material that ever existed in the family. Except in this case what Anita was looking at was an exact replica of a quilt in the spirit. Some of the patches were black, while others were hollowed out.

Anita had never seen anything like it in her seventy-plus years of peering through the layers of human beings. She had inherited the ability as a child, from a long line of Louisiana seeresses.

Never had she seen what she was looking at on Tracie Burlingame. Somewhere in the recesses of her memory an ancient religious myth was knocking around, but she couldn't recall it in detail. Anita did not like the black electrical current that swept through her body at the thought.

The hollowed-out patches of the quilt were raucous with activity, almost like a multitude of human hearts, many of them beating as one.

Then there were voices. The hollowed-out patches contained voices that spoke on their own. There were multitudes of them. In unison they screamed, loud, almost deafening. Anita was sure everyone on 125th Street could hear them screeching.

In reality no one heard them but her. "RELEASE US!" they begged, agonized. "RELEASE US!"

The black patches were seekers. They had the characteristics of humans in search of something. They were being hunted. They were also a symbol of death.

Anita peered into one of the black patches, trying to determine its origin. A sharp, lizardlike tongue whipped out, swallowing a host of people with one lap.

It was like watching the *Titanic* sink.

A symphony of screeching, crying agony rang out in one collective voice. Then there was silence. Anita jumped away from Tracie Burlingame, gasping. She made the sign of the cross; then she blessed herself.

Had she possessed holy water, she would have thrown it on Tracie Burlingame, the whole lot of it. What this woman contained in her spirit was unnatural. It was downright ungodly.

"There will be hell to pay," she muttered, not realizing that she had spoken the words aloud.

Anita Lily Mae Young backed away from Tracie Burlingame. "Don't come back, you hear, girl?" she spat. Her jaw was swollen with a wad of tobacco. She promptly swallowed it.

She pointed her finger in Tracie's face to make her point clear. "Don't you be coming back here to me, girl. I mean it."

She glowered at Tracie through beady eyes, which glowed with a strange light. Then the petite, turban-headed, brightly dressed woman turned away, abandoning her table on the street.

Anita sprinted through the crowded street. She muttered words Tracie didn't understand.

The words Anita had spoken earlier were the ones that echoed in the chambers of Tracie's mind. "Don't you be coming back here to me, girl. I mean it."

What had Anita thought she'd seen? She'd been a fixture on Harlem's streets for twenty-five years, peddling her psychic predictions. Never had she been known to act this queer. Besides, no one ever really took her seriously.

Did they?

Stupid old bag, Tracie thought to herself as she fumed at the audacity of the woman pointing her finger in her face.

She looked at the crystal ball, which, strangely

enough, was emanating a black stream of light. It should have been reflecting the colors of the rainbow on this sunny day.

She ignored it, turning her attention to the cards that Anita had left behind on the table.

Through no will of her own, unable to stop herself, she flipped one over. It was the ace of spades. The card beckoned to her. It throbbed with life.

Tracie shivered, although the heat was oppressive. The humidity was as thick as a blanket. She blinked and looked down at the card again.

There it lay placidly on the table. Tracie knew that the ace of spades represented death. She was not by nature a superstitious person. This was ludicrous.

It was ridiculous, she told herself. She was just paranoid. That stupid old woman must have spooked her. Maybe she wanted to get more money out of her by getting her to stop by again. But she'd told her not to come back.

Tracie laughed at the absurdity of the situation. Standing on a crowded Harlem street, she suddenly felt very alone.

"What a bunch of nonsense," she uttered.

Gathering her wits about her, she finally left the table. She tossed her hair back, held her head up high, and strolled down the street, donning her black Fendi sunglasses. Those who had witnessed the fiasco watched her strangely.

Tracie Burlingame was a mythical, ancient, haunting patchwork quilt. She passed along Harlem's crowded sidewalk with the past, the present, the future, and multiples of black patches cast and gathered together in her being. But only those with the vision could see it.

* * *

The dim streetlights cast shadowy, blurry streaks of light in the small room of the decaying Harlem building. The air was tight, humid, sweltering. It smelled like old mildew mingled with the smell of feces—human feces.

A strangled, gurgling sound caused the small child to cover its ears. The sight and smell of death layered itself over the room, a thick coating of it.

The beaten, withered man in the corner coughed. He looked at the child he could not help. He beheld the child for a last time as the light of life drained from his eyes. All over a horse and a dollar bill.

The men who had been sent to administer the beating laughed. They were small-time street hoodlums. The dying man was a notorious gambler who had ducked out on one debt too many.

Grayson Mounds, who controlled all the gambling activities in this part of Harlem, had ordered the hit after discovering he was not to be paid once again.

When he spoke, it was done. So Joe had played his last horse. They kicked him a last time for good measure. Briefly they considered the child. Then they discarded any idea of dealing with the child themselves.

They left the room. There was no threat—the child was too young to tell anybody a thing.

The whimpering child crawled over to the leftover carnage of the human being on the floor and put out a small hand to touch Joe's face.

Instantly the small hand was covered in a red, slippery substance. That was when it happened. It was a tiny, rushed explosion of a microcosm separating, splitting off into different beings—an open vessel for the domination of spirits.

The child could no longer emotionally inhabit this space where it had witnessed a man being beaten to death, tortured, and torn apart. No. It would leave this place for safer ground. Take flight and journey into a different realm.

It was a realm the average human being would never cross. Along the way it would satisfy its hunger and lust for the red, slippery substance.

Three days later, when the child and the remains of the man were found, the child sat happily slurping from a bottle of soured milk.

The child was a true orphan now, because its mother had died sometime ago from poverty and a broken heart. It was just as well, because this child's existence would not be predicated on human emotions.

The scene the child had just experienced would mold and create its future. It was the last nail in a coffin that would cripple as well as rule what would become a shell of a human being on the outside, and nothing but pure black malevolence salivating on the inside. In the absence of spirit there would be only darkness.

Tracie Burlingame. Her eyes were like a chameleon. They could change from a clear brown to shades of green and sometimes gray, depending on her mood, in the flash of a second. Occasionally they looked like pools of midnight black.

Tracie Burlingame was not your ordinary around-the-way woman. Nope. She walked to the beat of a different drummer. He played a rhythm that only she could hear, and she never missed a beat.

Tracie Burlingame was born and bred in Harlem. She was thirty-eight years old, sometimes going on the age of two and sometimes going on ninety. It all depended on which way the wind was blowing at the time.

On this day it was blowing due east as an agile, sensual, arrogantly proud Tracie ran alongside the traffic with a weight in each hand. On her right side the water stretched beneath the parkway. Her hair was windblown. She had a controlled, determined look on her face.

A few days ago she had visited and toyed with the old psychic up on 125th Street, but she refused to let that witch Anita crawl underneath her skin with her dour predictions. She should never have stopped there anyway. She had been raised in Christianity, though she was not a regular practitioner.

Heck, she wasn't an attendee in any sense of the word these days. But she knew better than to sample and frolic with the devil's wares.

However, she had been bored. She thought it would be a kick to toy with the old woman and play her games. Now she wished she hadn't. Still, she wasn't going to let it get to her.

Nor would she let the fact that she had drawn the ace of spades on her own bother her. It was just a card. Her life was a happy one with her boys. Well, maybe with the exception of Rashod. He had spread his doom. But still, she was happy, and she intended to keep it that way.

The devil be damned.

Tracie halted, breathing deeply. She warmed up with her calisthenics. She stretched and pulled with the agility of a colt. She ran again when she was done with the brutal mechanics of her workout regime. Her workout was enough to knock out a horse.

She paced herself through makeshift hurdles, over rocks, tree stumps, and overturned garbage cans. Anything Tracie could hurl herself over was fair game.

Then she ran, full speed ahead, eyes focused, adrenalin pumping. The muscles in her legs worked like a mountain climber's.

Her feet dashed through the streets of Harlem as though she had a victory to reclaim. Sweat glistened on her tight, lean body. The more she could feel the heat of it gliding down her body, the more she pumped.

Finally, satisfied with her effort, she slowed her pace to a gallop, then to a walk. Tracie spotted the ice-cream truck. A smile lit up her face. Yeah, frozen refreshment.

"Hey, Anthony. How ya doing?" Tracie said. Anthony could always be counted on to be in the right spot at the right time.

"I'm fine, Ms. Burlingame." Anthony beamed at the sound of her voice. Little did she know, he made it his business to be in the right spot whenever she worked out. He had her schedule down like a timer on a turkey. The man was infatuated.

"Give me a frozen yogurt. Strawberry."

Anthony shook his head in disdain. "Now, why you gonna play a brother out like that? You know I know your flavor."

Tracie smiled. While she waited, she took off her backpack and tossed the weights inside. Anthony handed her the frozen yogurt. She put the dollar in his hand. "Thanks, Anthony."

She left, slurping happily. She gave Anthony a dazzling thousand-watt smile as her well-coordinated body swished away. She was honed to perfection.

Anthony watched appreciatively as she walked away. She was what he considered one classy lady. She had a style that you didn't come across every day. She walked as if she knew a secret that no one else was privy to. Black grace, that's what she was. Simply, black grace. Anthony watched Tracie until the next customer arrived. She disappeared around the corner.

Tracie watched the balloon vendor hand a string of balloons to a little girl. She walked over, intrigued by the array of beautiful, vivid colors. They put her in a good mood, so she bought a string of balloons.

She strutted down the street, the balloons in her hand. Having second thoughts, she circled back, walking up to a little brick encasement that overlooked the dirty river.

Tossing her sleek sheen of hair back out of her face, she released the balloons in the air. She watched the separating colors as the balloons floated out over the horizon.

For a brief moment joy swept through her. She inhaled. Her beeper sounded; a car backfired in the distance. Tracie turned at the sound of it.

Screams ripped through the late afternoon, slicing through the stillness of the day, as a young man was hurled from a rooftop. His body hung suspended in slow motion for a fraction of a second, and then he plunged straight down, hitting the concrete with a dull thud. He lay with his neck broken and twisted.

When the screams sliced through the air, Sinead Watson looked up to see a body hurtling toward her with startling speed. It landed directly at her feet.

Sinead found she couldn't breathe. She reached for

her inhaler to control the oncoming asthma attack. She fumbled to get it to her mouth, then took long gulps.

The body lay at an odd angle on the sidewalk. The neck was twisted, the eyes wide open. The expression was frozen in helpless terror. Sinead trembled violently.

Suddenly, 135th Street and Malcolm X Boulevard was alive with confusion. People ran. Traffic was stopped in the street. A symphony of screams sang through the late afternoon air.

Across the street, in front of The Schomberg Center for Research in Black Culture, Souljah Boy watched the unfolding scene. His right eye twitched rapidly. Whenever something bad happened or was about to happen, his right eye always twitched.

A screaming, noisy crowd gathered around the body. A young man pushed his way through the confusion. Souljah Boy glanced up at the rooftop. He caught a glimpse of a profile, but it was barely discernible.

He shaded his eyes from the bright sunlight. Still he couldn't make out who it was from where he was standing.

Police and ambulance sirens sounded nearby. Andre Burlingame, Tracie's eighteen year old son, better known as Dre, the Image Maker, for his outstanding shots in photography, stepped in the middle of the action. Souljah Boy spotted his approach from across the street.

Dre was an intensely serious young man who exuded raw male confidence and a sort of graceful nonchalance in his tall, lanky frame. He had a camera case slung over his shoulder. He wildly clicked off pictures of the scene.

Excitement and adrenalin raced through his body. He loved it when he was in the right place at the right time. He would capture the image that had set 135th Street on fire. He would add another history-making shot to his already bulging portfolio.

Dre knew he would have the first shots, which would be shown on the evening news as well as in the *Amsterdam* newspaper. As luck would have it, he had been right there. His would be the first shots they saw.

His heart raced at his good fortune. The camera whirred. He clicked off shots in quick succession. Before a person could say, "Boo," Dre had snapped up the entire unfolding drama.

The streets were pure madness. People were screaming, hollering and crying. This only served to pump Dre to his peak while he clicked away, storing the horrifying portrayals on film.

Elbowing his way through the crowd, Dre reached the body on the ground for the supreme close-up. One click, the bulb flashed, and the camera slid down from his eyes as he looked down.

Shocked disbelief flashed across his handsome features. Slowly he dropped to his knees next to the body. A wail of electrifying pain burst forth from his lips. It echoed through the crowded street.

"Randi!"

An icy coldness replaced the excitement and adrenalin pumping through his bloodstream. Randi Burlingame was his brother. This wasn't some news item lying on the ground, broken and crumpled. This was his brother, his baby brother.

The only frame Dre could capture was the frozen expression on Randi's face. It swam in front of his eyes, as if encased in water. Dre's body had become statuelike. It was as though someone had thrown him into wet concrete. He couldn't move.

Souljah Boy, on hearing Dre shout out Randi's name, shot into action, running across the street. He was Dre's best friend. It couldn't be. That could not have been Randi's name that Dre had called out.

He made his way through the crowd until he reached Randi and Dre, who was kneeling beside him. Without a doubt this was Randi Burlingame lying broken on the dirty sidewalk.

Souljah Boy glanced once more up at the roof. His right eye twitched even more wildly now. Finally, he returned his attention to the two boys in front of him. His good eye roamed over the body on the ground, down to Randi's shoeless feet.

Two things struck him fast: Where were Randi's boots? And why wasn't there any blood on the ground?

Souljah Boy locked gazes with Dre. He knelt down, putting a hand to the pulse in Randi's throat. He knew it was in vain. Randi's eyes had no life in them. But he felt compelled to check anyway; he couldn't stop himself. His fingers reached out, hoping to connect with a spark of life. There was none.

He glanced at his friend Dre. Slowly he shook his head. "He's dead, Dre."

Dark, black, searing terror engulfed Dre on his hearing Souljah Boy's words spoken out loud. It was as if, because Souljah Boy had spoke it, that made it real.

"No," Dre said.

Souljah Boy's shoulders slumped. He bowed his head and whispered, "Yes."

Souljah Boy lifted his head to look at Dre. His throat was swollen in grief. His eyes pooled over with tears.

Dre stared at Souljah Boy across an ocean of pain, the waves of it tangible in the air. Their eyes locked in twin tunnels of disbelief and grief.

From the roof, the hysterical sound of high-pitched laughter could not be heard on the street. It had been three days since Tracie Burlingame had visited the old woman psychic and drawn the ace of spades, the card that represented death.

2

Hubert Noskog, MD, was a seasoned veteran. He had jowls like a hunting dog's. Craggy lines ran through his face. His eyes looked as though he'd seen it all and then some. By the year 2004, when Tracie Burlingame's son was murdered, he was the chief medical examiner in New York City, having worked his way up through the ranks.

He'd been on staff for thirty years, so his having seen it all was pretty close to the truth.

Two NYPD police detectives surrounded him. Monica Rhodes was a young, bright, tough, and ambitious detective. She was saucy, hip, and extremely intelligent. An average-looking girl, but what she didn't have in looks she made up for in sharpness.

Detective Alonzo Morgan was a tall, streetwise, fascinating specimen of male sleekness. He had a head full of long dreadlocks that were captured behind his head with a band. The dreads lay in neat locks and hung down his back, almost to his waist. He looked more like a reggae artist than a detective. Everyone called him Lonzo for short.

The two detectives were in sharp contrast as partners, but together their work was efficient. So far, they had managed to pardon what they each considered the shortcomings of the other.

Hubert stood at the head of the sheet-covered corpse. It was laid out on a slab of steel. The two detectives stood on either side. Lonzo's cell phone rang. He removed it from his back pocket. "What's up? Lonzo here." He nodded his head. "Yeah, we're on it."

He clicked off and looked at Monica. "Tracie Burlingame, Randi's mother." He lifted his chin in the direction of the corpse. "She's here to identify the body."

Monica cleared her throat. She glanced at the medical examiner. "I'll start the procedure. This isn't going to be easy for her."

The standard procedure was to show the family of the deceased a photograph. However, they were always **prepared in case** a family member requested to view the body in person.

Monica walked out the door with an air of authority. She was an extremely svelte young woman, brimming with confidence.

Outside in the corridor, Tracie Burlingame stood ramrod straight, arrogant and proud. She looked both beautiful and ravished, as though someone had invaded her secret territory.

Her light cocoa-brown eyes stared at Monica from a face hauntingly at odds with the pain engraved across it. Even in grief, Tracie Burlingame was an extraordinarily stunning woman.

Tracie's sons Michael Burlingame, seventeen years old, and Dre, stood supportively on either side of Tracie. Michael was an athletic basketball wonder.

Monica recognized his face from the newspaper. He was known as "Rebound" because of his extraordinary leaping abilities on the basketball court, and his incredible wristwatch timing.

Michael was an ambitious, shy, and compassionate young man. His heart was breaking for his mother and for the loss of his brother Randi, who had been the other basketball star in the family.

Raw pain glittered from his eyes. Dre, who had had time to compose himself, was much more laid-back. His face was an unreadable mask.

As Monica approached, Tracie pulled herself up a fraction of an inch taller. She tilted her head slightly in the air. The two women's eyes locked in an invisible battle. Opposition sizzled in the air between them.

"Mrs. Burlingame?" Monica asked.

Tracie's eyes flickered. *"Miss* Burlingame. But you can call me Tracie. These are my sons Dre and Michael."

Monica nodded a greeting, suddenly put off by the icy haughtiness of Tracie's tone. She handed Tracie a standard photo of her son, following the usual procedure for identification.

Tracie barely glanced at it, handing it back.

"I'd like to see him in person," she said in clipped tones, furious at the audacity of the City of New York in daring to hand her a standard photograph of her dead son.

"This way, please," Monica said, leading the way through the morgue doors. Tracie and her sons trailed behind her.

Tracie slowed her steps as she spotted the metal slab

with the sheet-covered mound in the middle of the floor. Dre gripped her arm.

He tilted his head arrogantly in the exact mannerism of his mother. Michael's face became a picture of pain so raw it shot from his eyes. It held those who glanced at him.

Lonzo stared at Tracie for a long moment. He looked at her sons. Then his eyes found Tracie's face once again. To Lonzo's eyes, Tracie was a ravishingly beautiful young woman with a hint of smoldering sensuality, gazing into his own dark liquid eyes.

The touch of a shadow on the beautiful features quickly vanished under his scrutiny. In the space of a second, Tracie's cocoa-brown eyes flashed to gray, hazel, back to brown, and finally settled on midnight black. Lonzo felt as though he'd been hit with a sledgehammer.

Tracie took one step closer to the table. Monica crossed her hands behind her back. She positioned herself next to the medical examiner. Lonzo gave an imperceptible nod of his head. The ME silently removed the sheet from the victim's face.

The only sound in the room was the audible gasp that escaped Tracie's lips. Michael grimaced. Tracie tightened her grip on Dre's hand. Her long, colored nails cut into his skin, drawing blood, but Dre didn't flinch.

Tracie took another step closer to the table. The other perfectly manicured hand reached out to stroke the dead boy's cheek.

The medical examiner had been kind enough to try to clean up the body, knowing that the mother would have to ID it. He was just a child, after all—sixteen years old. But even this kind courtesy could not erase the extensive damage to the body.

Nor had he been able to erase the terror frozen in the features. The one good thing was that the boy's eyes were closed, so she would never have to witness the stark fear along with the terror that was frozen in his eyes.

While examining him, the medical examiner had had a queer feeling. He'd dealt with a lot of deaths, but this one made him uneasy. The look in the boy's eyes had made him wonder, what the hell had he seen?

Slowly Tracie removed her touch. She gazed into Lonzo's eyes with a clawing, biting pain. Sparks of dark chocolate brown sprayed from her irises. Lonzo returned her stare unflinchingly. Tracie crossed her hands in front of her. She bowed her head.

Dre spotted Randi's clothing on a nearby table. His eyes lingered on a small gold cross lying forlornly against the stainless steel next to Randi's wallet.

Tracie finally lifted her head. Tears glistened in her eyes like jewels, but didn't fall. Lonzo was staring at her, completely awestruck. She was causing a deep animal stirring to rise up in him.

The ME slowly pulled the sheet back over Randi's head. Monica broke the silence. "Is this your son, Randi Burlingame?"

"No."

Startled looks ran rampant around the room. Tracie reached into her pocket. She pulled out her own photograph of Randi, handing it to Monica. It was in stark contrast to the one the City of New York had taken of the dead Randi Burlingame.

Monica looked at Tracie, then down at the photo of young, handsome, smiling Randi.

"That's my baby. He kissed me good-bye when he left this morning." Tracie shrugged. "I prefer to remember him this way."

Monica took a deep breath. "Miss Burlingame, you're aware that somebody might have pushed your son from the roof?"

"Tracie. Call me Tracie. I am aware that Randi may have accidentally fallen from the roof."

Monica tugged on her earlobe. She swallowed hard. Sarcasm crept into her voice. She did not like this woman. Tracie Burlingame rubbed her the wrong way. The woman was grating on her nerves for some reason.

"And he decided to remove his shoes before he fell? Which, by the way, were not found at the scene of the crime."

Dre stepped in. "That's enough."

Monica reached for her badge. She stepped forward, flashing it, up close and very personal, in Dre's face.

"I'll say when it's enough. Monica Rhodes, Harlem Homicide Division. Official business."

The medical examiner glanced at Michael sympathetically. Michael smiled his appreciation at the man. At least somebody in this room had the decency to show some sympathy.

Monica's voice sliced through the air. "So tell me, Tracie, what was Randi wearing on his feet the last time you saw him?"

"Footwear."

"Can you be more specific?"

"Karl Kani . . . boots. Gold and black hiking boots. Black hardware. Gold strings. Kani emblem on the side." The light cocoa-brown eyes shed a couple of teary jewels, which spilled and glistened on Tracie's high cheekbones.

"Excuse me. Hardware?" Monica said.

As though explaining to a child, Tracie said, "The eyelets in which you lace up the boots."

"You're a fashion expert?" The sarcasm dripped from Monica's voice without disguise.

"No. I'm a mother."

Dre gripped Tracie's hand. He glared his hostility at Monica. "My mom is tired. So, you're gonna have to do this another time."

Monica nodded at the arrogant young punk. She smiled. "Count on it."

Tracie looked at the medical examiner, her eyes filled with anguish. Her voice was barely a whisper. "What time did this happen?"

The ME reached for his chart, consulting it. He looked up at Tracie gravely. "Randi expired at approximately two p.m."

"Expired . . . I see." Tracie smoothly turned her back on them. She headed for the door with her two sons right behind her. Her heels clicked sharply against the floor. She sailed through the door. It slammed behind them.

Lonzo looked at the sheet-draped body. His eyes grazed the now empty space left by Tracie.

Hubert glanced at his chart. "There was one other thing I wanted to discuss with you." He looked at the two detectives.

"What's that?" They both said in unison.

"The blood, or perhaps I should say, the lack of it."

"Yeah," Monica said. "It was on our list to ask you how he removed it. It's the strangest crime scene I've ever been on. I kid you not. This boy is thrown from the roof, and there's barely a trace of blood on the ground, plus, his shoes are missing. Weird stuff."

"Have you determined how the blood was removed?" Lonzo said.

The ME peered over his glasses at him. "The old-fashioned way. He stuck a needle in his arm and simply drained his body of the blood supply. Maybe your guy has embalming skills. He barely left a trace as to his entry."

Lonzo laughed. "Stop it, Doc. This is serious."

The ME didn't budge.

Lonzo's eyes widened a bit. "Seriously? You're kidding, right?"

Dr. Noskog's expression never changed.

"You're serious," Lonzo finally stated.

"I am. Very."

Monica sucked in her breath. "What's he doing with the blood?" she wondered out loud.

Both Lonzo and Hubert looked at her, but there was no answer forthcoming.

3

After leaving the morgue on First Avenue, Tracie had the driver drop her off at 135th Street and Lenox Avenue. She stood in front of Harlem Hospital, under the canopy with Dre and Michael. She stared up at the roof of the Lenox Terrace apartments, from which her son had fallen.

Her mind refused to accept any other explanation. This was just a tragic accident. Not even a murderer could commit such a horrific, brutal crime.

She had been after Randi since he was a small boy about climbing rooftops. He loved to sit up there, staring down on the world. A tragic accident was what it was. That was all.

Tracie squinted in the fading sunlight. She pulled her shades down from her hair to cover her eyes. Something across the street drew her attention. Slowly the shades came down to the bridge of her nose. She stared over the top of them.

Rashod Burlingame, Tracie's nineteen year old son, her eldest, was racing across the street. Black twists sprouted all over his head, looking like black spaghetti erupting from his scalp. He weaved his way across Malcolm X Boulevard toward Tracie.

Tracie's skin crawled a bit at the sight of him. Lord help her. The mere sight of him had a way of churning her insides.

In Tracie's opinion, Rashod had one of the nastiest dispositions this side of the river. He was an extremely weak and emotionally unstable young man.

Yet he possessed a sensitivity that most people never got to see. He was also a veteran crack addict. He loved crack more than life, and woe to anyone who got between him and one of his coveted vials.

Motorists were blaring their horns, weaving around Rashod and yelling out of their car windows at him as he decided to slow his pace to a leisurely crawl while he crossed the street on a green light.

One guy yelled out of his window, "Yo, man? Can't you see? The light is green. You color-blind? Get a life."

Rashod ignored him. He swiped at his runny nose with the back of his hand. His pants slipped a little too low. He pulled them back up while taking another swipe at his nose.

Finally, he reached the safety of the spot in front of Tracie, on the sidewalk under the canopy. His face glistened with sweat as he focused on her and blatantly disregarded Dre and Michael.

"Mommy dearest," he said to Tracie, the sneer obvious in his tone.

Tracie swallowed hard. "What are you doing here, Rashod?"

"I want to pay props and respect to my dead baby brother. Harlem's grapevine don't know no end, baby."

"Don't call me 'baby,' " Tracie said in disgust. "The only respect you pay is to that pipe you be hitting."

Rashod laughed. He leaned in closer to Tracie. "Wrong. I also pay my respects to the Destroyer." He swept a low bow in front of Tracie's feet, paying mock allegiance to her. He glared once at Michael, then at Dre.

Rashod reached into his pants pocket. He pulled out his blunt. He put it to his mouth, searched for his lighter, lit it, and inhaled, blowing smoke at Tracie before turning on his heels and sauntering down the street in the direction of Sylvia's Restaurant.

Dre reached out a hand to snatch him by the collar for punking and disrespecting his mother. But Tracie put a restraining hand on Dre's chest. She pulled her sunglasses over her eyes.

She watched the back of Rashod as he glided down crowded Malcolm X Boulevard. Pain swelled in her chest as she watched the first child she had borne disappear into the crowded street. His hatred of her washed her onto the shores of failed motherhood and desolation.

Here she stood on a street named after a man who thought they should rise. Instead the street was full of boys, girls, men, and women who were sinking. It was as if some unseen force were swallowing their very souls whole. Rashod, her very own child, was only one of them.

Tracie shook her head at the thought. And that was only one of Harlem's disparities. A cruel twist of fate was laughing at them for daring to dream, on streets that possessed the whispering souls of a Harlem Renaissance long past. They were living in shadows. Rashod was her shadow.

The truth was, Randi wasn't the only child she had lost. In reality, she had lost Rashod a long time ago, in both body and spirit. He was as dead to her as Randi. Tracie let out a silent, wordless sigh.

Crack cocaine, the spiritless demon, had stolen him from her. The only difference was that she would not have to commit his body to the ground. No, he was a live ache that she would have to live with.

He was one of the living dead.

As Rashod glided through the streets that were like a second skin to him, his mother wasn't the only person who watched him.

The second pair of eyes not only watched, they absorbed him. Then they turned inward, swallowing the ghost of Rashod Burlingame whole.

After all, he was only one of Tracie Burlingame's black patches. Yes, she was a patchwork quilt, all right. She was full of black patches and hollowed-out places.

4

Graced. That's what those fools were. Graced. That would soon come to a crashing end.

Screech.

Those were the brakes, putting an end to things.

The people in Harlem were graced because he had not yet struck the streets of Harlem. But now he would, because he had his orders. Spirit and flesh, flesh and spirit—for him it was a game of "romp and let's play." In reality, it was not something to be played with.

He roamed the dark room. There was no need for light. He hated light and all things that were bright. He blew his nose, wadded up the tissue, and threw it in the growing pile, which was about three feet high in the room.

He coughed up phlegm, spitting that into the wad of tissues also. He rubbed his bald head, which looked like a shiny, brown globe. Then he stretched his tall frame.

Dirt caked the walls. The garbage in the room overflowed. He was pleased with himself for removing all the fresh meat from the refrigerator and setting it on the desk and tables in the room.

He watched as maggots and roaches fought for position on the uncovered meat. Then he laughed.

He was restless. He needed new spirit anyway. He was glad he was being dispatched to fresh territory. This mission was the most important of all. Harlem was considered the Black Mecca, the promised land. That made it important history-making grounds.

He'd made some trial runs. There were some territorial-rights issues, but he had his orders from the only power that mattered.

The one whose claim was already staked in Harlem was not moving fast enough. He was following a personal agenda. This was not personal; it was business.

The business of striking, hitting, destroying that which must be destroyed, was serious. There was a lot at stake. He must collect the gifts. It was time.

The primary show should have been on the road, and so far all he'd done was drop one boy from the roof. What the hell was he thinking?

He knew there was a much grander plan.

No, there was no more time. He needed to start collecting the spirits—now. He had received his orders.

He stuck the long shiny blade down into the sheath sewn to the inside of his pants. His breathing was shallow, just as it always was when it was time.

His arrival in Harlem would kick things into high gear. First he would observe his comrade in action.

Then he would stalk him. The next time his comrade struck, he'd be there; he wouldn't miss out. Spirit and flesh were sometimes uneasy companions.

He knew his invasion would not be welcomed at this time, because his comrade hadn't finished his own personal agenda. That was too bad. Time was of the essence. His comrade dabbled in flesh, but *he* excelled in spirit.

He looked at his biceps before pulling on his jacket. There they were: the faces of the ones already collected poked out all along his biceps and forearms. Their eyes stared at him. Some of them blinked at him.

Looking at them reminded him of faces with pronounced facial features poking out through a balloon, sort of as if a mask were being stretched over them—only it was his skin that provided the covering.

The faces writhed in the agony he had caused. Desolation, fear, and uncertainty peeked out at him. Sometimes they cried, particularly the very young. It was useless; they weren't going anywhere.

There was even one who always sneezed.

It didn't matter. It was a trap not of the usual making. They were contained in a spiritual housing, one from which they would never be released.

He thought about the death of Randi Burlingame and the missed opportunity to add him to his spiritual residence. This angered him because Randi Burlingame had been of high esteem. He could not miss again. He was the collector.

Quickly he grabbed his jacket, putting it on so he wouldn't have to look at them. He didn't want to look at them anymore just now. At times some of them spoke.

Sometimes they cried out in unison, wanting to be free. But only on a specific occasion, if someone had the sight to see. That reminded him: he had a visit to make. Sometimes those with the sight to see saw too much.

Today the residing spirits held their tongues. Soon he would add more to them.

And as soon as he made his visit, she would know his name.

5

That night Lonzo and Monica sat at their desks in the Harlem precinct station. Monica leaned back in her chair with her feet up on the desk. Lonzo sat running his hands through his long dreadlocks.

"All right," Monica said. "Let's go over everything we have."

"We did."

"Then let's do it again."

Monica was exasperated with Lonzo's attitude. He was getting on her last nerve. He glared at her, then shot up out of his seat, pacing the floor.

"We have a sixteen-year-old dead boy. And we're clueless as to why he's dead, because we have no motive."

Lonzo twirled in a circle and then threw his arms wide open in stage-show fashion. "Oh, and we have our star witness Sinead Watson, who, between wheezes, doesn't know a thing outside of the body hitting the ground in front of her." He took a bow.

"We ought to be able to use that, don't you think?" he said rather nastily.

Monica didn't answer the question.

Instead she said, "And we know for a fact that Randi has an ice princess for a mother." That took the air out of his sails.

He gave her a long, puzzled look. "Get a grip, Monie. The lady was grieving. Anyway that has nothing to do with this."

Monica swung her feet from the desk. "It has everything to do with this."

"Chill, okay? You're losing your logic."

She rolled her eyes. "I'm not losing a thing, but you might be." Her eyes arrogantly traveled the length of his body. Lonzo felt the heat rise in him.

"What the hell is that supposed to mean?"

"It means this is a homicide investigation, and everybody is a suspect." Monica tugged on her earlobe. She lifted an eyebrow in Lonzo's direction.

"We owe some respect to his mother," Lonzo said.

"I owe my respect to the people of the City of New York."

Monica walked up close to Lonzo. The physical attraction bristled in the air between them. A single electric, kinetic wave embraced them.

She paused before continuing. "And I owe my respect to the dead. In this case that would be to Randi Burlingame. Because I, for one, do not believe that he decided to remove his Karl Kani boots before he accidentally fell off the roof. Do you?"

Lonzo took a step back. He squared his shoulders. "Naw."

"And he certainly didn't decide to give blood before tossing himself over the roof." Monica searched Lonzo's eyes before adding, "I ain't buying accidental. Tracie Burlingame can afford to be in denial; we can't."

"Okay, look, I know where you're coming from. Let's call it for the night. We'll see what it looks like in the morning."

"Cool. That works for me." Monica retrieved her jacket from the back of the chair and left the room.

Both of them spent a restless night. They arrived at the precinct early the next morning. The first order of business was a meeting with Alexandra Kennedy, head of Harlem's homicide division.

Alexandra was tough. She was in every aspect of the word a ballbuster. Her manner was one of rigid coldness. She reigned supreme in the Harlem precinct.

She had tight blond ringlet curls plastered to her head, and bright blue eyes the color of a summer sky. She strode into their office, dropping a bag on the floor without a hint of a greeting.

She tossed a file on the desk. Then she stared belligerently at the two tired, weary detectives who looked as though they hadn't slept a wink.

"What's going on here?" Alexandra asked without preamble.

Monica stared at her unemotionally. Lonzo smiled engagingly.

"Murder," Lonzo said.

Alexandra took a pencil from her pocket. She chewed on the eraser. "Brilliant, Lonzo. Is that how you got to be in the top five of your class in the police academy? Just murder?"

A visible shade closed over Lonzo's eyes at Alexandra's tone. He sat down on the edge of the desk without answering her.

Alexandra pulled her gaze away from his. She moved over to the desk. Quickly she flipped through the file. She decided to direct her attention to Monica.

Sarcastically she said, "Well, now, Monie. Just murder?"

Monica flinched. She was stung by Alexandra's antagonism. She didn't appreciate hearing her nickname on Alexandra's tongue, either. Alexandra was a witch on wheels, and Monica was ever so close to hating her.

She shrugged nonchalantly. She wasn't in the mood to play Alexandra's games. She bit her tongue to keep from telling her so straight-out. Instead she said, "One eighty-seven. Why don't you tell us . . ."

Alexandra was irritated. She waved her silent. "This isn't the police academy. It's the real world. It's my world, and this case has the tracings of a serial killer on the loose. I don't like it."

Lonzo rose from his seat on the desk. "Now, wait a minute, Alexandra. There's only been one murder. You're chasing ghosts and creating chalk outlines where there are none."

Alexandra stepped up to Lonzo. She poked her finger in his chest. "That's one too many out of context. And I want to make sure the chalk manufacturers don't get too rich here."

"Out of context?" Monica echoed. "And exactly what does that mean?"

"Let me ask you a question. How many little black boys in Harlem have been hurled from a rooftop without their shoes on lately?"

She waved them silent before they could speak.

Chewing rapidly on the eraser, she said, "Particularly ones that live on Riverside Drive?"

Alexandra tossed a plastic bag on the desk, containing two pieces of a silver broken heart. Lonzo and Monica exchanged glances.

"Where'd you get this?" Monica asked.

"The killer had it delivered. A small courtesy of his. Along with this." Alexandra snapped open the bag. She tossed a black and gold Karl Kani boot wrapped in a plastic bag onto the desk.

Monica and Lonzo stared at the boot as though it were alive. It was exactly as Tracie Burlingame had described it to them.

"Oh," Alexandra said, "and he sent a note, too."

She pulled out a plastic-covered piece of paper. On it, letters were arranged in aluminum casing. She read aloud the one engraved word: "Atonement."

"Atonement—that's all?" Monica said.

"That's it. Don't bother dusting for prints. There are none."

Alexandra's baby blue eyes blazed at Lonzo, although Monica was the one who'd spoken.

"Find the other boot and we'll have the killer. This city is running out of burial space. Little black boys being dropped from rooftops isn't going to sit too well with the powers that be. Less so if they happen to be basketball legends, too.

"Randi Burlingame was better known as the Shooter. At sixteen years old he scored almost as many points per game as Michael Jordan in his day. The scouts were already looking at him. They were watching and waiting. He was primed for NBA glory, a legend in his own right. Now he's dead."

Caustically Monica added, "Well, Tracie's still got

Michael Burlingame, another basketball legend in the making. The boy with the wristwatch timing. They're calling him the next Earl 'the Goat' Manigault. Seems Ms. Burlingame has birthed more than one legend."

Alexandra pursed her lips, started to respond to the edge in Monica's tone, then decided against it and walked to the door. She stopped before reaching it.

"A mother tossing dirt on top of her son's coffin doesn't much appeal to me. So you see, not a damn thing is appealing to me about this case. Get me the killer. Harlem's a sensitive community. I want the killer—now."

Reaching the door, she walked through it and slammed it shut behind her.

6

A few days later Tracie Burlingame was in the cemetery, throwing fresh dirt on top of Randi's lowered coffin. The dirt landed with a loud thump, or at least that's what it sounded like to Tracie's ears.

At her side was Dre, who was firing off rapid shots of the funeral and its surroundings. Michael and Souljah Boy were also with her. Directly behind Tracie stood Renee Santiago, a close friend of Tracie's. She was stylish as well as bold, and quick with her tongue. The rest of the mourners were crowded behind them.

Renee stared at the back of Tracie's black-veiled head. Then she diverted her attention to Rashod, who was standing on the other side of the grave, across from Tracie. He was watching his mother. Open hostility and resentment flared from his eyes.

Surprisingly, he didn't look high. If he wasn't high,

it'd be the first time in years she'd seen him without the aid of ole crack cocaine.

Tracie stared down at the single rose lying on top of the dirt on the coffin. Souljah Boy had thrown it in after the dirt hit the coffin. Tracie looked over to where Rashod had stood, to find the spot where he had been standing empty.

At the curbside in a van, a camcorder was recording the services. The police photographer was snapping still photographs. His photographs included Andre Burlingame, for they found it curious that he was personally photographing his own brother's services.

Off in the distance, Lonzo and Monica observed both the services and the visitors. One by one, young men went up to pay their respects to Tracie Burlingame.

Sean Richardson, seventeen years old, was first up. "Randi was the greatest shooter in Harlem. I'm sorry, Miss Burlingame. I'm gonna miss him. He was my best friend." Tracie nodded serenely.

Next Jimmy "the Runner" Boyd, sixteen years old, made his way over to Tracie. "The NBA got cheated. Randi was poetry in motion." He imitated the shot stance that had made Randi famous in Harlem. "Swish," he said, "he was all that. He was my boy, Miss Burlingame." Tracie touched his cheek softly, wiping away a tear before it could fall.

Next came Little Rock; he, too, was sixteen years old. "My boy was a legend, Ms. Burlingame. This ain't right. If we find out who did it . . ." He punched his hand with his fist.

Tracie looked at him steadfastly. She lifted the veil off her face and kissed the boy's cheek. Her eyes changed colors three times in fast succession, affecting the grief-stricken boy. He blinked, unsure what had even happened. He'd never seen anyone's eyes change colors like that.

"That won't be necessary, Little Rock. Randi will live through our memories of him."

Little Rock nodded. "Whatever you need . . ."

"I know," Tracie said.

Renee Santiago hugged Tracie tightly. She looked at her pointedly. "Rashod could use some attention, Tracie." She lowered her voice. "Soon." She walked away. Tracie watched her make her way through the crowd.

Souljah Boy pressed in close to Tracie. He placed something in her hand before walking away. Tracie opened her palm to see a page ripped from the Bible, the Twenty-third Psalm.

That night, inside Tracie Burlingame's brownstone on Riverside Drive, the wars were inwardly raging. Randi was dead, and the emotions of her remaining sons were running high. She would have to deal with them sooner or later.

Michael was closeted in his room, incommunicado.

Dre lay in the middle of his queen-sized bed, fully dressed, with his booted feet on the bed. He pondered the airline ticket in his hand. One wall of the room was full of photographs and poster shots.

There were great ocean shots, sunsets, trees and mountains that Dre had taken during the hiatuses Tracie financed for him. There were lots of Harlem community scenes. The shots were bold, brash, and startling in their depiction of the streets of Harlem and its residents.

He had captured the stark reality of the borough in an ethereal way, a way that made one pause for thought.

Dre was a talented photographer. He had managed to capture the soul of the city and its people.

Every photograph had a grainy, misty quality. The rest of the shots were mostly black-and-whites of family and friends.

Camera equipment, video cameras, and leather satchel cases filled every available space, along with a ton of computer equipment and all its accessories. A miniature basketball court sat in one corner of the room.

Dre continued to ponder the airline ticket. Under "Destination" were the words "Los Angeles." Dre sighed. There was a knock on the bedroom door. He didn't answer. The knock sounded again, more persistently this time.

"Come in, Souljah," Dre called knowing it was him. They were close, so they had it like that at times, each knowing when the other was around.

Souljah Boy walked in. He closed the door behind him. Souljah Boy's real name was Daniel Thomas Caldwell. His instincts were razor sharp, and his intuition was not normal. He detected grief, as well as something else, in the air. He couldn't put his finger on it. His spirit registered it only as something nameless.

Where had that come from?

Since Daniel Thomas Caldwell was so formal-sounding, and there was nothing about him to suggest he be called Danny for short, his grandmother had given him the moniker of Souljah Boy, which was a perfect fit, and everyone he knew called him that.

His grandmother had declared that he was an old soul since the day he was born. She had flipped the Bible open in front of his face hours after he was born, and she told everyone who'd listen that that child had focused his eyes on the word and reached out to touch the Bible like he knew what it was for real.

From that moment on she had secretly dedicated him to Christ and given him the name Souljah Boy. It fit him like a glove. No one knew for sure if the story was true about Souljah Boy, but he was always walking around with the Bible.

His knowledge of scripture was astounding. And for sure he was Harlem's ghetto scribe.

Consequently, the only place you ever saw the name Daniel Thomas Caldwell was on a legal document.

Dre hit the ticket against his leg. He looked tired. Souljah Boy sat on the foot of the bed. Dre didn't bother to move his feet.

"So, what's up, Dre?"

Dre gave Souljah Boy a long look. "I don't know, man. Somebody flipped the script upside down on me. Threw shade. You know what I'm saying?"

Souljah Boy nodded. "What about L.A.?" He indicated the ticket Dre held in his hand.

Dre tossed his head from side to side on the pillow. "I can't leave my moms now, man. Maybe once things are straight." Dre held up the ticket. He stared at it as though an illumination to solve all his problems would appear.

Souljah Boy reached into his pocket and extracted a pocket-size Bible. He flipped to a page and started reading: " 'Yea, though I walk through the valley of the shadow of death . . .' " Souljah Boy stopped to give Dre a close look.

Dre leaped off the bed. He went over to the window. "Knock it off, Souljah."

" 'I shall fear no evil . . .' "

"I said knock it off, yo."

"Why?"

"Because this ain't the valley of death. It's Harlem."

Souljah Boy snapped the Bible closed. He stared intently at Dre. "Randi's dead."

"And I'm alive. I'm an image maker, Souljah Boy."

"All men are made in the image of God," Souljah Boy said.

Dre ignored him. He grabbed his camera. The flash exploded in Souljah Boy's face. Light surrounded his head like a halo. Dre clicked off a rapid succession of deft shots.

He had difficulty breathing as he turned and aimed the camera at the window. He took a shot of the full moon, hovering like a suspended ball in the sky. "The ultimate shot of all time. That will be me, Souljah. Images come from the living, man."

"Evil lives among the living, and legends are made bigger once they're dead," Souljah Boy said.

He rose, picked up the sponge basketball off the floor, and swished a shot into the hoop in the corner of the room. The ball dropped through the hoop in slow motion, in a perfect arc. Souljah Boy glanced at a smiling picture of Randi Burlingame up on Dre's wall.

"Men create images, Dre. Some they can't live with. Out of men's hearts sprouts evil. But only God can create a man. Only God can truly right a wrong. Remember that."

Souljah Boy walked out of the room, clutching his Bible. He closed the door softly behind him as Dre stared at the empty spot he had left behind.

7

Anita stood in the middle of her cramped apartment, with yards of colorful fabric draped across her arms. She twined the material across the mannequin that stood before her. It was busy work, and right now she needed to be busy. It had already started, just as she had known it would.

Sometimes her second sight carried a burden. Sometimes she saw things she didn't want to see. Disturbed, she worked quickly, wrapping the cloth this way and that way, the design draping itself across the mannequin easily from her experienced fingers.

She would stay off the streets of Harlem for a while. After all, she had accumulated a small fortune. It was not as though she needed to work every day. She did so because she loved being around people. She loved the streets and the electricity that filled the streets. She was in tune with the special harmony of the people that populated Harlem.

Nowhere else had she ever found the spirit that surrounded these people. She greatly appreciated being a part of that. However, she had decided she would cool her heels for a bit, stay off the streets and out of sight. Out of sight, out of mind, right? Or so she hoped.

Something was brewing just beneath the surface of Harlem, like a tidal wave that hadn't yet reached shore. She didn't know what it was, but she didn't like the feeling. It was queer.

And that Tracie Burlingame was like a magnet, attracting the wrong kind of things. She was a patchwork quilt. Anita didn't like what she had seen on her. It gave her a bad feeling, as if it were the tip of the iceberg. Yes, she would definitely stay off the streets.

Her apartment was littered with antiques and fabrics from every continent, and pictures of the famous graced almost every inch of wall space. Models, politicians, composers, musicians, and athletes—you name a famous person, and you would pretty much find them on Anita's wall.

All had been given their place, and space along her coveted walls. She loved people who possessed gifts.

Mannequins sat in every corner of the living room, all draped with their own designs. A rich array of vibrant colored fabrics covered the walls, sofas, and chairs. Silks, velvets, chintz, and soft transparencies littered the room.

There was also a scattering of Tiffany lamps. She was a collector. Crystal balls sat in brass holders; some dated back as far as the eighteenth century. Decks of cards sat in their designer cases, ready to be used at will. Ready to tell a story. Ready to reveal a secret. Sometimes ready to turn a life upside down. Oh, well. Their job was not to feel, only to tell.

Anita heard a noise. She looked down to find one of her five rabbits nuzzling an empty bowl next to the couch. She knew what that meant. It was time for them to eat. She had five black rabbits. Their coats were sleek and as shiny as velvet.

Anita had spoiled them shamelessly. They slept on the couch amid an array of colorful stuffed pillows. She fed them romaine lettuce. The little rascals loved music. They especially liked instrumental jazz, classical, and hip-hop. You name it, they were there. They loved a good beat. They would curl up on a pillow and listen for hours to the music, a contented look on their distinct little faces. Their whiskers would pucker in musical peace.

Anita smiled down at Pesky, the one who had brought her attention to the fact that it was dinnertime. He lived up to his name, because he was the one who kept Anita on the straight and narrow by nipping at her heels when she entered worlds that didn't include them.

But, that was all right, because Pesky knew what it took to bring her around. And right now he knew it was time to eat. He had her attention.

Anita filled the bowls with the fresh lettuce she had acquired from the market. She watched as they scrambled forth.

She was about to return her attention to the mannequin when the kitchen shutters banged open loudly. "Goodness," she said.

She walked toward the kitchen, intending to close the shutters. Something stopped her in her tracks.

The man standing before her was tall—huge. His

eyes gleamed brightly. His bald brown head glistened. It shone as though it had been dipped in floor wax. It looked like a brown, shiny globe.

He had the sort of disciplined posture of one trained in the military. She could see his biceps bulging beneath the army jacket he wore.

The strangest thing about him was, he stood silent, not speaking a word. But, Anita could hear voices emanating from him. A symphony of voices was swelling from within him, but he never moved his lips or spoke a word.

A clammy wetness broke out on Anita's palms. She rubbed her hands together. Suddenly the voices turned raucous. She recognized the tone. She had heard them before. She had heard those same voices emanate from Tracie Burlingame, the patchwork quilt.

Astounded, she took a step back without even realizing she had moved. She stared at him. She couldn't see through him the way she would have liked. For some reason, her sight had been blocked, and she couldn't dig beneath the layers of this huge thing that stood before her.

"What are you doing in my house?" she finally asked.

The bald mountain stared back at her without answering. Anita swallowed past the lump in her throat as she tried to design the next question. "Who are you?" she asked.

His deep baritone voice shook the room. "I am Me," he answered.

"Who is 'me'?"

"Me is Me," he said.

Anita sighed. She could see they were getting nowhere with this line of questioning. She decided to get straight to the point, although a part of her fearfully tried to hold back.

"What do you want?" she asked, all the while fearing the answer.

A voice spoke, but his lips didn't move. The voice was clear and distinct. "I have come for the gifts. The gifts in Harlem." His eyes roamed the walls, scanning the pictures of the precious, famed African-Americans.

Anita gasped, "No."

Another, very high-pitched voice spoke, different in tone this time. "We must all be gathered together." The bald mountain looked into her eyes. His gaze didn't waver.

Anita saw a slight movement in his biceps beneath his jacket. Someone sneezed, but it wasn't either him or her.

"Okay." Anita had had enough. "Don't you be coming in here uninvited, playing no games with me. I'm an old woman and I don't have time for games. State your business clearly." The Louisiana spunk she was so well known for found its way to the surface, and although she sensed imminent danger, she decided to face it down.

It was the only way. People who were too scared could be had. "Gone ahead." She slipped into her dialect. "State your business, I said."

"I came to collect the gifts. You have the sight." He removed the block to her second sight, allowing her to see. What she saw rocked her world. It rendered her speechless. She shivered in the cozy warmth of the room.

"I am Me. Do you understand?" he asked.

Anita nodded.

"Good. Now you know my name. You will see a great many things come to pass in the time to come."

He closed the shutters on the kitchen windows. He walked through the small alcove to the front door, opened it, and was gone. The door shut softly behind him.

Anita bowed her head in horror. He was the collector.

8

The night of the funeral, Rashod Burlingame sat next to the grave that held the remains of his brother Randi. He noticed they had covered the grave since earlier in the day, when Tracie had thrown the first dirt on the casket.

He dropped the cheap flowers he had gotten from a street vendor on top of the grave. Then he sat cross-legged on the ground with a sketch pad in his hand. He sketched the cemetery and the look of the grave, which held his brother.

It was hard for him to believe that Randi was lying all by himself in the dark, black hole covered with dirt.

But encased in the ground in the metallic blue box he was. Sometimes you never knew how things would work out.

He took a blunt from his pocket, lit it, and inhaled deeply. There. He felt better after taking a toke. The smoke swelled inside his lungs. A feeling of peace stole over him. Hell, the only time he felt peace was when he bought it in a vial or a blunt.

"Randi, I'm sorry," he said in the empty darkness.

There was no answer.

"I'm telling you, man, I didn't mean it. I didn't mean a lot of things."

Rashod was a highly gifted and talented sketch artist. His fingers flew across the pad, drawing in the eeriness of his surroundings. The charcoal seemed to take flight in his fingers, and magically they weaved the heartbreaking scene, capturing the essence of one having died.

Of one having been left alone, as Randi was in his patch of ground. His mind soared through the tragic, final event of death. To kill a man was a profound act.

He stopped sketching. His eyes scanned the grave site. He took another toke on the blunt. Then he stubbed it out in the ground. He'd need to save some for later, especially since he had spent some of his money on flowers for Randi.

He'd needed to come back that night, once the crowds were gone, because he couldn't talk to Randi with them there. He couldn't explain things. Besides, he was tired of looking at that Tracie with her fake face of grief pasted in place.

Sometimes her phoniness made him want to heave. The witch was a money lover and nothing else. Money was like a religion to Tracie. All she ever thought about was how to get more of it. She was a sleek clothes-horse, so glamorous on the outside and gluttonous on the inside. She made him sick.

He stood up. Thinking about her felt as if he had summoned her spirit to the place. He definitely could do without that. But he needed to say good-bye. He needed to say it in his own time and in his own way. Tracie didn't deserve Randi. He was good. Talented. He was too good for her to own. They were all just trophies to her.

Well, now he was dead. Tracie didn't own him anymore. She couldn't own Randi anymore, because now he was gone. That was good. It was over. It was one less son for her to hurt and hide things from.

Maybe it would be good if they were all gone. If they were all dead, then there wouldn't be anybody left for her to show off or play with. Bitterness welled up inside Rashod. He spat on the ground.

Not wanting to say good-bye, because it was too final, he thought for a moment. Finally, he said, "So long, Randi. So long, baby brother. Rest in peace. See ya."

He walked out of the growing darkness of the cemetery. Out on the street he relit his blunt and inhaled deeply. The eyes watched him, absorbed him, and swallowed the ghost of his spirit whole.

Though Randi Burlingame was dead, he had escaped the absorbing of his spirit. He had been spared this particular fate.

But there was a new kid on the block, and thus the rules of the game had changed. It was now time.

9

The day after Randi's funeral, Tracie was reigning queen at the helm of her empire. Her main place of business was her salon on the corner of 135th Street and Seventh Avenue. Although it was located in an old, worn-out-looking building, the inside of the salon was in stark contrast to its outside.

The inside was elegantly decorated. It possessed an air of sleek sophistication. It was one of many salons Tracie owned around Harlem. A sign above the door read, "Tracie's Place."

The salon was full-service. Hairstylists as well as braid stylists, makeup artists, pedicurists, and manicurists filled the place. The other salons Tracie owned were braiding stations only. They were purely cash businesses, where she hired the African girls to run the places and braid hair.

The African girls were the best in the business, hands

down. Some of them had come over directly from Africa. They had skills when it came to braiding hair. The art of braiding was a strictly cash-and-carry business. Tracie had been smart enough to recognize the trend at the right time. It was one of her better investments. Women came to her salons from as far away as D.C. and Philly to get their hair braided in her shops.

She had hired some of the best African talent in the city. The other thing was, these women were disciplined. They could stand on their feet, braiding for hours without tiring or needing a break. They worked hard, and they were loyal to a fault. Tracie had never met anyone like them. Under their skills, her braiding salons were raking in the cash.

A huge percentage of the braiding styles parading around the streets of New York City were obtained in her salons. All her salons were named after her: Tracie's Place One, Two, Three, Four, and so on. She loved it. The shop on 135th and Seventh Avenue was her baby. It was her first shop. This was where her headquarters was located.

At the Seventh Avenue salon she accepted credit cards as well as checks. In this salon the clientele sometimes tended to be a bit more exclusive. She serviced a lot of professional women with high incomes who worked in Manhattan.

She had to accommodate them because these weren't the type of women who walked around with wallets full of cash. Their credit card status was part of their esteem. It was part of their professional package. They expected to flip out titanium, platinum, and gold cards and use them for services rendered.

Plus, these women were into caring for their manes, which they wanted to look healthy and shiny. They were also into weaves of every sort and variety. So her main salon was of a different feel from the braid sweat-shops Tracie owned.

The inside of the salon had an ultramodern look, with black and silver color schemes. There were eighteen hair stations. Each was doing a brisk business. Ninety-eight KISS FM dominated the room with its golden classic sounds. There was lots of laughter and lighthearted chattering going on. The cappuccino and coffee machines were pumping.

The makeup stations were busy as usual, scattered with an array of colorful hues and makeup in every shade. Mirrors covered every angle, so a woman could admire the contours of her facial features and examine her coloring in different shades of light.

The nail booths were pumping out glittery, shining jobs; not one drop of polish was out of place. There wasn't a color that had ever been created that Tracie's shop didn't carry. The nail designs were cutting-edge. Customers fought for a seat here—particularly the young girls who changed their nail design every couple of days to keep ahead of the others, and who had taken airbrush to a different level.

Eight pedicure booths lined the wall. Each booth was designed with heavily cushioned seats, laid out for pampering and comfort. The foot sinks gleamed and sparkled, boasting the best-smelling scents in the city.

Bottled perfumed scents sat in antique holders. They were of the highest quality, to keep a woman's feet smelling good and looking like a creation in art itself. An array of stainless steel instruments complemented each pedicure booth.

Each seat had its own occupant, looking down upon the head of the pedicure stylist, who would churn out her pedicure as though she were a princess come to visit from a foreign land.

Yes, it was business as usual, Tracie saw as she looked out from behind the glass-walled office. This was her domain, built from scratch. She had built her business from the ground up, with plenty of hard work, imagination, and a flair for the beautiful.

Her goal had been to make beauty a sensual experience. When a woman left her shop, she left covered in the sheen of glamour. It wasn't just physical beauty. Tracie's salons poured it on so it reached the emotional recesses of a woman's psyche, leaving her feeling like a queen.

Tracie Burlingame had tapped into a secret, coveted place inside the black woman's emotions. And she had come out shining. Visiting Tracie's salon wasn't just maintenance; it was an experience.

The salon also boasted private rooms for those women who desired to pay for the exclusivity of services. The music was always pumping. She had runners who would go out for food, drinks, or many of the other desires of her customers.

She employed shoppers, who would run into Manhattan for that last-minute forgotten item if a customer required it. She also kept a stock of liqueurs, natural juices, mineral and spring waters, on hand for those women who required her exclusive services.

Yes, she had thought of every need. She had catered to the whims of black women in ways they hadn't been accustomed to. Her attention to detail was legendary, and it paid off big-time. There were personal spas and masseuses to attend to every ache a customer might have. She had created a silken lap of luxury for these women.

Tracie couldn't have been prouder of herself. She was seriously having trouble counting the C-notes she was raking in. However, she had resolved that problem by purchasing some well-oiled money machines to count the cash. Yes, business was good, but her personal life was rapidly falling apart.

10

Out in the front of the salon the door opened and chimes tinkled. Pete Jackson, better known as "Whiskey" to the neighborhood, due to the extreme amounts of alcohol he could down without getting drunk, stepped into the foyer.

Whiskey was a tough-looking man with a knife scar running the length of his ear to his mouth. He was suave and well built and possessed dark good looks. Whiskey was also Harlem's most prominent underground arms dealer.

A good sixty percent of the guns floating between Brooklyn, Harlem, and the Bronx were supplied by Whiskey. He was good at what he did. He was discreet and dangerously well-connected. He was also a sometimes lover of Tracie Burlingame.

Whiskey was the kind of man who commanded instant attention upon entering any room. He had the kind of persona that swept over people. He left them feeling as though they should be bowing and scraping. Most of his associates did. So did many of his enemies. The dark aura that surrounded him scared most people. So when he entered Tracie's salon the day after she had buried Randi, Whiskey commanded instant attention and got it.

Upon his entrance, Tiffany, the twenty-one-year-old receptionist, had looked up immediately. She cupped her hand around the telephone receiver. "Whiskey, she's in her office." She waved him through without hesitation. He nodded his appreciation at the coffee-colored perfection of a girl.

He looked through the busy salon and spotted a sultry-looking Tracie behind the glass window, dressed in classic black. She looked stunning. Her skin was shining and flawless. Her eyes were hazel-colored lights beneath thick, brown lashes.

In the flash of a second they changed to cocoa brown, connecting with Whiskey, drawing him in like a magnet. She flashed him a smile.

He headed to her glassed-in domain while reminding himself that dancing with Tracie Burlingame was an experience in sensuality. It would serve him well to remember that, because it was easy to get caught up in the silkiness that was Tracie Burlingame.

Tracie's office played off the same black and silver color scheme as the rest of the salon. A state-of-the-art computer, Persian rugs, Monet prints, a television, VCR, DVD, and a stereo completed the office. Off to one side a mannequin was draped in cloth with stickpins in it. The mannequin stood next to a sewing machine. Sewing was just one of Tracie's hobbies.

Generally she sewed when she really needed to blow

off steam. Her real love was playing piano and the organ, hence the expensive organ sitting in the corner of her office. On those black and white keys was where Tracie poured out her real feelings.

With every stroke, key, and melody, this was where she vented her anger, cried her tears, bared her soul, and left haunting melodies hanging in the air.

Every item in the office was neat and in place, including the stacks of cash, sorted by denomination and lying on the desk.

Whiskey knew he had to get straight to the point when he went into Tracie's office. After all, business was business. Stepping through the door, he closed in on Tracie. He leaned close to whisper in her ear, "I have another shipment. I need immediate storage. I haven't heard from you."

Tracie pulled her ear away from his whispering range. "I know. I just lost my baby son and—"

"Business is business, Tracie. The guns have to disappear from the street. There's not much time."

He raised an eyebrow. "You're a big girl." He touched a lock of her black, silky, wrapped hair. "And you're a survivor," he told her. He moved closer to her and brushed her ear with the soft whisper of a kiss.

"I don't think I can," she said.

Whiskey touched a finger to her lips. "Shush. There is nothing a beautiful woman like you cannot do, Tracie."

He reached into his pocket and pulled out a black velvet box, placing it in her hand. Tracie stared at the box, not speaking. Whiskey walked over to a plush chair in her office and sat down crossing, his legs. "Go ahead. Open it."

Tracie flipped open the lid. A pair of glittering pear-shaped diamond earrings twinkled at her. She estimated they were at least five carats each. She sighed. "Whiskey, I'm afraid I can't accept these." Distressed, she ran a hand through her silken hair.

Whiskey stood up. He was not in the mood to be toyed with. Her boy's death had already kept his goods on the street longer than was safe. He would not wait one minute longer.

"Yes. Yes, you can. And you will. Those diamond earrings have a lot to measure up to." Whiskey's voice was deceptively soft. He gave her a pointed look.

Tracie took a deep breath. She finally shook her head, hitting him with a sultry, seductive smile. Sometimes dealing with Whiskey was extremely trying. His spirit was black, but it was covered in a veneer of rough charisma.

She knew she had to be careful. Whiskey was a dangerous man. Playing with him was not an option.

He reached over her. He hit the button that lowered the silver blinds over the glass window in her office, effectively shutting out the salon. He reached into his inner jacket pocket and pulled out an envelope bulging with cash. He held out the envelope to her.

Tracie accepted it.

"Tonight," Whiskey said. "The usual time."

"Tonight," she agreed.

Whiskey walked to the office door and turned the handle. His gold pinkie ring flashed rainbow hues, playing against the office lights. He looked at Tracie. "It's too bad about Randi. Maybe one day there'll be other babies. Say hello to Michael and Dre for me."

The scar on the side of his face pulsed against his skin. He swept Tracie from head to toe with his gaze. Then he was gone.

Tracie went back to her desk. She immediately began

counting the cash from the envelope. Satisfied, she stored it according to denomination into the already neatly stacked bills. Softly she caressed the bills as she sorted them.

Money was the only thing in her life that made her feel powerful. It had lifted her out of the projects. Taken her away from other people's jobs, and it had made a great many of her dreams come true. It was the only thing in life she trusted.

Because she knew that with money most things, possessions as well as people, could be bought. But most of all, what money supplied for her was power. It was the greatest symbol of power she had ever received. It had an all-knowing eye. Money was the great equalizer.

Tracie finished counting the money. She turned her thoughts to the night ahead.

II

Later that night, after the drop-off, Tracie watched from the back door of the basement as the truck pulled out into the street. In the darkness of the alley-way Tracie, too, was being watched.

They watched her watching the truck. They watched as she slowly closed the heavy door. The hard-rock gaze bore into the slender figure of Tracie Burlingame as though it might burn a hole in her very being.

After securing the basement that now held Whiskey's shipment, Tracie headed back upstairs. Just as she passed her office, the phone gave a shrill ring. She jumped in the shadowy darkness.

Startled, she frowned, hesitated, and then decided to answer the ringing phone. She walked into her office, not bothering to flick on any lights. Standing in the eerie darkness, suddenly the room had an off feel to it.

She reached for the phone and spoke quietly into the receiver. "Hello, Tracie Burlingame."

Tracie heard a muffled sound on the other end of the phone. Finally, a man's voice, which sounded distorted on the crackling wire, floated into Tracie's ear. It was weird. It sounded as though the voice were coming from under water.

She heard a low, deep, throaty laugh. Then he spoke. "Well, well, well. Tracie Burlingame. *The* Tracie Burlingame."

Tracie gripped the receiver tightly. She frowned into the darkness. A streak of moonlight streamed through the window, casting shadows in the office. "Hello. Who is this?"

There was no answer. Tracie was about to hang up the phone when the voice burst forth loudly.

"I wouldn't hang up if I was you."

Slowly Tracie returned the receiver to her ear. She looked around the room, peering into the darkness. The streak of moonlight allowed her some light. She didn't see anything out of the ordinary.

Still, a slight trace of uneasiness crept into her voice. "Who is this? What do you want?"

"That question is a little bit late, Tracie. Just a wee bit." Softly the voice began to hum, " 'Rock-a-bye, baby . . .' "

Tiny beads of sweat appeared on Tracie's forehead. She gripped the receiver even tighter.

"What?" she said.

On the other end of the line, the man's voice was singing softly and distorted, "Rock-a-bye, baby, on a rooftop; when the wind blows, the body will drop. When the bough breaks, the body will fall, and down will come Randi with no boots at all." The man laughed.

Tracie dropped into the nearest chair. Her eyes opened wide. Her body shook. Her hand quivered on the telephone receiver. The whites of her eyes glowed in the darkness.

"Stop it. My God. You killed my baby? Why? Oh, God. Who are you?" she asked, the questions tumbling over one another in her confusion. It was one thing to lose her son, but for some maniac to call her up making a nursery rhyme out of his death was crazy. She was chilled to the bone. She didn't quite know what to make of it.

The distortion of the voice grew stronger on the line. "I freed your son, Tracie. I needed to be endowed. You should be licking my feet. Let's just say I have alleviated a certain weight for him. That sounds so much more pleasant, don't you think?"

Tracie couldn't find her voice. Her shallow breathing was the only sound in the room.

"I'm a collector, Tracie. I'm a collector of very fine things. Things that are rare, you might say. I'm also fair. I beeped you just before Randi was thrown from the roof. You never bothered to answer the page. You are a very self-absorbed young lady. Maybe we could have talked . . . entered into a little bargaining. Perhaps you could have saved his life, but I guess it's just a bit late for that now."

Tracie's body shook more violently. She felt a stream of water gliding down her armpits, soaking the sides of her body. She struggled with a memory. Suddenly, she recalled her beeper going off on that day.

When she worked out, she really didn't like to be disturbed. Everyone who knew her knew that. So she hadn't really paid attention to the page.

"Oh, my God," the strangled words erupted from her lips.

"Don't bother to call God, Tracie. He's too busy for the likes of you. Oh, and don't bother to call the police, either. They couldn't follow a clue if I taped it to their foreheads with an arrow pointing them in the right direction.

"I watched them from the roof that day. Took them at least a half hour to get around to coming up on the roof to see what was going on. They were too busy counting broken bones—in the absence of blood, of course. That, I added to my collection."

Tracie took in a sharp breath. He didn't miss it.

Arrogantly and forcefully his voice shot across the wire, saying, "Oh, you didn't know."

Tracie wept. He was not moved.

"How inefficient of the police not to tell you the body had been drained of its blood. You might say that I am possessed of many skills. Embalming is only one of them. I'm self-taught, so to speak. A legend in my own right."

Tracie tried to block out what he was saying; there was a deafening roar in her ears. It grew with the magnitude of a tidal wave.

"You got that side business to think about, too," the voice continued. "Whiskey has been known to be an unpleasant man in matters of business. I do love a parallel world, Tracie. Sort of makes things tidy by my estimate."

There was a pregnant pause.

Then, "Little Caramel?" he licked his lips. There was a distorted smacking sound.

"I love the sound of that name. It fits you. Makes me

think of your soft, caramel-colored skin. You look so soft and chewy. I think this will be my special little nickname for you. A little deference between friends. What d'you say, Tracie?" Reckless, hysterical laughter shot through the wire.

"Don't talk about this to anyone, Little Caramel, or I'll mail another one of your sons to you in bits and pieces. Eeny-meeny-miny-mo. Catch a son. Which one will go?"

Tracie's heart skipped a beat. "Why? Please. Don't do this."

Her whining pissed him off, made him very angry. "Shut up, Miss Burlingame. I detest whining. I also don't like repeating myself. I already told you why I snuffed out your egg. What are you, stupid? I'm wearing the pants here, and I'm calling the shots. I'm in charge. That's something you don't want to ever forget. If you keep your mouth shut, then maybe I'll send a clue to the police."

More laughter crackled across the line. "Instead of mailing one of your sons to you . . ." He paused for a moment. "Maybe I'll send them enough clues to help you find me, Little Caramel. In the meantime you and I are going to engage in the rules of the street. A little street warfare, you might say. The first rule being, nobody likes a snitch."

Tracie's trembling increased. She managed to swallow past the lump in her throat and stutter out, "I . . . won't tell anybody."

"Oh, I know you won't, Little Caramel. You and I are the same in many ways. You're a collector of fine things, too."

The voice turned singsongy again. " 'Rock-a-bye,

baby . . .' " It dropped to a whisper. "Check, Little Caramel, so soft and chewy. Till next time." A resounding click went off in Tracie's ear. The voice was gone.

Tracie heard a sound near the steps outside her office. She listened closely, peering into the darkness. Sweat was dripping from her chin. It ran down the cleavage of her blouse. She slowly and carefully opened her desk drawer and pulled out a handgun. She reached for the clip and slipped it into the gun.

Not too far away she heard it again. Something scraped against the floor. Tracie walked out of the office. She pointed the gun in the direction the sound was coming from.

The hairs on her arms stood up. She didn't hesitate. She pulled the trigger. A shot rang out.

Immediately Tracie flipped the switch, flooding the room with light. She looked across at her target. She hoped it was the maniac on the phone and she had gotten lucky. She knew that thought was extreme, but she was desperate.

She had not gotten lucky. Scurrying across the floor was a rat. Tracie's shoulders heaved. She didn't **know if** she should be relieved or not.

Outside on the street, Whiskey flipped his cell phone shut. Mission accomplished. Everything was secure. His gold pinkie ring glistened under the streetlamps. He had one thing on his mind. She had been on his mind all afternoon. Her name was Tracie Burlingame.

Try as he might, he couldn't get her out of his system.

12

Right after Tracie Burlingame received the worst phone call of her life, a strange phenomenon bestowed itself on Harlem. Beneath the ground, underneath layers of soil, a shaking began. It was really just a light tremor to begin with. But it built itself into a full-scale quaking before anyone really understood what was happening.

It shook the borough of Harlem so thoroughly and quickly, it left reams of doubt in its wake. It was over almost before it had begun. Strangely enough, it left not a trace in its wake, save the actual experience.

The mystifying effect was only felt in Harlem. None of the other boroughs—Brooklyn, the Bronx, Staten Island, Queens—or even the rest of the borough of Manhattan was affected. Therefore, Harlem would have a hard time reporting this phenomenon.

After a while the people of Harlem began to be unsure if that was what they'd really felt. After all, this was the East Coast, and earthquakes happened out west. There had never been one recorded before in Harlem. It left not a trace, although it shook them so thoroughly it would have rocked on the Richter scale had it been recorded.

The quake became an inside joke. In some circles it became taboo even to speak about it. The truth notwithstanding, it couldn't be proven or explained.

People would be thought crazy, or just trying to reclaim a spotlight they had been slowly losing with each generation. The only attention they had these days was when politicians descended upon Harlem to kick off the African-American vote or to raise money.

Maybe it was a sign. Who knew? People were beginning to be unsure it had even happened.

But there was one man who knew what it was. He knew it was definitely a sign. He knew it meant it was time for a shift in the balance of things. That was why he was in Harlem. It was time to collect the gifts.

He stood watching the killer of Tracie Burlingame's son playing phone tag with her. Tiring of this and knowing it was a good thing that he had come when he did, he decided to move on. He would scour grounds for the night that were more fertile, far more fertile.

He needed to take care of the gifts. He would start with the minor ones and build up. Like the Legos he played with. He loved Lego because he could start out with one colored little block and build and build, until it was towering far above the ground.

Tracie Burlingame was worth much more than the talents of her sons. Inside her, unknowingly, she carried the pattern of many of the gifts to come in

Harlem—and one very powerful gift that must be prevented at all costs.

When the time came, he would suck the gifts right out of her being. Yes. He knew Miss Burlingame was a spiritual patchwork quilt. He also knew that she waxed prophetic.

This fool, his comrade, wanted to play with her and toy with her. He was playing with her flesh. Me would take down her spirit. He would not play with her. When the time came, he would destroy her.

What she carried in her being was valuable beyond words. It could alter the course of history. What she carried was also dangerous, because it reflected out to people with the vision, such as the Louisianan seeress.

But just as he had told the seeress, she would see more than that before it was all over. Then she would die. That he hadn't told her.

Well, he knew for a fact that Tracie Burlingame would only be allowed to hold on to what she had for so long. After all, Tracie was nothing more than the host, so to speak. Satisfied with the greatness and wisdom that had been granted him, he walked the streets of Harlem.

He walked with his tall frame hunched over. His huge hands were stuffed in his pockets. His bald brown globe of a head gleamed under the streetlights as he ducked into the shadows to avoid the glare beaming from the lights.

He decided he would begin with a small gift. He headed over to 125th Street. The woman who owned this bookstore was a disseminator of information. He watched the woman as she began the process of closing down the dusty old store.

As he watched, he noted the certificates and little gold plaques hung on the walls, which reflected her achievements and those of others. Her little shop was chock-full of books. She had black history books. There were books on theology and the seminary, African-American books, memoirs, biographies, and autobiographies as well.

Even the ceilings of her store depicted the gifted and famous. Posters hung with pride from the sagging ceiling. There wasn't an inch of space that didn't reflect black pride.

He smiled ruefully to himself. All the books crammed onto the shelves of the dinky, dusty little shop reflected pieces of him in one way or another. That was the puzzle he could not allow some smart-alecky know-it-all to try to figure out. That was one of the reasons he needed to collect the gifts.

He watched the old woman with the silky gray hair, every strand laid in place. No doubt she was one of Miss Burlingame's elite clientele. Her carriage was erect. She carried herself proudly, tall, with a hint of arrogance.

Her air was like that of the great professors who, once they had taught their students the astuteness and wisdom of how to arrange the words of the English language to create vision, preened at their own images. They preened at the continuity of vision they had pumped out.

Oh, but he knew. This woman had taken up space here in the hopes that, between the pages of the knowledge she sold to the public, there would be one who would string together the truth about him. Well, she would not see it in her lifetime. It was time for her to join the others. They must all be gathered together.

He walked into the shop just as Ms. Virginia, as she was known through out the borough, had closed out the register. He stood with his brown, bald head gleaming under the single bulb she had left on while closing the shop.

He found the light irritating, but it was necessary for now. Later he would crawl and hunker down into his little room of darkness, where all was right with the world . . . where he could recuperate from the light.

Ms. Virginia looked up at his entrance. "I was just closing, young man."

She was a nice woman who always wanted to help someone in need. Sometimes just as she was ready to close her doors, someone would run through needing that last-minute item. Students looking for research, or others who just couldn't wait till the next day. She was always accommodating. She loved books. She could talk about them for hours, even when she was about to close.

The man didn't respond.

"Well," she said, "if you really need something, just go ahead; I'll spare you the time." She smiled engagingly at the man.

He didn't move. So she asked, "What's your name?"

"Me," he said.

She looked up from marking the cash-out envelope. "Young man, I meant your given name." She knew about all the strange names the kids gave themselves these days. She personally thought it was ridiculous. Why didn't anyone like to use his or her Christian name these days?

"I know what you meant," he said. The hairs on the back of her neck prickled. Something in his tone was downright disturbing. She peered through her bifocals at him. Suddenly his being erupted in raucous laughter, but his mouth never opened. A symphony of voices swelled up from within him. But his lips didn't move.

He decided he did not want to kill this old woman in a way that would bring them running just yet. But die she would. He already had a place picked out for her. Besides, this shop needed to be closed down. Her death would provide that. He saw the fear well up in her eyes, bulging behind the bifocals.

She looked out onto the street. Ms. Virginia was shocked that she didn't see anyone. This was a 125th Street in Harlem. There were always people on the street when she closed her shop, but not on this night. He wasn't moved by her search. He knew he had the area locked down.

She thought about the secret button that had been installed in case she was in trouble. All she had to do was hit it. The police would be immediately summoned. As she discreetly tried to reach for the button, she discovered that her hand was struck with a paralysis, and she could not move it, try as she might.

The man stood stock-still, watching her. His face was a mask devoid of any expression. His features molded together, forming a sort of blandness. He wanted to get this over with. He was still standing under the single lightbulb. He could feel the rays beaming down on him. Beads of sweat popped out on his head and face. He hated the light.

Slowly as she watched him, she felt the tentacles of his being absorbing her. It was a weird feeling, like being sucked in by a sponge. She began to understand that she was dealing with something sinister, dark, not of normal understanding.

The man was giving her the creeps. The shock of this information rooted her to the spot. And while her mind screamed in protest, not a single word or scream left her lips.

The man watched her steadily. He could actually be merciful at times. There were times when he handled things in what he called his gentle way. He liked this woman. He liked her strength and her dignity despite the circumstances.

She would be a welcome addition. Still, that didn't change anything. He would have no choice but to swallow her gift; he would just do it mildly. He would spare her the vengeance that he sometimes struck with.

He slipped off his army jacket and showed her his biceps. The faces immediately began to speak to her. They rose up under his skin, their features live and animated. Some of them travailed in great agony. All of them were well trained and under his command for when he needed to use their voices.

And they spoke to her about things past and present, things she could identify with. Spoke to her about the mysteries in her books, all of which would be recorded in her mind, then erased as information not needed.

The man opened his mouth, and Ms. Virginia beheld an unimaginable sight. The words stored on the many pages in all the different books floated off the pages and into the mouth of the man who stood before her. He swallowed the words whole.

Unable to fathom or hold up under such an unholy sight, Ms. Virginia felt a small explosion in her chest, like a tiny fire being ignited. Then she fell to the floor.

The man checked her pulse. There was none. Ms. Virginia had died on the spot of massive heart failure.

Me opened her mouth. He put his mouth to hers, sucking out her spirit, along with her gift. He absorbed them inside himself, and Ms. Virginia took her place in his biceps along with the others who had gone before her.

Her gift tasted sweet. It was the gift of intelligence.

13

Still shaken by her spooky telephone conversation, Tracie sat between Michael and Dre on the plush sofa in the living room of her brownstone. The entire room was done in white and silver. The room was sleek with angles. The entire brownstone was prewar, boasting high ceilings and long windows.

Tracie looked at the old-fashioned hourglass sitting on top of the fireplace mantel. The sand in the hourglass was at the bottom. Tracie tried to empty her mind of all thought, but she was having difficulty achieving this.

She took Michael's hand in hers. She pressed it to her lips, kissing the blue and gold class ring. Dre and Michael were very precious to her. This fact had been rammed home with total clarity since the loss of Randi.

"Hey, Rebound," she said to Michael. "You were on the court today, right?"

"Yeah, Mom. You know I was." As good as Michael was, he was somewhat shy, and sometimes it embarrassed him the way people acted over his basketball skills. He was often compared to Earl "the Goat" Manigault because of his extraordinary leaping skills on the court.

For him it was just something he did. He loved the sport. It was second nature for him, as it had been for his brother Randi. But for Harlem he was an Earl "the Goat" reincarnation. The community loved its own stars.

Even his Mom flipped out over his skills at times, the same as she had with Randi. He sometimes played on the same court the Goat used to play on, and the crowds came in great numbers at the sound of his name.

It saddened him that he would never be able to play with his brother anymore. He and Randi used to put on quite a show for the neighborhood over on the 135th Street courts. The crowd went wild because they were brothers.

Afterward they would always go to Sylvia's Restaurant to eat barbecue ribs, macaroni and cheese, and collard greens, to replenish their energy.

Tracie turned to look at him. "Good. Never neglect being on the court. Because you, baby, are going to be the greatest rebounder basketball has seen for a long time. But they already know it," Tracie said with pride lilting in her voice.

She turned to Dre, careful to keep the fear that was creeping up and down her spine out of her voice. She said casually, "Dre, I think you should still leave for L.A. You've got your ticket. I don't want this to—"

"I ain't going right now, Tracie. I ain't leaving you. That's all there is to it."

Michael jumped into the conversation. "Dre's right. Now isn't the time for anybody to be going anywhere."

Tracie hesitated before speaking, keeping her tone cool and nonchalant. "Actually, I think it's the perfect time. Michael, you can go to that basketball training camp we were talking about. Dre can go to L.A., where he can shoot sunsets and mountains. There aren't any mountains in Harlem. Rashod. Rashod needs to go somewhere, too . . . " her voice trailed off.

A soft click invaded the silence. Tracie turned toward the sound to see that the red dot was lit on Dre's camcorder. The boy videotaped and recorded everything. He was a fanatic.

Tracie was annoyed, but she decided now was not the time. One day he was going to videotape something that shouldn't be taped. He needed to learn some discretion. She was proud of him, but she didn't like the idea of him always recording things at random in the house.

Dre looked at Tracie. He stood up, looking down at her from his great height. He was mad as hell. He knew what she was trying to do. It wasn't going to work. Things were not normal. He wasn't going for her playing hide-and-seek, pretending, that they were.

Randi was dead. His death was not an accident. It was murder. As much as he couldn't stand that toy detective Monica, he had to admit she had some real points. Somebody was throwing shade. Something was wrong. Who would want to murder his baby brother? So, in his opinion no one needed to go anywhere until they knew what the hell was going on.

Determinedly he said, "Ain't nobody leaving you right now, Tracie, so forget it."

Tracie knew he was angry, because that was the only time he called her by her first name.

"I mean it," he said. He turned his focus on Michael. "Michael, get in touch with Rashod. Tell his dumb ass I wanna see him."

Dre stormed across the room, intent on leaving, when Tracie jumped up from the sofa.

In a pained whisper she said, "Expired. They . . . told me Randi expired. How the hell does one do that, damn it? He's not a canned good. I mean, he wasn't . . ." Tracie looked off to a faraway place that only she could see.

The vision insinuated itself right in her face, the memory so painful it cut off her breath. It wouldn't budge. There was no avoiding it. She saw herself when she was younger. She leaned over a man's broken body. Her eyes roamed the man's body, stopping when they reached his feet.

There were no shoes on his feet. And there was no blood on the ground. But there he lay, broken and dead. A scream erupted from her throat, shattering the memory.

The pain of Randi's loss swelled in her heart. Tracie's eyes swam with unshed tears. "When a woman has a baby, it's her job to protect him. Do you know what I'm saying?" Michael and Dre exchanged looks.

Suddenly she saw Rashod sweeping a low bow in

front of her and saying, "I also pay my respects to the Destroyer."

She blinked away the image, struggling to bring herself back into focus. Dre and Michael exchanged confused looks this time.

"Ma," Dre said.

"Ma," Michael parroted him.

Tracie didn't acknowledge them. Instead she began to sing a lullaby " 'Rock-a-bye, baby, on a treetop; when the wind blows, the cradle will rock. When the bough breaks, the cradle will fall . . .' "

Dre ran over to her. He gripped her by her shaking shoulders. "Stop it."

Tracie hiccupped. "Randi . . . rock-a-bye, baby . . . Randi . . . rock-a-bye, baby," she repeated over and over again.

She was like a scratched record that was stuck in a groove. In a flash she pulled out of Dre's grip and grabbed the poker from the fireplace, smashing the glass table sitting in front of the sofa. She sent glass raining clear across the room.

" 'Rock-a-bye, baby . . . rock-a-bye, baby,' " she sang as she smashed the glass to smithereens, hitting the pieces over and over again with the poker.

Dre and Michael were stunned. They had never before seen their stylish, classy, sophisticated mother out of control. Her eyes looked wild; her hair was disheveled— that definitely never happened—and makeup streamed down her tear-stained face.

They witnessed her breakdown with pain in their hearts. It was not a pretty sight to behold. They both wished they had not been present to witness such private grief. Dre was about to stop her again, but Michael held him back.

He shook his head. He knew it was better to let her vent than to stop her. It couldn't do anybody any good just letting her rage build up inside. Better she got rid of it. Although the sound of her calling Randi's name in connection with the song she had always sung to them when they were babies and little kids was not only eerie but was causing an internal meltdown inside him.

Later, after she was settled down, he would cruise the village to get his nerves under control. He would slip into his second life just as a ballerina slipped into her slippers before a performance.

Tracie continued to sing and bang on the smashed glass with the poker.

In his tiny, dark room saturated with the spirit and gifts of Ms. Virginia and the others, Me's body shook with the raucous voices, which were acting out Tracie's rage.

The patchwork quilt floated before his eyes, grabbing him, trying to smother him. He had to fight his way out. He struggled out of the army jacket, to free his biceps. He needed the wisdom of the faces.

It was the newest of the lot, the spirit of Ms. Virginia, that came to his rescue and spoke. Her eyes were keen behind the bifocals bulging from his biceps. "Don't be afraid, Me. Soon she will be here, and you won't have to be frightened anymore. There, there," she soothed.

Me calmed down a bit. He had known she would be a good addition, an old woman with a wise head. His breathing was shallow, but he began to calm as he curled up into a tight ball in the small, dark closet space in his room.

* * *

Anita, who was stretched out on her sofa and sipping from a cup of Celestial Seasonings lemon tea, looked out her window to see a patchwork quilt floating in the wind. One of the black patches detached itself and floated free of the others.

The black patch was a seeker in a state of discovery. Seek, and it would find. It was being hunted. The hunter was right behind it. Anita closed her eyes. She moaned at the sight of it. She knew, if the hunter caught up with the one who was represented by the black patch, that he would be the next one to die.

Tracie Burlingame, spent from her rampage, sat in the corner of the living room, weeping, with her sons huddled close beside her.

14

Later that night, after they had finally managed to get Tracie settled down in bed, Dre and Michael went off on their separate ways. Before Dre went in his room, he said, "Michael, call Rashod and tell him to meet me at The Lenox Avenue Lounge in an hour. That fool is gonna have to get in line; I'm sick of him."

"Sure thing. But you know what, Dre? Don't be too hard on him. This is a lot on him, too. You know how sensitive Rashod is."

Dre snorted. "Yeah, well, he's got a funny way of showing it, son."

"People are different. But still he's our brother, so you've got to respect his boundaries," Michael said.

"Aw, I'm gonna give him some boundaries, all right, and if he crosses any of them, I'm gonna smack him around like I'm the new Ali."

"Come on, Dre, hitting people ain't ever solved a thing."

"Maybe not, but it sure as hell will make me feel a lot better." Dre took off down the hallway. He'd call Souljah Boy and tell him he'd meet him after he squared things away with Rashod.

Michael shook his head at the futility of it all. Rashod was the black sheep of the family, self-designated. There was always some sort of feud brewing about him.

Michael actually got sick of it sometimes. But Tracie and Dre wouldn't leave him alone. Whenever he stuck his head out of the hole for a minute, they were on top of him, starting the crap all over again. Michael knew that no matter how many recriminations they threw at Rashod, it didn't matter. A man was what he was.

Only that man could change it.

Sighing, he went to his room. He called Rashod with the information, then set out for his own charted territory. He dug down in the bottom of his drawer, removed the false bottom, and selected several hot, black pieces of leather-and-chain clothing. He threw them in his duffel bag and headed off for Chelsea.

Normally, he would go on down to the village, but he had changed his mind. He was in the mood for something new. He would cruise Eighth Avenue and see what he could get into.

He jumped on the C train, got off at Fourteenth Street, and headed down Eighth Avenue. The moment he hit Eighth, he was in his stride. He hadn't gone two blocks before he was hit on. He found himself sitting at a corner table in the bar with a gorgeous light-skinned woman, with the clearest brown eyes and longest natural eyelashes he had ever seen.

She was a bodybuilder, toned and well muscled. After one drink they both knew they had scored for the night. The only thing left was where things were going to take place.

The light-skinned, brown-eyed wonder knew just the spot, so that worked for Michael just fine. The instant he was suited up in the black leather and chains, two things happened. The first was a delicious thrill of anticipation that coursed its way through his body, leaving a trail of sweet sensations.

The second was dark, black despair. What was he doing? He felt as though he were entering the dungeons of hell.

Yet he couldn't stop himself. He was drawn to this world like a fish to water. Maybe that was why he needed the punishment. He was dancing with darkness. He needed to feel the pain.

An unrecognizable voice rose up and cried out of Michael's mouth as the first lash landed across his flesh. "Oh, yes." Then Michael was tunneling—spiraling, actually—down into a deep, dark well.

Randi was dead, and the well was there. It was a huge, gaping black hole waiting to swallow him. It was waiting for them, his family. It was waiting for all of them, the offspring of Tracie Burlingame.

There was a strange twist inside Michael, and something happened that certainly had never happened before.

Michael awoke as though from a slumber. He hovered outside his body in the black leather and chains, and he watched the light-skinned, brown-eyed wonder salivating at the next strike.

Before he knew what was happening, he heard the

following words fly out of his mouth: "Lord, forgive me, for I know not what I do." He backed away, stunned, into a corner of the room. He watched his own body sag at the weight of the pain on the bed.

The light-skinned, brown-eyed wonder was startled at the words, and the whip literally flew out of her hand at the sound of them. The chains slid from Michael's shoulders and from around his neck, onto the bed.

Red, bloody teardrops began to fall from the ceiling, landing on top of Michael's head and dripping down the sides of his face. That was all the brown-eyed wonder needed. She backed out of the room in stunned fear, leaving the door open behind her.

The spot where Michael was huddled in the corner, watching, shook. Before he knew it, he was back in the aching body on the bed. "Lord!" he called out again. "Lord, forgive me, for I know not what I do." He collapsed weeping onto the bed. A wind swept through the room. The door closed.

Michael looked at the door. Down on the floor he noticed a black ashlike substance being sucked underneath the door. Silver crystals sealed the opening.

A feeling of peace permeated the room. Michael lay down on the bed, exhausted. He fell asleep, but not before he noticed one lone, red teardrop on the back of his hand.

In her bed, Tracie Burlingame tossed restlessly from side to side. Unseen hands were grabbing at her, pulling at her. She was fighting them, but she couldn't get away. In front of her was a big, black, gaping hole trying to suck her in.

She fought against the currents that pulled her body toward the hole at warp speed. Up in front of her were her sons, and the current was sucking them toward the hole, too. Randi was dead, and she couldn't see him. She sobbed out loud, but she never awoke.

15

Anita was in a deep, unconscious state of mind. Sometimes when she entered these states, there were others who would visit and talk to her. Right now she was alone. "Master, where are you?" she cried out, but there was no answer.

Sometimes the old wise one would help her out, but he was not to be found in this realm. All she could hear was the echoing of the atmosphere.

There was the patchwork quilt again, floating through the air. The quilt was her haunting. She couldn't seem to distance herself or back away from it, as she sometimes did when she received unpleasant sights and revelations. The manifestation of the quilt would not be deterred.

As she watched, one of the black patches transformed to a silky white. It was the purest white she had ever seen. It quivered in the breeze.

Anita was being pulled down deeper into the realm. She had never been as deep as this before. She struggled but couldn't regain consciousness. Her gift allowed her the knowledge of knowing when she was in an alternate state of mind, and usually she could bring herself out.

However, this time she couldn't.

As she descended, she saw babies. "Oh, my God," she said. Dear God, there were a lot of them. So many little black babies. A force was snatching them and then wrapping them, bundling them up. Her eyes opened wide in amazement. The babies were being wrapped in pure, silky white swaddling. Anita shivered.

She entered the second realm. Here, there were women, crying out from their given tasks. Their wombs opened up, bursting forth with more babies, who were immediately snatched, wrapped, and bundled in the pure, silky white swaddling.

She entered the third level. Suddenly a white arrow shot through the air, descending with the speed of light. Where was it going? Anita didn't dare blink. She watched as it pierced the realms and landed in the soil that was Harlem. Anita gasped.

She thought of the patchwork quilt that was Tracie Burlingame. She thought of the huge bald-headed man, and as she did, she received a vision. Books upon books upon books floated past her. The cover art and the pictures were intact; however, all the books had no words in them. The pages were all blank . . . save one.

Tracie Burlingame could no longer fight the currents, and she was whisked down into the black, gaping hole. Her screams went unheard as she fell through the realms.

As she descended, she saw babies. "Oh, my God," she repeated exactly the same words as Anita. Dear God, there were a lot of them. So many little black babies. A force was snatching them and then wrapping them, bundling them up. Her eyes opened wide in amazement. The babies were being wrapped in pure, silky white swaddling. Tracie gasped.

She entered the second realm. Here, there were women, crying out from their given tasks. Their wombs opened up, bursting forth with more babies, who were immediately snatched, wrapped, and bundled in the pure, silky white swaddling.

Then she saw someone she recognized. "Oh, no. No!" What was happening to her? Tracie screamed, a hollow sound that bounced off the atmosphere.

A woman was looking at her. When Tracie peered across the atmosphere, tiny electrical shocks seized her body.

The image that had appeared before her was her own. The woman spread her arms, opened her legs, and so many little black babies dropped from between her legs. They were falling into the atmosphere and disappearing. She couldn't see where they were going. Tracie howled. She screamed until her throat was raw. It was to no avail.

She entered the third level. Suddenly a white arrow shot through the air, descending with the speed of light. Where was it going? Tracie didn't dare blink. She watched as it pierced the realms and landed in the soil that was Harlem. Tracie gasped.

Then she saw a patchwork quilt quivering in the

wind. She was treated to a sight of a huge bald-headed man. The biceps on the man were stunning. As soon as she saw him, she was treated to a vision.

Books upon books upon books floated past her. The cover art and the pictures were intact. However, all the books had no words in them. The pages were all blank . . . save one.

Tracie Burlingame and Anita Lily Mae Young were entwined in identical visions. And this was only the beginning.

16

Dre watched Rashod enter The Lenox Lounge from a back table. It was too bad they weren't here to enjoy some of the jazz the lounge was famous for. Dre in particular had a real ear for jazz. Rashod, on the other hand, didn't know a thing about jazz; all he knew was hardcore hip-hop. He didn't listen to the soft stuff.

One way or the other, it was a moot point, because the brothers were here in direct opposition to each other, so neither of them would notice anything other than their antagonism.

Spotting Dre, Rashod made his way over and took a seat. The two young men sized each other up without speaking.

Finally, Rashod said, "So, what do you want?"

"I want you to show some respect to my mother," Dre replied nastily.

Rashod rose from his seat. "You know what? I don't need this."

In a flash, Dre covered the distance between them and slammed Rashod back in his seat. Rashod hit the chair with a dull thud, the air knocked out of him. "I'm not playing with you, Rashod. This is a family meeting, minus the rest of the family."

Rashod jerked out of Dre's grasp, but he didn't move from the seat.

Satisfied, Dre took his seat again while the bartender eyed them nervously, hoping there wasn't going to be trouble.

Rashod turned his seat around so he could watch the bar. He took out his little mini sketch pad and a small piece of charcoal that he used for tight situations like this one. He intended to trace the bar and its occupants. His fingers had nimbly begun to move across the pad.

Dre looked at him. He was going to say something and then chose not to. He really didn't care if Rashod sketched, as long as Rashod kept his behind plastered to that chair. In a softer voice Dre said, "Rashod, Tracie's hurting over Randi. She has three sons left. You're one of them. You need to knock off the bull."

Rashod's fingers had mysteriously taken on a life of their own, and they now traveled across the pad with the speed of light. Rashod had absolutely no control over them. It was strange. He had never quite sketched with this depth before. He didn't interfere, because he couldn't.

Instead, he decided that as long as he was a prisoner in this chair, he might as well converse with Dre. He loved his brother, although Dre was a pain in the ass at times. And in Rashod's opinion, Dre had no sight at all when it came to Tracie. "Tracie is what she is, man."

"What she is, is your mother, son." Dre lapsed into the code of speech of the New York City streets. Rashod didn't care. He refused to be sucked in by some meaningless, street maternal code meant for bonding, like two animals in a mating dance.

"What she is, is a destroyer. She destroys everything she touches. That's why Randi's dead. She should never have touched him."

Dre sighed. There was just no reality when it came to Tracie and Rashod. Sometimes he wished he had been born into another family, one without the drama.

"Look, Rashod, all I'm saying is, Tracie is worried about all of us now that Randi's gone. You're making it harder. She's your moms. You could at least stop by the house to check her out. Or not be so damned cold when she talks to you."

Rashod's fingers still moved across the pad. He looked at it and frowned, still unable to stop the flight of the charcoal. "Dre, look. The chemistry just ain't right with me and Tracie. You know that. Why the hell you think I hit my pipe? So I can forget about her. Besides, she doesn't care about us; all she cares about is money."

"That ain't truth, man, and you know it."

"What I know is that you're blind when it comes to Tracie Burlingame, Dre, and one day it could cost you." Rashod looked down at the completed sketch. His fingers had ceased moving of their own accord.

Generally, he traced whatever was in his line of vision at the time. He had set out to trace the bar, along with its occupants. He had also intended to trace Dre's crazy face. However, that was not what he had produced. In fact, he wasn't quite sure what he had produced, but it was definitely not what had been in his line of vision.

Seeing the strange look on Rashod's face, Dre leaned over the table to look at the sketch. Rashod was a talented artist, he knew. He had a way of capturing things in a certain light.

What Dre saw on the pad made his blood run cold. A man was chained to a bed, outfitted in what one would take to be black leather and chains. His face was a picture of raw agony, his head was thrown back, his mouth was opened, and a spirit rose up, hovering just above him.

Around his neck and shoulders were chains. Drops of rain, descended from the ceiling of the room, pelting the man. The body of the man looked as though it was surrounded and caught up in a haze.

The man in the picture bore an eerie resemblance to their brother Michael Burlingame.

17

The following morning Tracie was dressed in her workout clothes, poised and back in control. She had shaken off her dream the way a construction worker shakes the dust from his clothes.

Not being able to handle what she'd seen, her consciousness had simply discarded the information. Tracie had absolutely no recollection of the dream.

The doorbell rang. Tracie opened the door to see Monica and Lonzo standing on her porch.

She looked beyond them to see that an early morning jogger was out. Her next-door neighbor was walking her little Pekingese dog. Other than that, the neighborhood was just waking up, with the exception of the two wide-awake detectives who were standing before her.

Tracie brought her attention back to the two of them. She stared at Lonzo. "I don't believe I caught your name the last time we met, Detective," she said to Lonzo. "Of course, I know yours," she told Monica.

Lonzo smiled seductively at Tracie while drinking in every inch of her. "I'm Detective Alonzo Morgan. Most people call me Lonzo," he said. He extended his hand. Tracie didn't bother to shake it. After a moment of hanging his hand in the air, he felt foolish and pulled it back with a sheepish grin.

"What do you want?" Tracie hadn't moved out of the doorway, nor did she invite them in.

"We need to talk to you again, and we'd like to search Randi's room," Monica told her.

"Why?"

Lonzo jumped in. "There have been some new developments, and we need you to identify something for us." He hoisted the duffel bag on his shoulder.

Tracie hesitated, then decided to let them in. They looked at the broken shards of glass from the table all over the floor, then back at each other. Finally, they looked at Tracie.

Tracie, observing their reactions to the broken glass, said, "I dropped my coffee cup."

Monica shook her head. "Hmmm," was all she said.

Monica took in every detail of the room, including the video recorder with its red light on, recording every move. She was tempted to ask Tracie to turn it off—it made her uncomfortable—but then again, they had nothing to hide, so she said nothing.

Lonzo got right to the point with Tracie. "We've got a note that we think is connected to your son's death."

A chill found its way up Tracie's spine.

"It was an accident. Why would someone send a note? Somebody's probably playing games. Randi was known for sitting on rooftops and meditating. It's part of what made him a great ball player."

Monica was not going to play the game again with Tracie. She was growing tired of Ms. Denial. "The note said 'atonement.' What would Randi need to atone for?"

Tracie stalked to the door. She had no tolerance for this. She couldn't talk to them. These fools were going to get another one of her sons killed. "I've heard enough. I want you out. I don't have time for this."

Lonzo opened the duffel bag. He removed the plastic-covered Karl Kani boot. "Do you recognize this, Miss Burlingame?"

He held the boot up in front of Tracie's face. She was unable to hide her shock. She was visibly shaken.

"The killer had it delivered to us, along with the note," Monica said. "They enjoy these little games. Is it Randi's?"

Tracie couldn't find her voice, so she nodded.

"He only sent one boot. This isn't a game, Tracie. Nor was Randi's death an accident. Someone murdered your son," Monica said. She watched Tracie steadily.

"The medical examiner said there was stark terror in Randi's eyes, Tracie. His windpipe was clogged with sunflower seeds. The bastard most likely asphyxiated him, then drained the blood from his body, for God's sake, before flinging him from the roof." Monica paused, out of breath because she was so upset. She was trained to stay in control, but between the horrific nature of this young boy's murder and his mother's aloof, supreme manner, she was definitely losing her cool.

"I don't suppose you think Randi did that to himself. Do you?" It was all she could do to keep from screaming at Tracie Burlingame. Monica was completely exasperated with her.

"Somebody wanted him to atone for something. Any idea what that might be?"

Tracie didn't answer. Monica advanced on her slowly.

"He drained the blood from your son's body, Tracie," Monica stated once again for effect.

Normally she would have withheld this type of information from a grieving parent, but Tracie Burlingame was not being on the ups with her, and she sensed it.

In fact, Tracie was making her sick to her stomach, so there would be no mercy here. She wanted answers.

Still, there was no answer forthcoming from Tracie.

Monica reached into her pocket and pulled out the plastic bag holding two pieces of a silver broken heart. "Do you recognize this?" she asked.

"No," Tracie said.

"Damn it, Tracie, do you know what we might be dealing with here?"

Tracie's expression was remote. It was very clear there would be no answers coming from her.

"Okay," Monica said with finality.

If Tracie Burlingame wanted to be the ice princess, so let it be. She knew there would be a definite price to pay for her iciness.

18

In her office, Alexandra was on the phone with the mayor of New York. She told him, "I think we might have a serial killer on the loose in Harlem. Seems he possesses the traits of a modern-day vampire.

"He likes to withdraw blood from his victims before tossing them over the roof. There's only been one victim so far, but my gut is telling me there's going to be another one." Alexandra stood up. She paced her office with the phone in her hand.

"Rarely do killers kill with this type of shock effect and then just back away. I just wish I knew when and where he's going to strike next. We don't know why he killed Randi Burlingame, so it's difficult to anticipate his next move.

"All the signs are there, as far as I'm concerned, that he will make another move, though. It fits the profile of all the classics. He's grandstanding and collecting little trophies for himself in the process."

Alexandra ran a hand through her gold curls. She allowed herself a deeply disturbed sigh that filtered over the line and into the mayor's ear.

"Listen, Alexandra, I appreciate your keeping me up on things. But you must understand that Harlem is a community that is recognized around the world. It is not like the rest of New York. That means no serial killers or vampires allowed.

"Do you know that all kinds of implications could come of something like this? I will not tolerate it. Randi Burlingame was a legend in Harlem. My phone has been ringing all day. Now, there are lots of deaths that take place in Harlem that I never hear about, but this is not one of them.

"I want you to put a stop to this. There's only been one murder, and I don't want to hear anything about serial killers and vampires. Understood?"

Alexandra began to nod, remembered to whom she was speaking, and then answered, "Yes, sir, I understand."

"Good. I also don't want to see those words in the newspaper, hear those words over the radio, or glimpse those words being spoken by a television newscaster. Get me the murderer straightaway. He'll never see the light of day again, and then we will close this case. Good day, Alexandra." The line disconnected in her ear.

"Damn," she swore while replacing the receiver in the hook.

Before she could recuperate from her call with the mayor, her assistant, Maya, stuck her head in the door.

"I just thought you'd like to know that Ms. Virginia was found dead in her shop this morning."

Maya knew that Alexandra was paranoid about Harlem and wanted to know every little tidbit of information, even if it didn't relate to anything in particular. She just wanted to be up on things. Maya was competent as well as nosy, so generally she had no trouble accommodating what she considered Alexandra's fetish.

Alexandra frowned in puzzlement, wondering what Maya was talking about.

"Ms. Virginia, the old woman who owned Visionaries, the bookstore over on 125th Street," Maya said.

"Oh, yeah," Alexandra tuned in. "She was a very sweet lady. What happened to her?"

"Looks like she died of a heart attack," Maya hesitated. "But there was one strange thing."

Alexandra's eyes turned to slits. She glared at Maya. "I don't want to hear any strange things. She died of a heart attack; that's a very natural way to go."

"Yeah, I know, but that's not really it. Well . . . I don't know how to say this . . ."

"Just say it," Alexandra spat the words at her. If there was one thing she hated, it was procrastination, and Maya well knew that. It was a waste of valuable time. What the hell was wrong with her?

"It was the books in her store."

"What about the books, Maya?"

"Well, all the books in the store are missing the words."

Alexandra began to laugh; she couldn't help herself.

"Is this a joke? There's never been a book printed without words in it, Maya. That's what makes up the books—the words, get it?"

"Yeah. That's why it's strange. The covers of the books are all there, only the words are missing on the pages of every book in the store. Every page, inside every book, is blank. There are no words on the pages," Maya enunciated every word for emphasis.

Alexandra, for once in her life, was speechless. Maya took full advantage of this. She actually enjoyed it, even though she was unhappy about the circumstances. Ms. Virginia would be missed. She was like the heart of Harlem.

"I bought a book from her just yesterday morning, Alexandra. My book has all the words in it."

Maya took a last look at the shocked disbelief on Alexandra's face and backed out of the office, closing the door behind her.

For the second time that morning, Alexandra ran a hand through her blond curls. How the hell could the words be missing on every page of every book, in a bookstore that sold books for a living?

That was impossible.

19

The unmarked car flew over the roadway of the Hudson River Parkway. Monica's hands gripped the steering wheel. Her knuckles were turning a dull pink.

Lonzo looked at her face, which looked as though it were carved out of stone, and decided he might as well kick off the tantrum that was brewing. No sense in wasting time.

"What the hell was that all about at Tracie Burlingame's house?"

"What?" Monica asked through clenched teeth.

"Don't play me, Monica. I ain't seen you playing hardball with a dead boy's mother before."

The car raced over a ramp, and Monica's eyes flashed dangerously.

"That's because I haven't seen that many dead boys asphyxiated, with their throats stuffed with sunflower

seeds, and the blood drained from their bodies before."
She pushed the gas pedal to the floor.

"Gunshot wounds and stabbings, yeah. But somebody tossed that boy like a bag of potatoes over the
roof. After draining his blood, like they were collecting
some kind of sadistic souvenir. The blood wasn't found
at the scene, and it damn sure wasn't in the body. So
what the hell is he doing with it?"

She blew the hair out of her eyes.

"Damn, Lonzo. I mean, he really stuffed his windpipe with sunflower seeds. What the hell is that all
about? Even the ME couldn't come up with a rational
explanation for that one, and he has the whole damn
medical and scientific community at his disposal. So
why the hell did he do that?"

Lonzo glanced sideways at her. "How do we know
it's a he?"

Monica looked at him like he was crazy. "What the
hell? Didn't you read the criminal profile report?"

Lonzo snorted. "Textbook theories. Could be anybody on the street at this point."

"Well, 'anybody' also had the balls to remove his
boots first."

"Yeah," Lonzo replied.

"A damn street psychopath. Come on, man, you know
it's not a woman. No woman could do that kind of
damage to a strong, healthy male without shooting him
first. Look, psychopaths and profiles aside, this is probably a street killing," she speculated.

"Why the hell would he take his shoes?"

"They're jacking and killing each other for their
damn sneakers, for goodness' sake. Whoever did this
probably thought he was cute, adding a bit of a serial

twist to it. Most likely he's a very clever, MTV-bred, Michael Jordan sneaker-wearing baby. All the signs are there. And you would notice them if you'd stop day-dreaming about what's under Tracie Burlingame's skirt."

Monica wheeled the car off the ramp. It flew under an overpass, hitting a couple of speed bumps. The car leveled off on a side street. Lonzo held tight to the door frame as he slammed against it, feeling Monica's fury at the wheel.

Pissed off, he said, "You want me to daydream about what's under your skirt instead?"

He hated working with women cops. Why the hell hadn't they given him a man for a partner? He didn't need this grief from this wannabe female.

At his words, the car jerked to a halt. Monica threw it in park. In one swift motion she backhanded Lonzo in the mouth and jumped from the vehicle. She had to-tally lost control. A second later she couldn't believe she had hit him, but it was too late.

To her surprise, Lonzo jumped out of the car after her. Instead of being angry, he was actually contrite. "I'm sorry, Monie. Maybe I deserved that."

She pushed him. He stumbled backward. "You de-serve a lot more than that, Lonzo. Tracie Burlingame is a liar. Point-blank. She's holding back—I feel it. Who-ever killed her son is a monster." She grabbed him by his jacket and shook him. "Do you get it?"

"Yeah."

"A monster. Monsters have to be taken down or they grow into bigger monsters. I'm not going to let the killer get away, Lonzo. That boy was only sixteen years old. He was in the prime of his life."

Lonzo eyed her, shrewdly tapping into a place that she

would rather not have gone. "This isn't about your father's murder, Monica. And finding all the murderers in Harlem won't make up for not finding his."

Monica's father was a slain police officer, killed on the streets—case never officially closed, murderer never found.

Monica took a step back as though he had slapped her. She withdrew. "Just do your job, Lonzo. Do your job. Because daydreaming can get you killed. And if you blow this case, Alexandra Kennedy will have one of your balls for lunch and the other one for dinner. My girl ain't about to get played out of lunch with the mayor of New York. You'd do best to keep that in mind." She whirled on him and sauntered to the car in a languid motion he had never seen on her before.

Women.

However, she was right about Alexandra Kennedy, and his balls were something that he always had under protection. You never knew when someone would come along and try to cut one of them off.

20

After getting rid of those two damn pests of detectives, Tracie definitely needed to run. If she didn't blow off some of her pent-up energy, she was going to hurt somebody.

When she reached the park, she pushed her body through hurdles and then broke out in a fast run, whizzing past trees, other joggers, roller skaters, and skateboarders.

She was breathing harshly from the sheer speed of her run, but she didn't care; she pumped and pumped, and pumped. She ran until she felt like dropping.

She couldn't pace herself. She needed to feel the pain. The muscles in her legs screamed in protest as she pushed herself to an astonishing degree never before reached in her running. The sweat dripping, the focus, and the discipline were exactly what she needed.

When she was finished running, she headed home.

She spotted the ice cream truck. She just waved to Anthony. Disappointment flashed across his face when he realized she wasn't coming his way. She wasn't in the mood for any frozen refreshments or the banality of a conversation with Anthony. She didn't want to cool off her body; she wanted to feel the suffering. In fact, she was slightly dazed and confused. She wasn't even sure she could string together two sentences properly.

So, it was best to avoid Anthony today. Besides, she didn't want to hear one more word of sympathy about Randi's death. If she did, she was going to scream. She just couldn't stand to hear it anymore. All it did was ram home the reality to her that he was gone. She was having a hard time dealing with that.

As she walked along, she could hear the killer's voice. It reverberated in her memory as though it were on automatic remote. She remembered him saying he would send clues to the police. Just this very morning they had shown up with Randi's Karl Kani boot, a note, and that damned silver heart.

There was only one person she knew who could be connected to the silver heart. The thought was just too incredible. She wouldn't even consider it. What was wrong with her?

Tracie pulled the scrunchie from her ponytail, letting her hair fly free. She ran trembling fingers through it, trying to think. Her thoughts were all over the place. How the hell could she be expected to think when her world was crashing in? This was crazy.

She stood up and stretched. She knew what she needed. She needed some good old girlfriend chatter to calm her nerves. She had to talk to somebody, or she would go crazy. Renee was just the person she needed, and she was trustworthy. She hadn't really been able to talk to her at Randi's services. Maybe she wouldn't go home after all.

Tracie punched in her number, willing her to be home. She was probably caught up in the throes of some brainstorming or otherwise hot concept. Tracie knew she would either be on top of the world or totally down in the dumps, depending on the circumstances.

Renee was one of Tracie's closest friends. She was a screenwriter. Her workplace was at home. Renee answered on the third ring. "It's your quarter; speak," Renee said flippantly into the phone.

"Renee, it's Tracie. Listen, I wanted to stop by for a few minutes. Can you spare the time?" Tracie was respectful of her schedule because she knew Renee hoarded time the way some people would hoard gold pieces.

The flippant voice changed to instant warmth. "Girl, you know I'll make time for you; get your behind on over here. What are you waiting for?" Renee was a fast talker, partly due to her Hispanic heritage.

Her father was Hispanic and her mother was African-American. She spoke fast and fluently, and whatever came to her mind usually flew out of her mouth, such as her reference about Rashod at Randi's burial.

Tracie smiled. "I'm walking, girl, as we speak. If you've got any Rémy Martin, break it out. I know it's early, but I need a stiff one. No ice, straight up."

Renee frowned. "Just call me Dr. Renee. It'll be sitting on the bar when you get here."

"Thanks, girl, you're a real friend." Tracie hung up.

As promised, when Tracie reached Renee's apartment on 138th Street in the Old Strivers Row section of town, she found a snifter full of Rémy Martin waiting for her.

Spying it from the doorway, Tracie didn't even greet Renee. She headed straight to the bar, perched on a stool, and downed the hot brown liquid in one swig.

Renee closed the door, walked behind the bar, pulled out the bottle of Rémy Martin, and set it in front of Tracie, saying, "Help yourself. There's plenty where that came from."

She took a seat at the bar, next to Tracie. Renee swigged from a bottle of V8 juice. She watched Tracie closely, pain welling up in her chest for Tracie's loss.

Renee decided that her course of action would be not to treat Tracie any differently, because from what she could see, this might send her into a collision course of no return.

Renee was a snazzy, jazzy, light and lively sort of person, so she hated depressing scenes anyway. Unless, of course, she was writing a script in which she needed to make people cry buckets of tears on her way to box office success.

That wasn't the case here, so she would stick with bright. "Okay," she said. "I'm the number one girlfriend, so what's on your mind?"

Tracie determined that Renee must have been having a good writing day from her attitude. That was good, because it meant the whole of the conversation could center on Tracie's problems, without her having to bolster up Renee because of some job she didn't get or because some director was trampling over her creation and turning it into pure trash.

Tracie poured a healthy amount of Rémy Martin in

the snifter, took a more tentative sip this time, and decided it was girlfriend time in the hood. "The police are telling me Randi's death wasn't an accident. They believe somebody killed him."

Renee raised her eyebrows in speculation. Her line into the neighborhood was pretty good. She had connections just about everywhere, as every good writer does—including in the police precincts, but she hadn't heard a peep about this. "Get the hell out of here. You've got to be kidding me," she said.

"No. I'm not. I wish I was."

"Where did them fools ever get an idea like that? Everybody loved Randi."

Tracie took another sip before answering. "Randi didn't have his boots on when"—she broke off, hesitating and stumbling over the words—"when they found him on 135th Street," she finished lamely.

Renee considered this. It didn't make sense. "Why? Where the hell were his boots at?"

Tracie shrugged. "That's what the police want to know."

"Okay, you got me there. I'll admit that's a little strange, but maybe he took them off to air his feet or something. You know how Randi loved freedom. He's been like that since he was a little boy. That's why he was always sitting up on the roof."

Renee put her chin in her hand. "Hell, he was one of the only players in the city who sometimes played on the court without his sneakers. It's an inside joke, girl, you know that." Renee choked back the mist that rose in her throat.

"Yeah. I know. But the problem is, the police have one of the boots."

The mist cleared as a jolt of anger from Tracie's words bolted through Renee. "At the risk of sounding stupid, Tracie, where is the other one?"

Tracie sighed. "Hell, I don't know. They showed up at my door this morning with one of the boots, claiming the murderer sent it to them with a note."

For some reason that Tracie didn't understand, she decided to leave out the part about the broken silver heart. She didn't feel like sharing that with Renee.

Renee leaned back on the bar. She didn't like what she was hearing. "This is bad stuff, girl. What are you going to do?"

"I don't know. Outside of perhaps strangle that Monica Rhodes. She's a first-class dog in my opinion, and I'm sick of her snout sniffing up my behind."

Renee laughed at Tracie's choice of words. She was such the proper lady most of the time. "What's her angle?"

"She doesn't have an angle as far as I'm concerned. She's just a hound looking for a scent. Probably looking to get promoted on my son's death."

Renee stood up. "Well, I don't know anybody who can handle that type better than you, that's for sure."

Tracie smiled for the first time. "Yeah, you're right. I'm a bad-mutha-shut-your-mouth when I wanna be."

Renee laughed heartily, showing her white gleaming molars. "That you are, girlfriend, that you are. Hey! Did you hear the latest?" Renee had decided that a turn in the conversation wouldn't hurt while she had Tracie laughing, although what she had to say was far from funny.

"No. What?" Tracie's curiosity was piqued. No one delivered a hot piece of gossip better than Renee Santiago. The girl was plugged in, and her stuff was usually delicious, hot off the wire, and for the most part pretty accurate.

"What? Tell me already," Tracie said when Renee still hadn't spoken.

"You know old Ms. Virginia?" Renee had turned solemn.

"Of course I do. She's one of my oldest, most elegant customers."

"Humph, not anymore," Renee said.

Tracie set down her glass, deciding she'd had enough Rémy Martin for one day. "What do you mean, not anymore? I know there's not a salon in Harlem who could have stolen her from me."

"Nope, you're right. A salon didn't steal her—death did."

"What?" Tracie was beginning to feel like a parrot.

She hated the way Renee always strung out her stories a little bit at a time, so she could have you chomping at the bit, although, Tracie conceded, this was probably what made her a good writer.

"Ms. Virginia is dead. Died of a heart attack. You know Visionaries will close down now, cuz she didn't have no living heirs. She was always fretting about that. Threatening to leave her store to somebody from the community, so her legacy of selling words, and black literature could live on. I wonder if she ever got around to that."

Tracie's mouth was open, but nothing was coming out.

"Anyway," Renee continued, "that's not all of it, honey—might just be the least of it."

"What do you mean? How could her death be the least of anything? It looks like the biggest of it to me. There are other bookstores in Harlem."

"True, dat," Renee lapsed into complete street slang.

"However, all of the books in those stores have words in them."

Tracie laughed wholeheartedly this time. Visiting Renee had been just what she needed to get a grip on things. She hadn't laughed this much since Randi died.

"All books have words in them, Renee—in every bookstore. That, my dear, is the point to most books. Sorry to be the bearer of such startling news."

Renee did one of her famous ballerina twirls around the room. She had studied when she was younger, and it was one of her lost vocations.

"Very funny, Tracie."

Tracie was still laughing.

"But way off the track. You see, the books in Ms. Virginia's shop are just a little bit different. All the cover art and pictures are on or in the books. In fact, all the pages are in the books, with one small exception."

"What's that?"

"There are no words on them!" she shrieked emphatically. This time Tracie heard her. Really heard her.

"Not a single word, on a single page, not in a single book. Now, how weird is that?"

Renee completed her pirouette, ending in a graceful bow in front of Tracie. Tracie shivered as her memory opened up like a wide-screen television with all the glory of Technicolor.

The number one girlfriend, of the Hispanic ancestry, with the thick mane of hair, scriptwriter extraordinaire with the savvy Saks Fifth Avenue credit card, had just unknowingly landed another blow to what was Tracie Burlingame.

Tracie just stared at Renee while a very weird feeling rattled around inside her at the sound of Renee's words.

"There are no words on them. Not a single word on a single page, not in a single book. Now, how weird is that?" The words echoed against the chambers of Tracie's mind.

The dream she had blown off like so much dust had reared its head and come crawling out of the recesses of her memory. It was not to be forgotten.

"In your face," it seemed to say to Tracie.

21

Inside a crack house up on 133rd Street, Rashod sat with his back to the wall, in a cocaine haze. He had abandoned his charcoal and sketch pad. He just didn't want to touch them right now. He inhaled slowly on his pipe.

Genie sat next to him on the dirty, stained mattress. He loved cocaine as much as Rashod. They were crack buddies. They shared what they had, and they looked out for each other when one of them didn't have. Both of them were oblivious to the drug-induced atmosphere that surrounded them.

Lovers of the trade were sprawled around the room, creating their own havens. Each inhabited his or her own space, not encroaching on the space of the others.

Those were the rules of the house, and the rules were strictly enforced. If you broke them, you'd be out on your behind looking for a new house, and this was one of the better houses around. The security was tight. The crack, cocaine, and heroin were the best grades in town. If you were out of supplies or works, you could buy them here.

They even sold clean needles. And sometimes they would look out for you if you were a regular and short or a little down on your cash luck.

The house even had its own name.

Some fool who equated the myth of Santa Claus with the distribution of white, mind-destroying candy had dubbed the crack house "St. Nick's." Anyway, the name had stuck, and since you could buy whatever you needed here and rent your own little space in a room, breaking the rules was not an option.

After a few more pulls on the pipe, Genie turned to Rashod and asked, "Rashod, tell me what you see."

"What?" Rashod blew smoke clouds into the air.

"You heard me, man. Tell me what you see. You know, like me, man. I see a world surrounded in glass. It's a big glass ball. I keep trying to get out, but the ball keeps spinning and spinning in circles." Genie inhaled deeply.

Genie's question disturbed Rashod—conjured up pictures he didn't want to see. Rashod peered at him through a cloud of smoke. "I don't see anything, Genie; there's nothing to see."

Genie laughed. "Is that right? If you weren't seeing nothing, you wouldn't be killing yourself with that pipe. None of us would."

Off in the distance a church bell tolled, announcing a new hour. Rashod's voice was a soft whisper over the sound of the bell. "Doesn't matter. I'd be dying anyway. I was sprung from a seed with the shadow of death on it."

The heat of his words penetrated Genie's haze. Genie looked over at Rashod, seeing an aura covering him. However, he was unsure if it was the smoke from the drugs or a different kind of haze.

Uncomfortable, Genie decided to drop the conversation for now. Some days Rashod scared him, and this was one of those days.

22

Tracie walked into her brownstone, shutting the door firmly behind her. She was still shaken by her conversation with Renee regarding Ms. Virginia and the wordless books.

A heavy feeling was settling right in the middle of her chest. She didn't know what was going on, but suddenly she felt as though she had been thrust into the twilight zone.

Before she could shake the feeling that had come over her, a basketball bounced into the room. There was no ballplayer behind it. "Michael?" Tracie called out.

There was no answer. "Randi?" she caught herself. How was she ever going to stop doing that?

"Dre?" Dre didn't answer, either.

Slowly she walked across the room and looked down the hallway. It was empty. She walked to her bedroom. Her nightgown was lying on the bed. She hadn't left it there. Lying on top of the nightgown were two pieces of a broken silver heart and one lone sunflower seed.

Tracie backed out of the room, pulling the door shut. She turned and bumped into a rock-solid figure. A soft moan escaped her lips as a bolt of fear shot through her. "No."

Tracie looked up as Michael grabbed hold of her.

"What's the matter, Ma? Are you okay?"

She quickly composed herself. "Uh, yeah, baby. I'm fine. I . . . I just have a bit of headache. I think I'll take some Tylenol."

Michael eyed her closely. "Are you sure?" He was still quite shaken from his own experience, but he definitely would not allow Tracie to key into that.

"Yeah. I'm sure," Tracie said.

Michael released her. The phone rang. "I'll get it," he said.

"No!" Tracie shrieked at him. Calming herself, she lied, "I'm expecting a call, so I'll get it." She left and went to pick up the extension in the living room. "Hello."

The distorted voice greeted her again. "Hello, Little Caramel. You're doing very well so far. I guess I won't have to be mailing you a package. I was just about to enjoy your sweetness when I was interrupted. I left you a present, though. Did you see it?"

Tracie wrinkled her nose as though she could smell the scent of him.

"Yes."

"Just the thought of you, Tracie, is soft and silky. I wanted to play ball with you, but I ran out of time.

Maybe next time. You're doing well with rule number two, and I haven't even told you what it is yet."

At his words, a cold draft swept through the room where Tracie was standing. She shivered.

"When I call, you jump. But just like the smart girl you are, I see you've accomplished this on your own. It's your move, Tracie."

Emboldened by his audacity and her anger, Tracie said, "Why don't you show yourself the next time instead of running away? Only punks run away."

He laughed. She couldn't provoke him. Didn't she know who he was? "Come on, Tracie," he said. "You're a more worthy opponent than that. Don't disappoint me. You were doing well. Don't be impatient. Believe me, you and I will dance when the time comes."

Tracie heard the soft click of him hanging up in her ear.

The caller ID registered a spooky "Unknown."

23

Whiskey sat mesmerized before the blown-up portrait of Tracie Burlingame. Her image occupied almost the entire length of his bedroom wall. He was absolutely obsessed with her haunting beauty. The photograph had been taken one gorgeous spring day when he and Tracie had ventured down to the shoreline in Connecticut.

The stunning replica reminded him of what they could have been, not what they were. Taming a woman like Tracie Burlingame would be a full-time occupation or preoccupation, whichever one wanted to call it.

Even through the still photograph the sheer beauty she possessed was hypnotic. The depths of her eyes that changed colors like a chameleon seemed to flash and transform even in repose.

Tracie's eyes twinkled. He turned away from looking at the photograph while swigging directly from a fifth of Jack Daniels, although he still felt her over-whelming presence.

He was the type of guy that came from a background that said a man like him could never have a woman like Tracie Burlingame. Even though Tracie had built her image from scratch and clawed her way out of the projects, she had built an image that screamed, "untouch-able."

She was crème de la crème.

Whiskey had grown up as a hood rat, basically. His father had been a notorious gambler, and he wasn't any good at it. His mother cleaned other people's houses to keep food on the table. Not that it worked—his father had pissed away every cent she brought into the house, chasing the next dream.

Whiskey had vowed he would overcome. When he was young, he took from those who were weaker. When he grew older, he took from those who were strong.

He took, stole, banged heads together, and built his image on the back of black, dark danger. He was always more dangerous and more daring than the next man; that's why he was the most prominent arms dealer in New York City.

He'd never wanted for anything since he learned how to hustle past hunger pains, until Tracie Burlingame. Whiskey wanted to possess Tracie. She occupied his thoughts most days and nights, to an extent that was scary. He could smell her perfume even when she wasn't with him.

Speaking of smells, Whiskey turned his thoughts to the scent Tracie had given off when he'd talked to her about his shipment.

Being a predator of sorts, Whiskey had smelled a stench on Tracie that far surpassed any perfume she'd been wearing. It rose up from her pores, permeating the very air between them, creating vibes that were felt but unseen.

Her boy Randi Burlingame, Mr. NBA himself, was already in the ground, covered over. She had to deal with that. So what was the problem?

Staring once again at her photo, Whiskey identified the scent that was rising up from the pores of Tracie's skin, seeping out like molasses being poured from a bottle. Yes. It was seeping right out from the strands of her perfectly coiffed hair.

Fear.

Tracie Burlingame, Ms. Thang, was scared. It was a foreign emotion that he'd never sensed on her before.

"Fear." He said it out loud, savoring the word on his lips. Then he threw his head back, roaring in laughter; in fact, he howled with laughter as he took a long swallow from the bottle of Jack Daniels.

Tracie Burlingame was running scared; that meant it would be an interesting chase.

Whiskey was not the only entity that had Tracie on his mind. A little farther uptown on 135th Street, a man sat drinking the last cup of her dead son's blood.

He drank slowly, savoring each drop of the remnants of Tracie Burlingame's seed. He licked his lips, loving the feel and the smell of it. His blood craving was critical, and he could not afford to run out. He prowled the basketball court restlessly.

It was late at night, so he was the only person on the court. He would need more blood, and he would need it very soon; otherwise he would be sick. The beast would rise up in him, refusing anything less than total saturation.

His compulsion for drinking blood was growing. He

knew he would have to feed at a much faster rate than in the past. He was drawing out his own withdrawal symptoms by playing tag with Tracie Burlingame, but his craving for her went much deeper.

Tiring of his thoughts, he got up and dribbled the basketball down center court, trying out his newfound skills. Swish, swish, and swish. It felt good—exhilarating, actually.

In drinking Randi's blood he had acquired the boy's skill, superstar skills, and his moves on the court were now pure poetry in motion. Just like the dead legend.

He ran the ball downcourt again, caught up in the joy, the run, and the feel of the ball in his hand. He was in total command. Hell, maybe the NBA would recruit him. He ran the court a few times, and on his last trip down, he found Me standing in front of the basket.

Just as the ball flew out of his hand and up toward the basket, Me's hand blocked it, bouncing it back downcourt to him. The two comrades were finally face-to-face.

Unadulterated hatred coursed through his veins at the sight of Me. He threw the ball at him. He only tolerated Me because they were bonded in a higher calling, but he found him to be an extremely disturbing individual.

The man walked around chatting with the spirits of his dead victims. Hell, once they were dead, they were dead. Me was downright creepy. And he was out of his territory.

"What the hell are you doing here?"

Me ignored his question, asking his own. "How come you're not doing your job?"

He laughed. He had a lot of damned nerve. "This ain't Jersey. In case you haven't noticed, you're on New

York soil. More specifically, you're on the promised land, Harlem. That means you're out of bounds and on my turf."

"We have to collect the gifts," Me said.

"I'm collecting the gifts."

Me shook his head. "You're playing with the girl. It's not the same. That's personal, not business."

"You know what? Why don't you get up and out of my business. Your timeline's a little early here. I'll do what I need to do. So why don't you hop on back over to Jersey and let me handle my business."

"No."

"No?"

"No," Me repeated. "I have already started. Here I will stay."

His blood ran cold. Then, with startling clarity, he realized that Me had kicked off a serial marathon. "Ms. Virginia . . . the bookstore . . . Visionaries. It was you, wasn't it?"

Someone sneezed, but Me's lips didn't move.

He rolled his eyes in disgust at Me. "Don't get in my way, okay? Just don't get in my way. And stay away from Tracie Burlingame. She's hands-off, and I mean it."

Me shrugged.

"Give me the ball."

Me threw the ball awkwardly to him.

"And take your ass back to Jersey until the real time comes." With that he walked off the court, leaving Me to his own thoughts.

"You're not in charge!" Me yelled.

He kept walking.

"There's only one boss. You're not it."

He didn't break stride. When he reached the street,

he took a couple of pulls off his pipe, so he could erase the blot on his spirit that was Me.

He reached into his pocket, pulled out a glassine bag, and took a couple of hits of cocaine.

The rush of the potent white powder was good.

24

The following morning Tracie stood in the steamy shower, letting the hot water pour over her. She hadn't had a good night's sleep, and her very bones felt weary. She was going to call into the shop today and have her manager run the salon.

She just didn't have the energy to face people. She wouldn't be able to get away with that for long, because Whiskey's shipment had to be moved out. But that was for another day.

Stepping out of the shower, she went to the mirror. She rubbed the steam off the mirror so she could see. She began her facial with a special cleanser she had. As she cleansed her face, eyes of desolation stared back at her from the mirror.

Her usually bright eyes lacked luster. She lightly rubbed her hands over them, trying to massage in some life.

Suddenly she frowned. She put her face in the sink and splashed pure, cold water on it. Then she dried it quickly. She didn't have time for a leisurely facial.

A thought had been plaguing her that she couldn't shake, so she needed to put her mind at ease. She dried herself, put on her thick velour robe, and walked out of the bathroom, down the hall to Rashod's old room.

The boy hadn't slept in the room in so long Tracie couldn't even remember when. There was a cocky sign on the door that read RASHOD'S PLACE. An arrow was taped underneath it that led to the words DO NOT ENTER IF YOU AIN'T BEEN ASKED. Tracie shook her head at his usual brashness.

Turning the knob, she went into the room. A smell of musk hit her in the face as soon as she opened the door. The room was dark and musty-smelling. She could kill this boy. He knew damn well that she didn't keep her house like this.

She rarely ever went in the room, because it was just too painful since their relationship was so estranged. However, if she had known he'd turned it into a pigsty, she'd have gone over to that damned crack house he hung out in and kicked his behind until the cows came home.

Frustrated, she stepped over the clothes, electronic gadgets, and shoes strewn all over the floor, to go to the closet, when she felt something crunching under her feet. What the hell could be crunching under her feet when the room had wall-to-wall carpeting?

She flicked on the light and closed her eyes at the disaster of a room that loomed up in front of her. She went to the edge of the carpet, pulling it up and back from where it had been tacked down.

She gasped. There were hoards of sunflower seeds,

mountains of them. Rashod had a fixation with those damned seeds, and it looked as though he'd been collecting them under her rug.

A memory flashed, hot and painful. A sunflower seed had been lying on the nightgown next to the silver heart.

Tracie got up and went to the closet, yanking open the door. She was having a fuming fit. She just started pulling things off the hangers, down off the shelves, and throwing things around. From high up in the closet, a shelf shook from all her shaking, and something fell down, hitting her on the top of the head.

Startled, she rubbed her head and looked down at the other black and gold Karl Kani boot belonging to Randi. Spent from her tirade, and aghast at seeing the boot, Tracie Burlingame sat down on the floor and wept like a baby. This was too much. Why the hell was that boot hidden in Rashod's old closet?

25

Lonzo and Monica sat in the coffee shop on 135th Street and Malcolm X Boulevard across from Harlem Hospital, sipping coffee. The shop was crowded to distraction, but it suited Lonzo's state of mind. His thoughts were in a jumble.

For Monica's part, this case was bothering the hell out of her. They literally had no leads. There were no prints. The one witness was a joke. Actually, she couldn't even really be called a witness just because the body fell at her feet. As much as Monica hated to admit it, just as Lonzo had, voiced, the girl Sinead was a trembling, non breathing mass of a mess. And she was everything they had.

Her total testimony: "The body fell at my feet." Period.

That's all they had. It was hard to believe, but it was truth. There was no DNA and no motive, and the killer was toying with them. It was a totally senseless murder.

Monica sipped her coffee and ate a bagel slathered in cream cheese that she really didn't need.

Lonzo's phone rang. He clicked on, listening to the voice on the other end. When he was done, he said, "That was Alexandra. The final report on Randi Burlingame just came in."

"And?"

"The sunflower seeds crammed in Randi's throat were what actually killed him. The official cause of death is asphyxiation. His windpipe was blocked. The ME says he died of obstruction of the respiratory apparatus. The seeds cut off his air supply. He was dead when he hit the ground. He drained off his blood after he was dead."

Monica grimaced. "Now, why would he stuff his throat with sunflower seeds? It doesn't fit well with the rest of the injuries he inflicted. I mean, he drains his blood, takes his boots, tosses him off the roof, but before he does, he stuffs his mouth with sunflower seeds, essentially choking him."

Monica realized that was what was bothering her. Clearly the sunflower seeds were part of the killer's distinct signature. But what did they mean?

Lonzo stood up and threw some money on the counter. "Come on, Monie. Let's visit the funeral home that handled the burial services and see if we can find out why Andre Burlingame was photographing his dead brother's funeral. That's really been bothering me. Most relatives wouldn't want to be the one to do that."

"If there were something in particular you wanted to capture, maybe you would."

An electric vibe shot between them.

26

A Hundred thirty-third Street was crowded and busy. The traffic was hectic; horns were blaring. Kids were running and playing, and the drug dealers were out in full force. Apparently their trade started earlier than Tracie remembered, because they were definitely out clocking dollars.

Tracie ran down 133rd Street as though her life depended on it. She ran in front of cars, not paying attention to the traffic or the signals. Once she had gotten over her weeping jag, pure fury had swept through her body and propelled her out into the streets.

She headed to St. Nick's, the crack house that was Rashod's home away from home. She didn't have time to play. Knowing about the security procedure, she used her visibility in the community plus five crisp one-hundred-dollar bills to gain entry.

The young boy handling security lowered his nine-millimeter. He pocketed the money, waving her through. She wasn't worth a hassle, and he knew she was Rashod's mother.

Every once in a while some mother had been known to show up, trying to save her child, although not usually with hundred-dollar bills in hand, and not nearly as fine as Tracie Burlingame.

He'd have done it for three hundred. Tracie Burlingame was fine with a capital "F."

Tracie stepped over people in the smoky, crowded room. She spotted Rashod, sitting in a corner of the room with his back to the wall. Lying next to him were his sketch pad and charcoal. Tracie immediately noticed that he wasn't sketching. Rashod usually sketched no matter what he was doing. Tracie knew that getting high wasn't an exception.

When she reached him, she knelt in front of him. Rashod was high as a kite. He groggily tried to focus on the kneeling figure in front of him. He hoped it wasn't the man in agony from his sketch, with the raindrops pelting him, although, the way things were going, he wouldn't have been surprised.

Slowly he came to his senses, and Tracie's image weaved in front of his eyes. This was worse. He wished it were the man in the sketch, the one who looked like his brother Michael.

Rashod shook his head in disgust as he focused in on Tracie. "Get out," he said.

Tracie swallowed hard. "Rashod. I want you to come home. You need some help. I can help you."

"I'm at home," Rashod told her. He waved his hand around the room and started laughing. "I don't need your help. Don't you have money to be made or something? Go clock somebody else."

"Making money is not more important to me than you, Rashod."

Rashod fumbled to light his pipe, got it to his lips, lit it, and took a long pull. His morning was definitely heading downhill into complete ruin, and he was not about to face it without his fix. He took out a glassine bag, stuck in a little silver spoon, and took four good hits right in front of Tracie's face.

Feeling more fit to continue the conversation, he told Tracie, "You could have fooled me. I thought clocking bank was everything to you, since that is what you spend most of your time doing—that and trying to control other people's lives, baby."

"Don't call me 'baby,' Rashod. And you know that's not true."

"You calling me a liar?" he said. He gave her a sharp, focused look.

"No," Tracie said, trying hard not to fight with him.

"I ain't interested in replacing Randi the Shooter for you, Tracie. He's dead and he ain't coming back." Rashod laid down the pipe, suddenly more interested in tormenting his mother than smoking crack.

"That's not what I want."

"Oh, really. Then what do you want? It ain't me. After me you had . . ." Rashod's voice trailed off for a moment as he counted off on his trembling fingers.

"Let's see, you had Dre, the Image Maker; Michael, the Great Rebounder; and Randi, the Shooter. Mr. Poetry in Motion. I guess I should say, the Dead Shooter, all motionless now. All you ever did was sing to Randi."

Rashod mimicked Tracie's singsongy voice. " 'Rock-a-bye, baby . . .' " he sang.

Tracie stared at Rashod in shock. Through no will of her own, she found her hand flying through the air as she slapped him viciously across the mouth. Immediately they both rose to their feet, and the room around them awakened. The slap had resounded throughout the room, echoing across the bareness, catching everybody's attention.

The boy who had been on guard with the nine-millimeter stepped into the room, assessed the situation, and then stepped back out into the hallway. He wasn't about to interfere with nobody's mom. He might be a drug dealer, but still some forms of respect hadn't died. He went back to his post.

Rashod stared at Tracie, livid with white-hot hatred and rage. He shoved her so hard, she stumbled backward. "You ever put your hands on me again and I'll . . ." He stepped right up in Tracie's face as people scrambled to get out of the way.

Tracie hissed at him and took a step back, pulling her gun. The clicking off of the safety reverberated through the air. She flipped the trigger back in one smooth move as she pointed the gun at Rashod's forehead, dead center. This happened within the space of a second.

"You'll what, Rashod? Come on, punk. You want to try me? What the hell will you do?" She screamed.

Her breathing was shallow. Her chest heaved in and out as though she couldn't get enough oxygen.

"I brought you here, and I'll take you out. What will you do? Did you kill my baby, Rashod? Come on. Tell me. Did you?"

Tracie's voice had turned into a high-pitched, piercing scream, and it scraped like a siren gone wild. "I asked you a question, damn it."

Tracie kept the gun trained on the middle of his

forehead. She never wavered. "I'll blow your head off and scatter your brains around your new home—what's left of them. Now, I'm gonna ask you again, boy."

Her tone was gutter nasty. "Did you kill my son?" The room had gone totally still. There was not a sound to be heard except for Tracie's harsh breathing.

Rashod looked at her, crumbled, and broke down before her eyes. Tears streamed down his face as he stared at the mother he had tried so hard not to love. Her anger and doubt in him sliced like a hot arrow through his being.

The tears poured, and he tried to wipe them with the back of his hand. "I didn't kill him, Mama. I didn't. The only one I'm killing is me."

It was the word "Mama" that broke through the icy insanity that was covering Tracie like a glassy sheen. This was her son, and it had been a long time since he had called her that. And she couldn't remember the last time she had seen him cry.

Tracie stared at him for a long moment before lowering the gun. An eternity seemed to pass. She loved her son. She must be losing it. How could she even think about taking him out? But for one totally insane second she had intended to do just that: take him right out of his misery and let hers go with him.

Tracie reached out a hand, wiping the tears from his eyes. She put the gun back in her inside jacket pocket. She pulled Rashod close to her, loving him and missing him all at the same time. Although she had had three other sons, none of them could take his place or be him. He was her firstborn.

She missed him in her life so much that the realization of that one thought swamped her in pain. It was a visceral physical reaction. Her body trembled and shook. "You can come home, Rashod. My door will always be open to you."

Rashod shook his head sadly. He hugged her for the briefest of moments, feeling her warmth, the sweetness, and the love he never had but had always craved. All he had ever wanted was for her to hold him and love him. But he knew he couldn't buy into it. It just wasn't meant to be.

"I know about Raymond, Tracie. I know. I can't come home. I'd be a walking dead man. Your door has the shadow of death on it."

Upon Rashod's words there was a time warp. The two of them were frozen in it. They were locked in, solid. Stark, cloying fear rose up and sprayed out of Tracie's eyes.

She hadn't heard Raymond's name spoken aloud in many, many years. Raymond was her children's daddy.

27

Michael Burlingame stood in front of the garbage chute in the Abraham Lincoln apartment projects, on the fifteenth floor. He listened as the last of the clothing and paraphernalia of his other life tumbled down to join the rest of the refuse.

He felt secure dropping these items in the projects, since none of them would surprise any trash collector or superintendent who might happen upon it. Also, no one would be able to link it to him. He didn't even live here.

He pressed the button for the elevator and waited for it to creak its way up to the fifteenth floor. Good thing he wasn't in a hurry, because this could take a significant amount of time.

While he waited, a kid who looked to be about six years old came running out of one of the apartments, dribbling his basketball, and lost control of it. The ball was almost as big as he was. Michael stopped the ball and dribbled it back to the little boy. Recognizing him, the little boy beamed. "Mama, it's Rebound; look!" He pointed at Michael excitedly. The mother smiled. "Can I have your autograph on my ball?" the boy asked.

Michael smiled at him. "Yeah." He turned to the mother. "Do you have a pen?"

"I'll get one," she said.

"Tell you what, little man. I'll do you one better than that. How about two tickets for you and your mother to the benefit game that I'm going to be playing with the Harlem Globetrotters?"

"Are you for real?" the boy asked.

"Oh, yeah."

"Yes!" The boy jumped up and down excitedly, and his mother smiled her gratitude at Rebound. She retrieved the pen. He signed the ball. He reached into his pocket, giving them the tickets just as the elevator finally arrived.

"Thank you," she said.

Rebound looked at the boy. "Naw, thank you. That's a cool little man you've got there."

He remembered when Randi had been the same age. He had been so excited about playing basketball. Michael couldn't believe he would never hear the echo of Randi dribbling downcourt again, and that he would never hear 135th Street screaming as Randi ran up and down the court barefoot.

He rubbed his hand across the boy's head and then stepped into the elevator.

"See ya at the game Rebound," the boy called. "I hope you win," he added. "But you know the Globetrotters are good, too."

"That they are, little man. Enjoy the game."

The elevator door creaked closed. Michael waved good-bye. On his way down in the elevator, he wondered if meeting the little boy could have been a sign. The boy was young. Considering what had happened to him, maybe that meant he could get a fresh start.

The usual anxiety and anguish he walked around with inside had started to fade. That was a good start. Understanding what had happened to him would have to be next. He knew that, for the life of him, he truly didn't understand. He just knew that somehow things were different.

Michael stepped off the elevator. He looked at his watch. Shoot, he was already late for school. Stepping outside, he decided he would ditch for the day. Sometimes being a star athlete had its advantages.

He attended Stuyvesant High School over on Chambers Street. His team was called the Running Rebels, and he was proud of their record. They had finished in the league, largely due to his performances, at twelve and two. Last year they had earned the Manhattan Division III-B crown. The first-place finish had given them a bye in the first round of the playoffs.

They played to a packed house in Stuyvesant's gym when they played their archrivals from the north, Hunter High. With a crowd of support from the community of Harlem, they had gone on to beat Hunter 72–60. They had now advanced to the quarterfinals, where they would meet Central Park East High School next.

The scouts were already looking at him, and his coach was pleased as punch. He had a good chance at a full scholarship, and he knew it. He would be recruited, no doubt. In fact, an agent had already approached him off the record. So his little foray for the day wouldn't be a big deal.

He decided he would visit Rashod. He flagged a taxi. Rashod lived in a residential hotel over on 111th Street. He had a small studio in the hotel. Michael was taking a huge leap of faith in hoping to find him there instead of at St. Nick's.

At St. Nick's he would have to pay a runner to go up and get Rashod for him. Anyway, he decided to try him at home, since lately his faith seemed to be a bit more restored. He had a spare set of keys, so if push came to shove he could let himself in and chill for a while.

The gypsy cab stopped, and Michael got in. Not ten minutes later he was knocking on Rashod's door. To his great surprise, Rashod answered it.

"Rebound. Hey, man, whatcha doing here?" Rashod clapped him on the back. He opened the door wider to let him in.

"I was in the neighborhood. I decided to check you out," Michael told him.

"Yeah, right. And I was at NASA last night, and I decided to shuttle on up to the moon to check things out." Rashod laughed. "Want some OJ?"

"Yeah. I could use a glass of vitamin C."

Rashod went to the small refrigerator, took out the orange juice, and poured Michael a healthy glass. Michael took a seat on the worn, squeaky sofa and watched Rashod closely.

It took him a minute to digest the fact that Rashod wasn't high, for a change. He wondered what had brought that on. Usually by this time of day he already had his groove on.

Rashod saw him observing him. "So," he said, "Mommy's gonna kick your butt from here to Brooklyn when she finds out you skipped school."

Michael tried not to show his utter amazement at

Rashod calling Tracie "Mommy," but he wasn't that good at hiding it.

Rashod didn't miss a twitch, so he said, "Well, she is my mother, too, you know."

"Yeah, I know, but you're the one who usually doesn't acknowledge that, big brother."

Rashod shrugged. "Sometimes things change."

Michael took a long swallow from the glass, enjoying the cold liquid. "So, tell me. What changed?"

Something flickered across Rashod's face. For a moment he was silent. But he and Michael were tight. Michael knew and tried to understand how he felt, unlike Dre. And Michael always looked out for him. Often he brought him money and food. Even if he wasn't there, Michael would leave it for him.

Rashod was unemployed, so sometimes he ran low when he didn't sell enough of his sketches on the street. The rent wasn't a problem, because Tracie paid that even though she was always threatening to cut him off. So far she hadn't.

Rashod picked up his charcoal and pad. He started sketching. Michael was silent. Finally Rashod said, "Tracie came to see me and blew a perfectly good high."

"Why?" Michael asked in a cold tone that indicated he was surprised at Tracie's visiting Rashod. Rashod looked at him. Michael really hadn't meant that to sound so cold and distant.

But given their history, he was somewhat surprised. He knew that generally Tracie just mailed Rashod a check and was done with it.

Rashod decided to shake up Michael's complacent little world, so straight up he said, "She came because she thinks that I killed Randi."

Michael choked on his juice. He sputtered, and juice went sloshing all over his clothes and the sofa. "What!"

"You heard me. She wanted to know if I offed Randi."

Rashod got up and handed Michael a rag so he could clean up the mess. Michael used the time to get his thoughts together.

Then he decided to do what he did to his opponents on the basketball court. He twisted them up in knots, leaped into the air, and then swished the ball into the basket from the other end of the court.

"Did you?" he asked.

Now it was Rashod's turn to be shaken. Rashod gave him a queer look. "You're kidding. Right?"

"Yeah," Michael said. "So what's this really about?"

"Seriously. Tracie somehow got it into her mind that I might be responsible for Randi's death. Don't ask me how, but she did. She came to St. Nick's. She had no trouble, of course, penetrating security, and the next thing I know, she's in my face. Anyway, things got a little ugly. She slapped me." He decided to leave out the part about pushing her, because he knew Michael would get mad and couldn't handle that. The next thing he knew, the conversation with Rebound would be over. So he skipped that part.

"Next thing I know, she's got her gun in my face, demanding to know if I killed Randi. End of story."

Michael was puzzled. Tracie hadn't mentioned thinking that Randi's death had been anything other than an accident. At the morgue she had staunchly stood by that point. Suddenly he remembered the night when she kept saying something about how she should have protected him, though.

Come to think of it, she had been acting a little strangely, but he had thought it was grief. She was real jumpy these days. When did she begin to ponder the idea that somebody had killed Randi? The police had indicated it, but she had never given any sign that she believed them. He knew his mother, and now he knew she was hiding something.

"You called Tracie 'Mommy,' so that can't be the end of the story. What happened?"

"Nothing," Rashod said. "She believed me, and then she invited me to come back home. I said no."

"Why?"

Rashod decided the moment of reckoning was here. He got up from the sofa, laying aside his sketch pad, and went to a stack of sketches leaning up against the wall. He flipped through the heavy stack for a bit, finally coming up with the ones he wanted.

Rashod took a seat across from Michael, thinking about the weird drawing he had done that looked like him, but he decided to skip it. He didn't know why he had drawn the sketch; it was as if a hand other than his had drawn it.

He also didn't understand what it meant. He decided it didn't matter. He'd known his brother was into kinky, sadomasochistic sex for some time. He'd seen the videos as well as the black clothing and chains Michael hid in his room.

But he was also aware that Michael thought it was his best-kept secret, so it was best to let it ride. He didn't want to invade his privacy or shatter his illusions.

Rashod looked at Michael and said, "I know we didn't grow up religious, man, but sometimes I wonder if there's something else out there. Do you believe in dreams? Or in seeing things before or after they've happened? Even if you weren't there?"

Before Michael could answer, Rashod said, "Actually

this is probably a question for Souljah Boy, because weird and different is right up his alley. Maybe I should have Dre hit him up."

"I don't know. I never thought about it," Michael lied, because recently he had. "Anyway, what does that have to do with why you told Tracie you couldn't come home?"

Rashod handed the first sketch to Michael. In the sketch a man was on the ground with his neck twisted. His body looked broken. It appeared as if he had fallen from a great height. "What's this?"

"That's the reason I told Tracie I couldn't come home. Her door has the shadow of death on it. That man in the sketch is dead. Tracie knows him and was somehow involved in his death."

"Oh, come off it, Rashod."

Michael looked at his brother. He noticed a strange aura surrounding him. It almost looked as though the light was absorbing him. He was sort of disappearing into it.

Michael blinked away the imagery, but when he looked again, the aura was still there, misty and shadowy.

Michael struggled to hang on to his sanity. What the hell was going on? He had never noticed anything like this on Rashod before.

Lately he seemed to be seeing a lot of things he had never seen before. Maybe it was like a residual flashback from his strange experience. He decided it was best to ignore it.

"It's true. Death somehow surrounds her, Michael. That's probably why Randi is dead. It's not what it looks like, Rebound." Rashod resorted to the affectionate name Michael's basketball skills had earned him, in order to show love and respect.

Michael was quiet. He didn't say a word. Rashod handed him the next sketch.

This one was startling in its clarity and vision. It showed a man throwing a boy off a roof. Some kind of substance spewed from the boy's mouth. The man stood watching the boy fall. The boy didn't have any shoes on his feet.

And more than that, something was waiting for him to fall. Something or someone was waiting for the falling boy below. The image looked vaguely human, but there was something else there. Even through the charcoal sketch there was a spirit of demonic force, although Michael couldn't make out what he was feeling.

He was absolutely stunned. "Is this what you think happened to Randi?"

"No," Rashod said in a much more subdued tone than before.

"That's me. I ain't got long. It is what it is, Rebound. The picture depicts my upcoming death. I'm Tracie's first seed. That seed has the shadow of death on it," Rashod finished with hot conviction.

Michael could not find words.

There was no comeback he could think of for his brother's weird revelation. He sat back in his seat, staring at both sketches as they trembled in his shaking hands.

Rashod felt sorry for him. But Rashod had come to grips with this thing. He didn't know how he knew, but he did. He would be the next one to die.

* * *

Over in the Abraham Lincoln apartments, Souljah Boy awoke from a dead sleep after having a dream in which he'd seen the very same sketch Rashod had shown Michael Burlingame.

Very distinctly a voice had uttered, "Rashod Burlingame is the next one to die."

Souljah Boy sat stock-still, sweat pouring from his brow. He reached for the phone, then thought better of it. What was he going to say, "Rashod, you're going to die"?

Visions of Randi Burlingame's broken body lying on the street flashed through his mind. Something deadly was going on with the Burlingame family, and all he had were instincts and dreams, which wouldn't stop it.

His right eye twitched rapidly.

He knew better than anyone that even if you were given or shown something in spirit, it didn't always mean you'd be able to halt the circumstances—in many cases all you could do was watch it play itself out.

He couldn't fathom why he'd been given the dream, but he knew there was a reason.

All his life he'd yearned for extraordinary sight, sight that was beyond normal human comprehension. He possessed instincts that were out of the ordinary, and an uncanny ability to feel things that others could not, but sometimes it was a hard burden to bear. It wasn't easy seeing what others couldn't.

Maybe it was paranoia that made him have the dream, because of Randi's death. He feverishly hoped this was the right answer, because if it wasn't, they were in big trouble. His spiritual insight was sensing trouble of a major magnitude.

So Souljah Boy did what he knew how to do. He bowed his head in prayer.

* * *

Rashod Burlingame stared at the sketch of his death. Michael Burlingame didn't believe, so he blew his conversation with Rashod off like so much dust.

It would come back to haunt him very, very soon.

28

Lonzo and Monica arrived at the funeral home where the preparation for the interment of Randi's body had been done. They stood just inside the doors.

There were three chapels attached to the building. It was extremely well kept. They stood on plush beige carpeting in which their feet were sinking amid scores of pieces of antique furniture.

"Looks like a profitable business," Lonzo remarked.

"It sure does," Monica readily agreed.

Just then the very stylish Lawrence Washington, the city's oldest funeral director, joined them. He walked with a cane, but the man had a certain vitality that permeated his presence. He smiled at them. "Now, how can I help you two young people today?"

Monica flashed her badge. "I'm Monica Rhodes, Harlem Homicide Division." She pointed to Lonzo. "This is my partner, Alonzo Morgan."

He nodded at her official tone. "Lawrence Washington. What can I help you with?"

Monica took the lead. "Did you direct the services for Randi Burlingame?"

"I did."

"We need to see the guest list," Monica said.

The funeral director waved his hand at her. " 'Fraid not. Only the family can see it."

"I can secure a court order. It's your call."

Lawrence Washington hesitated. He shook his head sadly. "Such a shame. Closed casket on a sixteen-year-old boy. Those boys are Tracie's world. The girl dreams, lives, and breathes for their success. Now one of 'em's dead."

Lonzo stepped in. "Did you know the family personally?"

"For some time now," Lawrence told him. "Tracie owns a hair salon called Tracie's Place. She's also got a slew of braiding salons. She does most of the hair for my clients here. Beautiful work her people produce with lots of pride."

He smiled at his memory and rambled on as though to himself. Monica and Lonzo didn't interrupt. They watched him closely.

"Long time ago, when she was just starting out, she used to bring her sons here with her while she worked. She started out with what little money her mama left her. Tracie was raised in the projects.

"I used to have to chase that Rashod all the time for spilling sunflower seeds all over my rugs and coffins. Sometimes he'd climb into the new coffins thinking they was a great place to hide, getting those darn seeds all over the velvet and velour cushions. Lord help me," Lawrence Washington reminisced.

Lonzo and Monica exchanged swift glances. They couldn't believe their ears. Lonzo had been intent on finding out why Andre Burlingame had been photographing the funeral services; instead, Lawrence Washington had just handed them a vital link.

Lonzo had been fishing. However, Lawrence Washington had just handed them real bait, bait that was leading straight to Randi Burlingame's murderer.

Lonzo was having a hard time containing his excitement, but he knew from experience that it was better to let the old man continue talking. He risked another glance at Monica. That glance told him she was just as excited, only more contained.

Lawrence continued, "That's 'bout all he did. Outside of sketch and play with that silver locket Tracie bought him. The other three boys were fine. Dre with his camera, and—"

"What?" Monica brutally cut him off. She no longer cared about Andre Burlingame and his camera, just as she knew Lonzo didn't. This man had just identified two key aspects of their case in the space of a few sentences.

She knew in her gut that they'd just hit pay dirt with Lawrence Washington's recollection of the sunflower seeds and the silver locket.

Composing herself before she spoke again after having so abruptly cut him off, she said more softly, "What silver locket? Can you describe it?"

"Course I can. It was designed in the shape of a heart. Boy had more than anybody I know. Ever' time one broke, Tracie would replace it with another one for him."

Monica fumbled in her pocket and extracted the plastic bag with the locket.

"That's it. I'd know it anywhere. Ain't too many people in Harlem walking around with none like it. Rashod's had one or another since he was a kid. He loves that thing just because his mama gave it to him.

"When he was little, he told me it was just like carrying his mama's heart around on a string." For the first time he smiled in thinking about Rashod.

Then Lawrence Washington cleared his throat, thinking maybe he should clarify how he knew so much about the Burlingame family. "I been sort a like a father to Tracie over the years, you know."

Oh, yeah, Lonzo thought he knew, all right.

That was hood-speak for "he used to be laying down with Tracie's mama, so that was how he stepped into the surrogate-daddy role." Lonzo and Monica traded looks. Wonders never ceased.

A satisfied smile was making its way across Monica's face. She didn't really give a damn who Tracie's mama had slept with, but she did give a damn about wrapping Tracie Burlingame up in her own little games.

Monica had known she was playing them.

"Thank you, Mr. Washington, for your time." Monica extended her hand. "You've been a great help to us."

"Well, I just hope all this was a help to Tracie," Lawrence Washington said as some of his senility started to show through the surface. "She sure done had enough loss, losing her baby boy and all."

"Yes," Monica said, anxious to get away. "And again, thank you."

Just before they stepped through the foyer, Lawrence said, "Oh? Will you still be needing to see the guest list?"

"No. There's no need for it now," Monica told him.

He shook his head. "Good. Cuz I really don't be liking to deal with no house of the court and the likes. I run a nice, quiet business."

He smiled at the irony of his own words. "And I'd just as soon keep it that way."

"I'm sure you would. Good day, Mr. Washington."

Out on the street, Monica turned to Lonzo. "I'm gonna secure a warrant for Tracie's house. I'll call you, and we'll set up a time to meet there. Let's pay her a little visit tonight.

"Alexandra will make sure we get the warrant, because the mayor of New York is breathing fire down her neck. If there was a conflict brewing between Tracie's sons, then you can believe she knew about it. She's been trying to suppress that information. Tracie's a woman who keeps her finger on the pulse of things, only this time she's got it on a hot button."

"And that button is about to explode," Lonzo whispered.

It was not going to be a pretty sight to see.

29

That night Monica and Lonzo stood on the steps to Tracie's brownstone, waiting rather impatiently for her to answer the doorbell. The chimes resounded through the brownstone as though summoning a dignitary.

Finally, after what seemed like an interminable wait, Tracie opened the heavy, elegant brown wood door that looked as though it belonged on Fifth Avenue instead of in Harlem.

Before Tracie could open her mouth, Monica stepped to the plate. "Miss Burlingame, we need to talk."

"There's nothing else to talk about," Tracie replied, her veneer of calm hiding a kaleidoscope of emotions.

Monica's eyes flashed as if they would burn a hole through Tracie. Still she was unable to crack the supreme arrogance that surrounded Tracie like a halo. Monica sighed, enunciating her every word. "I'm afraid there is."

"We'll keep it short," Lonzo said.

Tracie gritted her teeth. A brief storm of rage shone through the arrogance and played across her face. She pulled the door open, turning her back on the cops.

Monica didn't pull any punches. "Where can I find your son, Rashod Burlingame?"

Tracie wheeled on Monica. Her eyes spit pure flames of fire. "Why?"

"Because I asked, that's why." Monica glided so close to Tracie, she could feel her breath on her face. Tracie didn't back up or flinch an inch.

"I don't know," Tracie said with a lift of her chin.

"I think you do." Monica served up a verbal volley.

Lonzo inserted himself between the two women, forcing some distance between them. "We ain't going nowhere with this," he said.

Monica reached into her vest pocket. She produced the search warrant, handing it to Tracie. She refused to waste precious minutes on the ice princess that was Tracie Burlingame. "I believe this will take us where we want to go."

Tracie stared at the paper without touching it. "I already let you search Randi's room."

"I don't want to search Randi's room. I want to search Rashod's room. This piece of paper says I can."

Tracie's first trace of real fear emanated from her. Monica picked up the scent like the true hunter she was. Like an experienced hunter, she waited until she had the prey exactly where she wanted her.

"Why?" Tracie asked.

Monica pounced. "I don't have to explain to you,

Tracie, but I will. We have reason to believe your son, Rashod Burlingame, tossed Randi from the roof."

In one swift stroke, Monica reached into her pocket and pulled out a handful of sunflower seeds, thrusting them under Tracie's nose. Tracie began to shake violently. It started as a small tremor that birthed into a physical quake, rising into a human tidal wave. Tracie's limbs had turned to jelly.

Lonzo took her gently by the shoulders to calm her. "Tracie, sit down," he told her. Gently, brotherly, he guided her over to the nearby sofa. Tracie obliged like a small child.

Monica headed toward the hallway in search of Rashod's room.

Tracie pulled air into her lungs in long gulps. She shouted out after Monica, "He didn't do it! There must be some mistake. He wouldn't . . . he couldn't do it. Damn you, I said he didn't do it!"

Monica halted. She turned back to Tracie. "Oh, I think he did, Tracie. I think one of your sons killed the other one, and I'm going to be arresting Rashod Burlingame tonight for the murder of Randi Burlingame. How does that play for you, Tracie? And what's more—"

Monica whipped out her cell phone. She punched in digits. She shouted into the phone, "Put out an APB for Rashod Burlingame."

She snapped the phone closed. "And what's more, I think you know it."

Tracie bowed her head between her legs, whispering, "Rashod, why did you lie to me?"

*   *   *

At the Harlem precinct station, police vehicles began pulling out with their sirens screaming into the night. They sped from the lot in search of Rashod Burlingame. Riot police jumped into police vans.

This search was to be a display of power. It was a stab into the consciousness of the Harlem community, that the powers that be would not allow the slaughtering of a little black boy without serious ramifications.

They would not tolerate this type of murder. It was too bold, too flagrant, too in your face, and it had the capability of tunneling the residents of Harlem into one sweeping and angry voice. That just could not be.

This action would serve as a political volleyball, and those who were really running Harlem would come up shining brightly for a change.

It was an opportunity not to be missed. And if it was brother against brother, it really didn't make a difference. The message was simple: no bloodletting and no emotional crippling in the Harlem community. The community itself was mentally docile for the time being, and there would be no rippling of the still waters.

Alexandra was gazing out of her office window at the scene taking place outside in the police lot. She flicked her pencil in and out of her mouth. "I think my serial vampire is turning out to be a case of sibling rivalry," she murmured.

The intercom on her phone buzzed. She hit the button. A male voice came over the speaker: "We've got a handle on the suspect. He was spotted in the vicinity of St. Nicholas and 139th Street. According to our sources he's still over there."

Alexandra smiled her pleasure. "Bring the little vampire in—now. I want him downstairs in holding immediately."

"Got it," the voice responded. Alexandra clicked off.

Inside Tracie's living room, Tracie sat alone at the white baby grand piano, banging away a dark tune. Lonzo had gone to conduct the search with Monica in Rashod's room. The notes rose and fell, rose and fell, until they felt like sweeping waves pouring over Tracie.

In the middle of Tracie's private symphony, Monica walked up to the piano and dangled a black and gold Karl Kani boot directly in front of her face. She held the boot with the tip of her gloved fingers.

"Recognize this?" Monica said.

Tracie's fingers halted, stiff and frozen. The notes came to an abrupt halt. Tracie stared at the hideous boot, regretting that she had been in such an emotional frenzy that she hadn't thought to get rid of the damn thing.

"I know you recognize these," Monica said as she let a cascade of sunflower seeds she had scooped up from Rashod's room drop over the piano keys.

Inside Alexandra's office, the phone rang. Alexandra snatched it off the hook on the first ring. She listened for a moment, her facial features turning to pure granite.

"Are you absolutely sure?" she said into the phone.

Taking a deep breath, Alexandra disconnected the caller and hit the intercom button on the phone. "Maya, get me Monica Rhodes on the line. Now!" she barked. "She's at the Burlingame residence."

Monica's cell phone rang, interrupting the cat-and-mouse game she was torturing Tracie Burlingame with. "Yeah. This is Monica."

An ashen look of disbelief crept across her face. She cupped her hand to the phone. "What? Are you serious?"

Suddenly there was a shift in temperature in the room, causing both Lonzo and Tracie to stare at Monica. "We're on our way," she said into the phone.

Monica clicked off. She looked at Lonzo. "That was Alexandra."

"What did she say?"

Monica pulled him out of Tracie's earshot without excusing herself. She glanced over briefly at Tracie, who was still sitting on the piano stool, staring in disbelief at the sunflower seeds.

Monica spoke barely above a whisper. "A body was just discovered on St. Nicholas Avenue . . ." Her voice trailed off.

She tossed a look at Tracie Burlingame.

"It's a positive ID. Rashod Burlingame. He was thrown from a roof on St. Nicholas. His shoes are missing. There are sunflower seeds stuffed in his throat. The blood has been drained from his body. Same MO as his brother."

"Son of a—"

Monica cut him off.

She stole another glance at Tracie. "There's a serial killer on the loose in Harlem. Maybe I was wrong about Randi's death being a street killing. There's a

profile emerging here. Whoever the killer is, the offspring of Miss Burlingame seem to have his attention."
Monica spoke the prophetic words without having any
way of being aware of their full meaning.

"We've got to tell her." As soon as Monica spoke the
words, Tracie rose instinctively, regally, from the piano
stool. Her eyes found Monica's.

Monica cleared her throat. For the first time she felt
a stab of empathy for Tracie Burlingame. "Tracie I,
ummm . . ." Monica closed her eyes, shocked at the
impact of her own feelings.

"I'm sorry to inform you . . ."

Tracie was caught up in a tidal wave. She felt as if
she were being smothered. Waves of water rippled over
her. There was a current of diseased information floating through the air. She could feel it. She could taste it.
She didn't want to hear whatever it was.

Maybe if she resisted it, it would go away.

She backed away, fighting against the disease of
truth that was reaching out its arms to her, trying to
spread its poisonous tentacles through the recesses of
her mind.

Lonzo touched Monica briefly on the shoulder. He
zoomed in on Tracie Burlingame. The only way to deliver bad news was just to deliver it. Period.

"We're sorry, Tracie—"

Monica regained her composure. She cut Lonzo off
in midsentence. She would have to finish what she had
started. She wasn't a runner.

"Your son, Rashod Burlingame, is dead, Tracie. We
need you to confirm identification for us, but we're
pretty sure it's him. I'm sorry."

Tracie stood like a statue. Monica's words closed in
on her mental recesses. They squeezed until there was

barely any air left. They squeezed until the only word she could hear was *Death*.

Death. Tracie accepted this. She now understood it was her mantle to wear.

Her seed had the shadow of death on it.

30

Tracie Burlingame, Monica, Lonzo, and the medical examiner stood in the morgue in the same positions they had taken earlier, when Randi was murdered. Their joining together in this room was starting to feel like a regular occurrence. It was an uncomfortable occurrence, to say the least.

Both Dre and Michael were blessedly absent. The ME slowly unzipped the black body bag. The zipper scraped with a loud sound that grated on Tracie's nerves. It made her want to screech.

Lonzo viewed the damaged body with a silent inward sigh. He marveled at the sheer audacity of the killer's handiwork.

The medical examiner shook his head without even being aware of the gesture. He was a trained professional. It was an unconscious move on his part, but between the damage Tracie Burlingame was witnessing and the depth of her loss, which hung in the air like a blanket, well, it was enough to move even a hardened veteran like himself.

Monica closed her eyes, then glanced at Tracie, nodding her head. Tracie looked at the damaged, skeletal-thin remains of her son.

He looked small and vulnerable to her inside the clinical bag. He had the wispy air of somebody who had lived and died without anybody caring. She knew that wasn't true, but she couldn't shake the feeling that swamped her as she stared at the visual ruins of her son.

She had tried time and time again to get through to him, but he had moved further and further beyond her reach.

Though she hadn't really wanted to admit it to herself, Rashod had been the one blight on Tracie's false sense of happiness. Now he was dead.

Worst of all, she couldn't even feel his spirit in the room. There was simply nothing left of him. He was gone, like ashes blown away in the wind.

Recollections of the last time she had seen him barged into her memory banks. Guilt gripped her, making her wish it had been different. She couldn't believe that it was only yesterday morning she had seen him. It seemed like an eternity to her.

Unlike with Randi, she didn't even reach out to touch him. She couldn't touch him even if she wanted to. It just wasn't possible. Despite everything, this was not the end she had envisioned for Rashod.

A part of her had always held out hope that one day he would come around, that one day things would be different. Now that last glimmer of hope had been wrenched from her grasp, stolen from her by a maniac, and she intended to exact retribution.

"I've seen enough," Tracie told Monica, and nodded in her direction.

Monica gave a slight, almost imperceptible nod of her head. The medical examiner zipped up the bag without hesitation.

"What time did—"

The ME didn't let her finish. By now he knew the question by heart. "Rashod expired at approximately seven p.m."

"I see," Tracie said.

Her long, polished nails cut into the flesh of her palm. She glanced over at Lonzo for a fraction of a second, giving him a small smile. She tilted her head a little higher, although it felt as though she were dragging a heavy object from the ground. She turned and walked slowly away.

When she reached the door, she turned back. Waves of hatred splashed from her. The target of her hatred was Monica Rhodes. "I guess you won't be arresting my son for the murder of his brother tonight. Will you, Miss Rhodes? How does his death play for you?" Tracie threw Monica's words back at her with a vengeance.

They didn't miss the mark. The words poured over Monica like acid. Before she could gather a response, Tracie raced full speed ahead. Insultingly, she shot verbal bullets at Monica: "You couldn't follow a clue if the killer taped it to your forehead with an arrow pointing you in the right direction."

Tracie found herself mimicking the voice on the telephone. My God, she was repeating the words of a killer. Not only was she repeating the words, but also she had found herself taking on the same intonation, as though the killer were controlling her words by remote.

"Maybe I'll have to catch him myself, since you're obviously not up for the job. But if I do, you can rest assured there'll be nothing left in this room for you to view. You have my word on that."

There was total silence. Monica had the decency to look properly embarrassed. Tracie turned again, to go out the door, determination set in her shoulders. Her heels clicking on the high shine of the morgue's waxed and sterile floor signaled her departure.

Monica looked at Lonzo. "If Rashod Burlingame didn't put Randi's Karl Kani boot in his room, and if he didn't kill him, then who did?"

Lonzo's eyes shifted to bore into Monica's.

The question simply hung in the air between them, unanswered. Their former theory, as well as their slim lead, had died tragically with Rashod Burlingame.

The pieces had fit so perfectly, yet they didn't fit perfectly at all.

All theories, as well as any illusions, had been completely shattered below another of Harlem's rooftops. Anything resembling a fact was a joke.

And the body count was tallying up.

31

The Ancient Book of Prophecies. There it had lain on the altar carved out of stone. It was just within his reach, the pages whispering, beckoning to him to come forth and partake of the gems, to partake of the threads of power that lay within its pages.

In the light of day Souljah Boy, or Daniel Thomas Caldwell, as he was rarely called, could hardly believe it, but he knew it had been so. For years he had studied to show himself approved before the Lord Jesus Christ.

When he had reached the ripe old age of twelve, he had set out on his own quest for the truth. He had diligently followed the path to it, although it had always set him apart. He'd never had the same interests as other young men, not even other kids when he was a child.

He and Dre had always been tight. Once he had tried to indoctrinate him with some of his learning, but it hadn't worked. Dre just wasn't in that particular plane of thought.

Harlem was famous for its churches, and as a kid, his grandmother dutifully made sure he was in his pew during the week and on Sundays.

Only, as he listened to sermon after sermon, he had begun to feel there was more. Much more. There was always this haunting, hungering feeling inside him, reaching, trying to embrace that which he could not see.

He had begun to observe the people in the church, and he couldn't help feeling that somehow the people were not totally connected to this deity. It was as if they praised, shouted, and Bible-studied, but they weren't connected on the ethereal level.

Finally he had hit on the truth. There was no power in their worship. There was no power, because there was no real faith. There was no real belief, not at the gut-wrenching levels or the deep emotional crevices they would need to tap into.

If the sweeping, healing power of Christ had ever entered the church, a great majority of the people who were in regular attendance would have questioned the source.

How could you receive a miracle if you didn't believe in its existence?

As a result, most churches he had been in were devoid of real spiritual gifts. The gifts of prophesying, faith that moved mountains, healing, and teaching were simply not in existence in the hallowed souls of a lot of people who attended church.

It was obvious in the lack of evidence of power in their everyday lives. It wasn't there, because they were not audacious enough to activate it.

The shock of this revelation had spiraled Souljah Boy on a course in life that had birthed great knowledge, and with that knowledge had come great pain.

He'd dedicated himself in the coming years to constant and meditative prayer for mercy and an increase in faith, so he could be a living participant in a higher learning—a participant who could connect to that power.

The power that Jesus had both demonstrated and promised during the time he had spent on earth. Jesus Christ was the most legendary man ever to have lived. And Souljah Boy wanted to be part of his legend.

He hungered to connect spiritually to the Maker, the Creator of mankind. It occupied his thoughts most nights and most days.

He desired to be at one with the spirit who had blown the breath of life, his own spirit, into man. And then, to top it off, had allowed his son to be slaughtered for the sins of the world. In short, Souljah Boy had dreamed of climbing the highest pinnacles to be obtained in the flesh and on earth, in the spirit. On this night he was not to be disappointed.

The discipline, enlightenment, and teaching he had received were not learned of men. For that, he was truly humbled. The gift of his salvation was a daily source of joy for him.

Souljah Boy was a researcher at heart, a spiritual researcher and a black ghetto scribe. He had spent many a year between the dusty, yellowed pages of books that most people didn't know existed.

He had been researching, seeking, studying, and yearning for a long time, and he had known that the Ancient Book of Prophecies existed. It contained the secrets, codes, and prophecies of things yet to be for the black people, ancient prophesies that were shrouded in the spirit and guarded by it as well.

Never in his wildest imaginations did he fathom his ever seeing or touching this book. Its rumored existence among prophets, scribes, spiritualists, African-American theologians, and religious scholars was pure legend and myth entwined into one.

Church leaders, ministers, bishops, archbishops, missionaries, priests, and laypersons alike were never blessed enough for the myth to reach their ears, nor would they have believed.

No, you had to be a very special person to hear the whisperings of its being. You had to be one who denied the flesh, the simple yearnings of man; one who was humble and honored the spirit, not the glory of men. You had to be one who was chosen.

That single book lent credence to many things to come and many things past concerning the spiritual roots of blacks the world over. In it were both good and evil.

The night Rashod Burlingame was murdered, Souljah Boy had been summoned as he slumbered, into a recess of the spirit that was one step away from death. He had been summoned because there were things he needed to see.

He received the same vision as Anita Lily Mae Young and Tracie Burlingame, only the wisdom of this was opened to him like petals on a flower blooming.

This vision was tied to the reason he had received the prophecy of Rashod's death.

He saw the big bald-headed man and all that was in him. Souljah Boy bowed his head in horror.

Finally, the pages of the book had beckoned him: *Come.*

He had done so. When he reached out a hand to touch the parched, sandpapery pages, he had been sucked into a void. That void was the *Unspoken,* and now he beheld many things, just as they had beheld him.

Once he had felt, he had been dispatched back to his own bed, back to his own consciousness, back to the consciousness of men. And that was why he had sat in the light of day, illuminated from the inside out.

He had been given a mission, and only through the levels from whence he had come would he have ever believed it about Tracie Burlingame. Only the truth of where he had journeyed in the spirit kept him firmly anchored.

Suddenly, looming up before his very eyes, there emerged a spirit that announced itself, saying, "I am Reverence."

Souljah Boy rebuked the evil, and the spirit immediately vanished. His spirit had been touched by the *Unspoken.* He was now one of the elect. As such he could not be deceived.

Curled up in a tight ball in the dark of his closet, he who called himself Me was deeply troubled.

Someone was treading very near his spirit.

Someone had been dispatched to follow his trail.

32

Me was spiraling again, totally out of control. The wind was whipping with the fierceness of a hurricane. He was twirling, twirling, caught up in the spirit of the storm, and there was nothing he could do about it.

He knew from past experience that it would take him where it would. When the hurricane stopped twirling, he found himself standing on dry desert land under the scorching brightness of the sun.

There was literally nothing he could see on the vast horizon. The earth had shaken under his feet. The wind roared in his ears like the voice of loud thunder. Then the world around him went pitch-black. It was just as if someone had come into a brightly lit room and turned off the light switch.

Me ran his hands along his biceps, hoping to feel the comfort of his spirits, but his biceps were smooth;

there was nary a ripple. He could not even feel the rims of Ms. Virginia's bifocals. He could not feel them, because they were not there.

She was someone he had come to rely on. Without her he felt coldness deep within him, not in his soul, for he didn't possess a soul in that sense, but in the inner parts of his being. Once he had possessed a soul, many eons ago. The price of having one, well, he couldn't allow himself to dwell on that right now. He knew the price. He knew it all too well.

Sometimes some of the spirits he collected writhed in anger and agony. But even that was better than not being there at all. Panic welled up inside him. He took deep breaths, psyching himself into controlling the wind flow of his body.

Then he heard it: a sound like a zillion scabs being picked at the same time. It rumbled from the pit of his stomach. It exploded inside him.

"Now!" came the rumble from inside him.

He was being pummeled, pummeled with spittle. It rained down on him, turning into baseball-size hail. As soon as the hail hit the ground, it turned into balls of fire that rose up, searing his feet, moving, moving and scorching his skin along the way, but he did not burn.

He was one livid motion of burning, searing pain. The Quest—that was it. He must move faster in order to claim the ultimate prize. There was a new spirit that had been added to the dimension. It was fast on his trail.

"Okay," came the echo of his acquiescence. "Okay." And the searing flames released him. The ground opened under his feet and bounced him through the realms, back into his own closet.

Once again he rubbed his biceps. Someone sneezed,

and he burrowed his body into a tighter ball. The sound of the sneezing gave him great comfort. As he rubbed, he felt the rims of Ms. Virginia's bifocals. Things were back to normal for the time being.

But he could not lose that which he was.

33

Michael Burlingame had stood rooted to the spot, fighting off waves of nausea as he stared at the corpse that used to be his brother, Rashod Burlingame.

The coroner, knowing who he was, had obliged his request to visit with his brother alone.

"The Burlingame family is one troubled lot," the coroner had mused aloud to himself after receiving Michael's call.

He had already dealt with the mother. Now here was Michael Burlingame. He wondered briefly if the other son would show up. Actually, there really weren't too many of them left.

The medical examiner had retreated to his office, allowing Michael some privacy, although he could see him through the glass partition. He would rather have skipped being party to the boy's sorrow if he could have.

He knew that the boy's street name was Rebound, a namesake of his basketball skills. But in his opinion he didn't seem to be rebounding too well from the well-placed blows to his family. Despite the detectives, the medical examiner knew that something dark and sinister had been unleashed in Harlem.

Something nameless.

Hubert knew they were not just chasing a psychopath. They were chasing an entity, an entity that was quite possibly foreign to them—or to any police force, for that matter.

Some of it he couldn't explain, but examining Rashod's body gave him the heebie-jeebies, for lack of a good solid medical term. There just was no term for what he was seeing and feeling.

And it was a good thing he had decided against mentioning it, because he would definitely have been at a lost to find precise words with which to explain it.

For instance, he hadn't highlighted in his report that part of Rashod's brain was missing. It was basically his memory bank. It was similar to what you saw in advanced Alzheimer's patients. Parts of the brain just disappeared—evaporated as though they had been absorbed.

But this was a young, healthy boy in his prime, with no previous medical or personal history of any memory loss. It was, well, bizarre, to say the least. It was like missing pieces of a patchwork quilt. Some of the pieces seemed to have been, well, somehow hollowed out. And, it wasn't only the brain—there were literally hollowed-out parts throughout different organs of the body.

He'd had an uneasy feeling about Randi Burlingame's death, too, when he examined him. Only the symptoms in his brother Rashod were not found in Randi, although the same feeling persisted surrounding both their deaths, if that made any sense.

The circumstances of both their deaths were the same. Both had been asphyxiated. Both had sunflower seeds stuffed down their throats. Both had their footwear missing. Both bodies were drained of blood. But here was where the similarities ended. Internally Randi Burlingame possessed the whole of his brain and innards.

Rashod Burlingame did not.

The ME glanced over at Michael. Michael's face had taken on a skeletal quality. There were dark-rimmed circles under his eyes, and his cheekbones stood out starkly against his skin, like sharp-pointed bones. His eyes had taken on the quality of a startled deer caught off guard in the bright headlights of a car. And he moved as though he had suddenly been afflicted with arthritis. His motions were stiff and awkward. He was barely a shell of the lithe, swift young man the coroner had met such a short time ago.

Michael simply stared at Rashod, unable to believe he had predicted his own death and had in fact actually sketched out the details in advance. It was too fantastic a thing even to contemplate. So were the events that led to his learning of Rashod's death in the first place.

Michael had been taking in a new high-action adventure flick at the Chelsea Theater on Twenty-third Street. He had arrived early, just as he always did, so he was comfortably ensconced in his seat with hot buttered popcorn, a box of Milk Duds, and a Coke while the previews were running.

He had no plans for cruising the streets or of ever suiting up in black and chains again—not after what had happened to him. His heart beat like a trip-hammer whenever he thought about the incident.

He could not get the image of red, bloody teardrops— falling from the ceiling, landing on top of his head, and dripping down the sides of his face—out of his mind. Blood had actually rained down on him.

Nor could he forget the piercing wail of his plea for mercy. He had lived an out-of-body experience, and it had shaken him to his very core. Hell, he had thought that only happened to freaks, like people who participated in those weird psychology experiments.

He hadn't known it was real.

So he had gone to the movie, trying to take imaginary flight from the stress levels that were building up in his head. A mind-blowing, fantasy-oriented, high-action beat-'em-down flick was just what he needed, or so he thought.

Just before the main feature was scheduled to run at about seven p.m., Michael had found Rashod, hovering in front of him in a dreamlike state, blocking his view of the screen. He looked mangled, almost like a balloon someone had sucked all the air out of. He was wheezing, and something was streaming from his open mouth.

He had reached out for Michael. When he did, Michael felt as though he were being wrapped in a soft, silky cocoon. It was a feathery-like feeling.

Rashod had leaned over and whispered, his voice rasping in Michael's ear, agony tingeing his every word, "This is it, little brother. Checking out. Time's up, just like I showed you."

Michael had sat frozen in his seat, not believing his

own eyes. Rashod had begun to flicker like a lightbulb that was not screwed in tight. Then pieces of him began to disappear, as though he were being absorbed.

It was the same type of aura Michael had witnessed on him when they were kicking it in his room.

The last thing Michael felt was a blast of frigid air, directly in the spot where Rashod had stood in front of him. He heard a sucking sound. Then he literally felt the spirit of Rashod evaporate, like mist into thin air.

And then he couldn't feel him at all.

He saw his brother lying broken on the concrete. Michael couldn't feel a thing. The theater faded from around him; it ceased to exist.

Michael witnessed the broken and shattered shell of Rashod Burlingame, lying dead against the hard sidewalk. The landscape of his death visually affected him as though he'd been hit with a sledgehammer.

Reality returned. Michael clutched the back of the seat in front of him. His heart thundered so loud in his ears that he couldn't hear the sound track on the movie.

He leaned over as he noticed what looked like a white sheet of paper that had been left on the empty seat.

If Michael had any doubt about what he had witnessed, that single sheet of paper told a story more powerful than any words. It was the sketch Rashod had shown him of his pending death at his apartment.

His brother had left him a legacy.

Suddenly Rashod's words reverberated through the recesses of Michael's mind: "Tracie's door has the shadow of death on it, man."

It wasn't possible. Yet as he stood staring at Rashod, the evidence was hard to deny. Rashod was in fact dead. Michael had felt him die. Then somehow Michael had been transported to St. Nicolas Avenue, where Rashod had drawn a final breath. He had seen his body sprawled on the street.

Rashod had left him something to be remembered. He had left him a message just as sure as Michael was standing there. Rashod had sketched a gruesome scenario, and in it he had been the key player. Or was he?

Michael reached inside the body bag. He ran five fingers down Rashod's bloodless face, as though Rashod might feel the tender gesture.

Inside his new home next to Ms. Virginia, Rashod felt Michael's pain. He shivered at the touch from the world he was no longer apart of.

34

Me wasn't sure he liked his newest resident. In fact, the more he thought about it, the more certain he was that he did not. Yeah, he had a few minor gifts: sketching and a strong sense of telepathic communication, for sure.

Rashod had managed to reach his brother Michael just before Me sucked out his spirit.

That alone was unusual. Me had never once had it happen before. Usually he was in total dominance. Rashod Burlingame had been an exception. But still, he wasn't of the caliber of the other residents in state.

Over time, Me had collected extraordinary gifts. In him resided artists, painters, sculptors, musicians, authors, singers, politicians, sports figures, and even some ministers of the clergy known the world over.

Rashod Burlingame was not of this breeding, and yet he had been stamped and profiled to be in residence. The boy was a junkie, plain and simple. To Me that fact alone had overridden Rashod's gifts. He had no discipline, no stamina. He had been corrupting and polluting his mind and his body while he lived.

He was a sack of nothing, despite his minor-league gifts.

In fact, Me had been watching Rashod all along. He had been absorbing pieces of him before his comrade killed him, and immediately afterward he had stolen his spirit.

Even though Me had absorbed parts of his brain and other organs in his body, Rashod's gift had still been strong. Pieces of his brain were physically missing, but his ability to perform was not.

The drugs had weakened Rashod and made him transparent, while he still possessed the spirit of life. But his gift and insight had been intact; he had grown in direct opposition to Me's absorbing him.

And it had not escaped Me's notice that the boy had extraordinary will. His strength was phenomenal. He had reached his brother, before the final execution as well as before the absorption of his spirit by Me.

That in itself was exceptional.

Me looked at him and saw the same sullen attitude and insolence the boy had possessed while alive.

"Don't get on my nerves, Mr. Burlingame. You are a guest—a temporary one, to be sure."

Me was almost exhausted from the stream of words he had spoken; generally he used as few words as possible. But this Rashod, he disturbed his spirit.

Rashod glared at Me from under the thick molasses of Me's dark skin. His lips stretched into a thin veneer of distaste. He looked at Me with what could not be mistaken for anything except disdain.

He was his mother's son, all right. "Go to hell," he told Me emphatically, without a twitch of fear.

Me viciously backhanded his left biceps. He watched Rashod's head whiplash from the blow. "Don't talk back to me, boy. You're here because you're the nurtured seed of the host, nothing short of that."

Rashod snorted but made no other response.

In that instant, Me knew that he would have to greet the other brother, Michael. He would have no time to waste. He knew that Michael would be at Rashod's very soon.

He had not counted on this; however, provisions would have to be made. His current plans would have to be delayed for the moment. He had planned to get around to Michael, sucking up the aftermath of his spirit once Me's comrade killed him.

Michael was most definitely on that hit list.

In addition to that, Michael Burlingame was another seed of Tracie Burlingame, the host. Me had already missed devouring the spirit of Randi Burlingame.

He would have to launch a counterattack thanks to Rashod Burlingame's brilliance. Well, it would be one of majestic proportions.

He would have to be very careful. He could not take Michael's life, because that would force a confrontation with his comrade. Michael was tied like an invisible umbilical cord to Tracie Burlingame. Therefore, it was not worth the risk of killing him himself.

His comrade was salivating after Tracie. Me knew he both needed and wanted the distinctiveness of Michael's blood. It would not do to force his hand too soon. The time would come.

He figured his comrade would tire of playing with Tracie soon. When that happened, Me would be there.

But it would not do to engage him in a personal vendetta at this time, upsetting the plan or the powers.

However, he would pay a little visit to Michael Burlingame. But he certainly would not go in his present form. No. This meeting would require a different entity. Rashod Burlingame had managed to leave a trail, a link that must be destroyed, erased at all costs.

Rashod glared at Me as though he could read his thoughts, causing an alien feeling to come upon him. A feeling that said, "formidable opponent."

That feeling, never before felt by Me and unbeknownst to him, would prove to be prophetic.

35

Tracie was in a dark, foul mood, and she knew she was facing a storm of humongous proportions. Even though Rashod was dead, she would still have to deal with Whiskey. There would be no time for mourning. As soon as he was out of the way, she would begin putting a plan in effect to learn the identity of the person who was destroying her life.

She would come straight to the point with Whiskey, who had no respect for her current circumstances. When he wanted to see her, he wanted to see her. Period.

Here she had another dead son, and she could not even attend to his memory until Whiskey's desires had been met. In that instant she hated him with a passion, but business was business.

She would tell him she wanted the guns moved now.

She arrived at the club on Malcolm X Boulevard and strutted over to the bar. There was an old jukebox spinning off sounds. Some things never changed in Harlem, and this place was one of them. The blue strobe lights flashed streaks across Tracie's features.

As soon as she sat down, the bartender approached her. "I'll have a double Rémy Martin," she spat before he had a chance to ask.

He looked surprised.

He pulled out the bottle and poured the drink. He had been working in the liquor business so long, he prided himself on being able to guess a person's drink from a mile away, but Tracie Burlingame had just put a stitch in his game.

She downed the drink in one gulp and handed him the glass. "I'll have another."

He poured. She gulped that one, too.

She handed him the glass. He poured again. Same drill. Again she handed him the glass.

It was becoming a ritual. This time he hesitated.

Tracie slipped a hundred-dollar bill from her bra. She put it on the bar in front of the bartender's face. Her gaze was unwavering.

He poured the drink. This time she took a sip and set the glass in front of her. He heaved a sigh of relief and hightailed it away from her to serve another customer.

Whiskey walked in. Tracie spotted him out of the corner of her eye. She gave no acknowledgment of his approaching presence. Upon reaching her, he ran his finger along her cheek. Her cheek was cold, smooth to the touch. Tracie didn't twitch a muscle.

She was one cool customer, Whiskey observed.

"I want the guns moved."

Whiskey sucked his tongue. "Ta,ta,ta,ta,ta. Do you think you can be involved with weapons of blood and vengeance?" He hesitated, then smoothly slid into his French accent: "Caro, without having it touch you?"

He leaned over and whispered in her ear while entangling her hair in his hand and turning her face smoothly toward him. "They stay until I say they're moved. I'll give the order soon. Oh, and you seem to keep losing things, Caro. I wouldn't want you to lose those guns."

Whiskey slid an envelope into her purse, disentangled his hand from her hair, and walked out of the bar. Tracie didn't acknowledge the cash or his leaving.

Lonzo breezed past Whiskey on his way into the bar. He was officially off duty and had decided he needed a drink.

He noticed Tracie Burlingame immediately. Quickly he moved into her sphere. He took the seat on the bar next to her. She glanced over at him, drained her glass, and then signaled the bartender.

It was getting to be a long night.

The bartender came over, and before Tracie could speak, he said, "I don't think—"

Tracie cut him off sharply. "I'm not paying you to think. I'm paying you to pour my drinks."

"It's all right," Lonzo jumped in quickly.

"Really, it's all right, Willie; I'll make sure Ms. Burlingame gets home. Give me a seltzer water." Seeing as Lonzo was a cop as well as a regular, Willie backed off. He tossed an exasperated glance in Tracie's direction before walking off.

When he returned, Tracie said, "I'll take another one; that way I won't have to bother you again in a few minutes." Willie bit his tongue, pouring another drink. The woman drank like a fish.

Lonzo stood, stretching his arms and legs. "Excuse me for a minute, Ms. Burlingame, I need to use the restroom."

Tracie didn't even acknowledge his words. First Whiskey, now this; they were like parasites draining her flesh.

Somewhere in the distance a phone rang. Willie answered and walked up to Tracie. "You're Tracie Burlingame, right?"

"I am."

"This is for you." He handed her the phone.

The now familiar distorted voice floated over the wire. "You can run, but you can't hide, Li'l Caramel. Oh, and I'm sorry about Rashod. His death and all, you know. Consider him another contribution to my endowment in my thirst for blood. You know?"

Tracie couldn't believe her ears. She hissed into the phone, "Screw you."

"Are you angry at me, Tracie? It's only a game. We could meet if only you'd be willing to travel back in time."

A loud click ended the call.

Tracie was fuming. She would find this child-eating monster if it was the last thing on earth that she did. He could count on it. She was so furious, she could hear her own blood supply pounding in her ears. Her blood pressure was skyrocketing.

First she would have to make sure that her other two sons were safely tucked away. The audacity! This maniac actually thought killing her sons was a game.

She would kill this bastard.

She stood up, steady as a rock despite the amounts of alcohol she had consumed. She threw another couple of crisp, new one-hundred-dollar bills on the counter for the bartender's trouble of having to deal with her tonight.

She left the bar before Detective Lonzo Morgan had a chance to return from the men's room. He was an incompetent dog of magnified proportions. He couldn't even find her son's killer.

Upon Lonzo's return from the men's room, Tracie Burlingame had vanished.

36

Michael arrived at Rashod's studio in the hotel in a foggy state of mind. He couldn't remember the last time he had eaten—or even slept, for that matter—and he was hungry. He was also exhausted. The emotional roller coaster he had been set on was draining him.

He had this weird sense of being a spectator, as though he were watching someone else go through the motions, but that someone else was not him. Somehow he was not really attached. He put one foot in front of the other.

He needed to take one step at a time. That was it. He could do this. He just needed to take one step at a time.

He flipped out his spare set of keys, the same keys he used to let himself in with, to leave Rashod food and money at times when he was skied out of his mind on crack cocaine.

"Hey, Rebound."

He turned, thinking he had heard Rashod's voice whispering to him. But of course, Rashod wasn't there. He was in the morgue. Michael knew that. He ran a hand through his thick, short dreadlocks and sighed.

He decided he would go home once he was done and have a serious chat with Tracie. He knew from the medical examiner that she had already been to view Rashod's body and that she was devastated over the loss of another of his brothers.

A sense of unreality settled over Michael, gripping his brain cells and squeezing tight. His head was pounding. The tension was starting to creep along just at the base of his neck. How could two of his brothers be dead?

Another day of school was being blown off. He couldn't play the benefit game with the Harlem Globetrotters. He felt as though his life in school and on the basketball court belonged to another person.

It didn't seem as if it was his life anymore.

He had another brother who had been put on ice. Surely that was a legit reason for missing school as well as basketball practices and benefit games.

Besides, he couldn't concentrate on anything. His focus was dimmed. All he could think of was the sketch that had portrayed Rashod's death, as well as his recent conversations with Rashod, although the last one had been more of a one-sided deal that he hadn't yet come to grips with.

Suddenly he recalled Rashod's words with stunning clarity: *"I know we didn't grow up religious man, but sometimes I wonder if there's something else out there. Do you believe in dreams? Or seeing things before or after they've happened? Even if you weren't there?"*

Michael slipped his key into the lock on the studio apartment, trying to keep the recalled words at bay. He had lied to Rashod because something had happened to him that he hadn't felt ready to talk about.

Michael shook away the thoughts. He needed to concentrate on the task at hand. He decided he would probably need to open the windows to get rid of the closed-in, musty scent of the place and let some sunshine in.

Rashod needed to air the place out more. When Michael was here the last time, the place felt stuffy and airless to him.

Rashod had been something of a slob in his own right, except with his sketches. He was known to throw his things around everywhere. His room generally looked like a cyclone had hit it. You could clean up his room, and hours later it looked as if it had been turned upside down by a tornado.

He smiled at the memory of Tracie screeching at the top of her lungs for Rashod to clean up the room. She had actually chased him through the brownstone with a broom handle once because she was so infuriated with his pigsty methods of keeping his room.

Michael couldn't stand disorder, so in contrast to Rashod's bedroom, when they both lived at home, his room had been neat as a pin. They were probably about as different as they could be, even though they were brothers.

They had all been tight as a family at one time, because Tracie was all they had—her and each other. Their father had died when they were young. There was little or no memory of him, except for the stories that Tracie had shared with them while trying to evoke a male presence in their lives.

Michael pulled himself from his reverie, deciding he would look at the sketches, search around for whatever else he could find that might lend some reality to the situation, and then later come back to put things in order.

He didn't want Tracie to have to deal with the pain of sorting through Rashod's room so soon after Randi's death. She hadn't touched a thing in Randi's room as far as he knew. Randi's room looked as though he would be back at any minute.

Michael opened the door to the studio, knew he was right about letting in some air, and flicked on the light switch. Before he was fully in the room, the first thing he noticed was another one of Rashod's sketches lying on the table in the small alcove that served as a kitchen.

That struck him as odd, because Rashod's sketches were the one and only thing he had kept in order. He had been meticulous with the keeping of his artwork. There was a sequence to Rashod's work; he had never liked it to be skewed. Michael sighed. He would need to go through the other sketches leaning against the wall, too. As far as he could see, only the one on the table was out of place.

A strange feeling shrouded him. He realized with a start that he did not want to see the sketch on the table. The feeling persisted, draping itself over him like a strong electrical surge. For no reason that he could explain, he just didn't want to see it.

But he was drawn like a magnet to the sketch on the table. He had absolutely no will of his own. His limbs were acting under their own influence. They drew him steadily and with fixed focus on his collision course. He couldn't have stopped himself any more than he could have stopped breathing.

When he reached the table, he stared down at the drawing. He reached out his hand to pick it up. The paper scorched his hand as though he had stuck his hand in fire. Michael pulled his hand back as a shocked gasp of air burst of its own accord from his lungs. His eyes misted over.

He was staring directly at a sketch of what had happened to him when he was cruising Chelsea—right down to the bloody raindrops falling on his head. It was unmistakably Rashod's work.

It was impossible. How could he have known? How could Rashod have sketched a picture of his shame in Chelsea? He hadn't been there. Michael stared down into the tracings of his own agonized image. His mouth was thrown open as a plea for mercy escaped his lips.

There was a tingling in his scorched hand. The pain in his hand receded as if it had never been there, as though he had only imagined that he scorched it. He needed air. He went to the windows snapped up the shades on each one, and opened the windows with a frightening speed.

He ran from window to window. He had to move. He could not stand still. His heart was pumping out an erratic tune he had never heard before. It was actually skipping beats. He hoped he wasn't having a heart attack. No, he couldn't be. He was too young to have a heart attack. Creepiness had clamped itself to his skin like a sticky slime he couldn't detach himself from.

He had the vague feeling that this was how a horse must feel when someone other than its owner was riding it. The alien rider was in control, demanding that the horse bow to his will. The other gave subliminal physical signals that the horse knew it must obey.

It also dawned on Michael that Rashod must have

guessed or known all along that he was sadomasochistic. Yet he had never mentioned it or treated him like anything other than the little brother he loved. The force of this knowledge staggered Michael.

Once the windows were open, he walked back to the table with the sketch on it. Suddenly every shade and window in the place snapped shut, one by one. Michael watched in fascinated horror as the room began to shut him off from the outside world.

His surroundings had come alive. A force of energy swept through the room, causing the very air to shiver in its wake. A resounding bang reverberated like a firecracker exploding as each window slammed shut.

The shades on the windows snapped shut with an eerie finality. Rashod had one of those old-fashioned police bolt locks with the long iron rod on his door. It slid into place, metal banging against metal. Michael turned and jumped at the sound of the clanging metal lock.

The floor shook, literally knocking him off his feet. His ears exploded as though he were being dropped from a great height.

And then he was. "Sweet Jesus!" he yelled.

He was falling through the air. He threw out his arms, and he could feel nothing to latch on to. There was nothing for him to grab. He was flailing, sailing through the atmosphere. His oxygen supply was being sucked away. He gasped, trying to gulp in some air. His chest caved in. He was hit with a sledgehammer blow.

It was just like the dreams he had heard people talk about, so he knew he couldn't land or hit the bottom. If he hit the bottom, he would be dead.

"God, no!" Michael screeched as he fell through layers of air.

"Please!"

A loud thump, and Michael was gripping the thread-bare rug on the floor of Rashod's studio. He lay on the floor like a beached whale.

The room plunged into total darkness. Not the same kind of darkness as when the shades were closed, but darkness that felt total in its completeness. This darkness was all-encompassing.

All along, Michael had felt that something was amiss when he stepped in the room, but he had not been able to put his finger on it. The dawning awareness of what that was made him grit his teeth in horror.

He could feel no trace of Rashod's spirit. It was as though he had never been there. But there was some kind of spirit in the room, and it was not a good one. There was a demonic force in the room.

Although Michael had no experience with it what-soever, he knew it was so. He identified it as the same force he had felt when he looked at the sketch Rashod had shown him. The force was alive. It was very, very much alive.

He also knew from his brief experience with Randi's death that you could still feel a person you loved when you entered their personal surroundings. He had felt it when he had gone to sit and mourn by himself in Randi's room—as though Randi's aura still somehow permeated the room.

But that feeling was completely absent in Rashod's studio. The studio was cold. In fact, it was downright frigid. Rashod's spirit was nonexistent.

He heard a sucking sound. Michael strained his ears. Oh, yeah, there it was. It started like the beginnings of a whisper. It was building to a full-scale wind tunnel.

It gathered speed.

Michael watched as it funneled into a whipping swirl of wind that contained itself in the center of the room.

As suddenly as it had started, it stopped. Abruptly. The sucking sound was gone. The wind tunnel was gone. There was nothing save the deep darkness that inhabited the room.

Michael tried to adjust his eyes to the blackness. He blinked. His whole body was trembling. It had turned into a mass of jelly. As he tried to climb to his feet, his legs unsure of what it meant to stand anymore, a slow, scrawling scribbling insinuated its warning on the wall, in crimson, glowing print: "Go."

"What?" Michael listened to the word torn from his throat, but it might have belonged to anybody else, so foreign did it sound to his ears.

The scrawling grew more furious, bigger, as though it were yelling at him: "GO!"

Michael was on his feet—unsteady, to be sure, but he could feel the floor, which felt solid and comforting.

"What are you?"

Another scribble on the wall: "I AM ME."

"Who's Me?"

Raw fear had taken control of his every word. He hated the tremor that was in his voice, but it couldn't be helped.

No scribbling this time.

In the instant that Me had hesitated, Rashod had scrambled full force from the bereft depths in which he was residing, and forced a projected picture of himself before Michael's face.

He had always worn his pants pulled low, below his belly, with his Ralph Loren undershorts showing the label just above the rim. Now he used the disliked fad of his black youth to his advantage.

Across his belly he scrawled the words, "Fight, Rebound. Fight. Tracie . . ."

Rashod couldn't speak; his windpipe was clogged, clogged with the damnable sunflower seeds.

That was all he could transmit before Me sucked his image back, clamping it into his biceps.

Me was stunned. He couldn't. Hell, no. He wouldn't believe Rashod had this type of capability. Aw, but he did. That kid was a pain in the ass. He had no gift, and Me didn't want him. How the hell did he bypass him?

However, there was little to nothing he could do right now about Rashod and his little bag of tricks. But he could do something about Michael Burlingame.

Michael grabbed hold of a chair that was in front of him. For one solid fraction of a second, he had felt Rashod's spirit. Rashod had broken through. He was trying to reach him, trying to tell him something.

Something about fighting. He was trying to communicate something about Tracie. He fought through the layers of sheer horror gripping him, trying to retain what Rashod had said.

Michael had been steeped in fear and disbelief, along with confusion. But he now knew that Rashod was in the room. He hadn't been able to feel him before, but Rashod had broken through. He was trying to help. Michael understood this on a basic, gut level, but he couldn't put it into the right perspective. The pieces were scattered. He backed up, trying to figure out how he could get out of the room.

Me struck with a vengeance.

Rashod had taken this to a different level. Me could

not allow Michael Burlingame to think that what he had seen was Rashod. He had to alter the image.

As Michael was fumbling in the dark, trying to make his way to the door by memory, a shape emerged before him. It looked almost like a watery illusion, except that it began to take form. That form reached out, touching him.

Before him stood his brother Rashod Burlingame.

Before Michael could utter a sound, the form changed shapes. The skin on Rashod turned to scales, like those on a fish. It began to peel slowly away. Writhing underneath was a black boa constrictor. It was not Rashod at all.

Rashod appeared in front of the snake.

It *was* Rashod.

The six-and-a-half-foot snake stuck out its forked tongue. The heat sensors on its lips located the invisible prey that was Rashod Burlingame. It lashed out, sucking Rashod in, suffocating him, and then swallowing him whole as Michael watched in terrified astonishment.

"Rashod!" he yelled, his vocal chords constricted from fear and shock. "Rashod!"

NO! It couldn't have been. That wasn't Rashod. "God, please. That couldn't have been Rashod. Oh, my God, a snake swallowed Rashod!"

Michael ran blindly for the door, groping in the dark. But the boa constrictor was not yet done. His tongue lashed out, ripping the sketch Rashod had left him from inside Michael's pocket.

Michael felt the slimy, thick wetness of the snake's tongue soak right through his shirt, saturating his skin. Disgust rose like bile out of his stomach. He heaved.

The snake's beady eyes watched Michael accusingly. Its tongue flicked. It swallowed the damnable sketch whole, just as it had swallowed the spirit of Rashod.

Then it turned to dust before Michael's eyes.

With that, Michael fell to his knees. "Sweet Jesus," he softly moaned. "Sweet Jesus. Save us, Jesus. Please, save us."

Immediately upon speaking the words, Michael realized with shell-shocked reasoning, like a man who had been to war, that he was religious. Yes, he did believe. He would seek out the grace of this man called Jesus, who would help them.

Me had had a time with Michael Burlingame, but it was definitely time to move on. Besides, in the instant that Michael Burlingame had yelled out to Jesus, Me had fled. He could not stand before the presence of the Son of God.

Michael had cried out from the depths of his belly with such sincerity that unknowingly he had evoked the presence of the Holy blood. Me had instantly disappeared from the realm.

Light returned to the room. The door opened before Michael Burlingame as he bowed low on the floor, drenched in sweat and soaked in the saliva of the loathsome reptile.

37

Alexandra was fuming. She could have spit nails. Moments ago, the mayor of New York had just chewed her out in no uncertain terms, and she was out for blood.

Pacing her office, she had screamed into the phone at one of the police consultants as Lonzo and Monica sat trapped in their chairs before her desk, wishing they were someplace else.

"I said no press. I meant no press. Not a word. What? Am I not speaking English? Get rid of them. Now." She slammed the phone down in the receiver.

Her gaze landed on the two detectives sitting before her. A purple vein was pulsating in the side of her neck. Her breathing sounded like the whistle on a teakettle.

Lonzo, who was used to these little displays of temper, pulled a nail file from his jacket pocket. He filed his nails, waiting for the storm to switch directions.

Monica quietly stared out of the window. She was still chafing from Tracie Burlingame's spiteful little verbal bullets and was not quite ready to cope with Alexandra's as well. But cope she would, because Alexandra was in rare form.

"I tell you to find me a single murderer, and instead this escalates into a serial killing, just like I suspected. I told you I didn't want chalk outlines all over this city." Alexandra reached for a pencil, a sure bad sign. She gnawed on the end of the eraser.

Lonzo was tempted to throw her the pack of cigarettes in his jacket pocket, but he resisted the temptation. He continued filing his nails instead.

"Let me cut to the chase here. Do we have any suspects that are still alive? Because obviously Rashod Burlingame no longer qualifies."

Lonzo looked up. His nail file came to a halt. "No," he stated without elaboration.

Alexandra's steely blue-eyed gaze took in Monica. Monica shook her head.

"No?" Alexandra roared. "Did you say no?"

Outside Alexandra's office, Maya put on her Walkman. She turned it up full blast as Alexandra's voice came rumbling through the closed door. She liked Lonzo and Monica. She didn't want to be a willing witness to their verbal demise.

Maya hadn't acted a moment too soon, because just as she turned up the volume, Alexandra kicked over the chair in her office. It went skidding across the office, banging into the wall.

Alexandra sighed. She had to get a grip on herself.

This wasn't going to bring in the killer. But she was under a tremendous amount of political pressure, and various community leaders had decided to put in personal calls to her, demanding to know what the hell was going on. The last call had been from the reverend of Harlem's best-known historical Baptist church, with a large congregation that read like a who's who list. Needless to say, he hadn't called to invite her to Sunday's sermon.

This was exactly the kind of circus she had been trying to avoid. She also had to keep the media out of the case, and that was blowing up in her face, because somehow they had received vivid blown-up, colorful photographs of Randi Burlingame lying dead and broken on 135th Street.

Whoever had shot the photographs had a keen eye and was gifted with a laserlike precision for the visual. The vivid clarity with which the photographer had captured the tragedy had made even Alexandra bow her head in horror. She could not imagine what the public would do if those photographs were published.

She would have to call in some serious markers. She had already put the mayor of New York on it. He was calling in his markers as well. He had not been happy or diplomatic in stating his feelings about it. Gone was his Ivy League, Princeton-educated I'm-an-all-around-guy tone. In its place was fury, pure and simple.

The mayor would have to go to great lengths to suppress the information and keep the press away from this case. He was certainly not thrilled at the prospect. Besides, if by any slim chance it leaked, then there would be political and personal hell to pay. He would have to use his utmost discretion.

Alexandra took a deep, calming breath. She went over to pick up the chair, sliding it back to the desk. She sat down in the chair, ran her hands through her short blond curls, and joined Monica in staring out the window. She really needed to attend her meditation classes more often.

Monica continued to stare out the window in a sullen silence. What did Alexandra think they were, magicians? If there was no killer, there was no killer. Period.

It was all she could do not to let this blond witch know a thing or two. Who the hell did she think she was? Monica's thoughts kept repeating in her silent fury.

Finally, Alexandra spoke in a voice that belied her anger. "The *Amsterdam News* has received some stunning photographs of Randi Burlingame's death. Close-ups of him broken and twisted on 135th Street. They are claiming they don't know who sent the photographs. I'm in the process of trying to restrain them from publishing them, given the circumstances. I don't want to help the killer grandstand."

"That's an understatement," Lonzo muttered under his breath.

Alexandra ignored him.

Monica was suddenly revived from her comatose state upon hearing about the pictures. "Are they being truthful about not knowing the source of the pictures?"

"I don't know. Generally speaking, they don't like to reveal their sources. In this case, the killer could just be toying with us."

Monica wondered if Andre Burlingame could be responsible for the photos. But she didn't have anything to go on. Besides, it really didn't matter who'd sent them—unless, of course, it was the killer. What did matter at the moment was whether Alexandra could keep them from being published.

"Can you hold them off?"

"For now. But I don't know for how long," Alexandra said.

The three of them sank into silence, wrapped in their own thoughts.

Finally Alexandra said, "Oh. In keeping with consistency, the killer was kind enough to send us one of Rashod Burlingame's Air Jordan sneakers. His boy, Genie, identified it. There was no note this time; I guess he's told us what he wants to say. A picture—or in this case a sneaker, I guess—is worth more than a thousand words."

She blew a harsh breath. "But then what the hell? It seems he may have pictures, too, of his little artwork."

"No doubt our boy certainly doesn't like to stray far from the rules. We already knew Rashod was dead, so what was the point to sending the sneaker? Unless he has a fetish for tidiness."

"That and blood," Alexandra said. "Rashod's body was drained of blood, too. Same MO all the way through."

"What if this isn't a standard serial killing?" Monica said.

Alexandra squinted her eyes at Monica. "What do you mean?"

"I mean, what if the killer isn't a standard-profile serial killer? What if his serializing is selected? What if he's only after Tracie Burlingame's sons? Her sons are the only ones being murdered in Harlem right now."

Monica had Alexandra's rapt attention. Feeling herself, she spoke more rapidly.

"He hasn't struck anywhere else. What if it's a personal vendetta but he's making it look like a serial? Fun and games, you know what I mean? What if his killing is only centered on her sons? For that matter, she may know the killer."

Alexandra's eyes brightened. A newfound respect for Monica appeared briefly on the horizon. She would have thought of that if she weren't so damned stressed out. Where the killer would strike next had been all that was on her mind.

True, she had been shocked when she learned it was another one of Tracie's sons, but the pattern indicated that it could happen to any other boy at any time. Because of the style of the murders, she hadn't been convinced, even with Rashod's death, that it was just Tracie Burlingame's sons. The killer could be trying to throw them off. But Monica might be onto something.

"Okay," Alexandra said. A pregnant pause, then . . . "Let's fly with it. We could narrow our scope. Maybe even discover which son is the next target before he strikes. Then we could be there when he does." Alexandra's voice was laced with excitement. Her chase instincts had been revived momentarily, pushing aside her political agenda.

"That's what I'm saying," Monica said. "Now you're feeling me."

Alexandra nodded. "All right, I want you two to dig up everything you can find on Tracie Burlingame's family. See who's holding a grudge. Who's jealous? See if we can pinpoint which of those boys would be the next target." Alexandra smiled for the first time that day.

The two detectives rose from their captive seats, relieved at the slim ray of light they had received, and ecstatic about getting out of Alexandra's presence.

They could not in their wildest imaginations or in all their police training have been aware of what a cunning, shrewd, powerful criminal entity they were up against.

They could not even have imagined that the person they were seeking had created deception—that in fact, he was the embodiment of deception.

How could they have known he who was history?

He who was called Legion? Legion had the distinction of being the best known, yet he was the least recognizable of any enemy.

The police had been trained to believe only what they could see. They used scientific weapons of engagement, and technological profiles of research.

They were trained in hand-to-hand combat. They were highly skilled at fighting in the air. And they relied on historical data that had been gathered by the hands of men. If it had a shape or a form, then they were on it.

But what if it didn't?

If the police had had any idea that by that same time the following day, Harlem would be swamped in a river of dead black boys, their blood drained from their bodies, the coveted sneakers missing from their feet, and sunflower seeds stuffed down their throats, they would not have felt the false sense of elation they were experiencing by ferreting out another angle to look at.

No, they would not have felt elated at all. Instead they

might have abandoned their respective posts, seeking refuge in any place other than Harlem.

And not one of them would have traded places with Tracie Burlingame.

38

Tracie Burlingame made her way to the House of Pentecost on 129th Street in Harlem. She stood staring up at the crumbling but somehow awe-inspiring structure of the small church tucked in a corner of an old brownstone. She could feel rather than see the spirit that generated from it.

Just looking at it had given her a sense of serenity. It washed quietly over her as she stood with her hands stuck in her jeans pockets, debating whether she had the courage to actually step inside the church.

It had been a long time since she found herself seeking for the roots of the Christianity of her past, but here she stood. She had opted not to go to one of the larger churches in Harlem, because she was too well known in the area to seek the anonymity of spirit that she needed there.

But this church, so unassuming that it might not

even have been noticed, drew her to it. Its wings of comfort reached out to her.

Tears streamed down her face. She felt overwhelmed as she thought about the deaths of her two sons. Who would want to kill them? Why? She didn't even know why she was at the church. She was far from what one would call a praying woman.

But she needed solace in her spirit, in the place she had always kept well guarded. So she found herself striding up to the doors while wiping the tears from her eyes. She had tied a linen scarf over her silken mane of hair. She wore dark sunglasses to shade her eyes from the early morning sunlight. She had cried buckets of tears.

Yet her pain was her own to wear, not for the world to see.

She pulled open the heavy wooden doors to the church and stepped inside. A hushed silence greeted her as she gaped at the beauty of the church in its absolute simplicity. Everything was done in simple hand-carved wood. Her high-heeled pumps sank into what appeared to be lambs wool covering the floor.

The muted lighting and the age-old draperies lent an air of solitude to the small church. An antique table stood in front of the altar in the center. It held the Holy Bible on a wooden stand. On each side of it a flame of fire shot up out of what looked like glass candlestick holders.

The sight of the Bible with the flames of fire held Tracie. She almost wanted to touch it, but she dared not put her hands on it. How could she? She pulled away from the very thought.

Looking around the church, it was almost as though

she had gone back in time, as though she had stepped into another era, another place and time.

The church was wrapped in a blanket of serene peace and things unspoken but felt. Although it was small, it felt enormous, as though it were bigger than it looked. The few stained-glass windows in the front of the church cast brilliant, colored rays of light across the pews. It was a breathtaking sight.

Tracie walked down the aisle. She entered one of the pews and sat down. The church was empty, so far as she could see. She stared ahead at the altar, her eyes roaming to rest on the crucifix of Jesus Christ. She stared at the holy relic, depicting the body of the slain Messiah. Briefly she wondered what his life must have been like. There were bloody teardrops streaming from his eyes.

Lost in her reverie, she didn't notice the old, dignified black preacher, his skin the liquid color of black tar, with the silvery gray hair and beard, who was clothed in layers of colorful robes, until he was nearly upon her. His hair and beard were so silvery, they were the color of silver tinsel that people wrapped their Christmas trees in year after year.

The silvery hair against his tar-black skin was a startling contrast. The eyes that peered out from the sharp, smooth bone structure of his face looked centuries old. They radiated both wisdom and peace.

Tracie ventured a brief, startled glance in his direction as he stopped beside her. "Does your God dwell here?" she asked.

"My God dwells in many places," the old black minister said with a quiet confidence that conveyed his faith.

Tracie nodded. "I . . . I . . . I don't suppose he would help a woman who bows her head but cannot pray."

There, it was out. She had said it. For many a year Tracie had bowed her head in supplication, but nary a prayer had fluttered up from the depths of her heart.

She was a woman who was blocked. She simply could not pray. Not even as she had stood viewing the smashed, ruined remains of her dead sons had she prayed. She had bowed her head in abject pain, but the prayer had not come.

Tracie rose quickly from her seat. She slid out past the preacher. She quickly walked back up the aisle, toward the doors of the church.

Suddenly she halted. She turned shakily to face the old preacher. He hadn't uttered a word. But he was watching her with fatherly, ethereal concern.

"Could . . . Could you ask your God not to let my remaining sons be punished for my sins?"

Tracie's composure broke. She trembled slightly, biting hard on her lower lip. "Pl . . . pl . . . please," she stuttered.

The minister nodded his affirmation. He continued gazing at Tracie as she turned, rushing through the doors. When she was gone, he walked down the aisle. He approached the altar; then he reached underneath, pulling out one golden candlestick.

He lit it, bowing his head in prayer. "Heavenly Father, according to thy will let your mercy and grace be upon this woman. And if it be in accordance with your will, let her plea for the remission of her sin not fall on deaf ears. In the name of Jesus Christ, I pray. Amen."

The preacher felt drained by this simple prayer.

He felt as he did at times when he was in fasting, prayer, and supplication for long periods of time, although it had been mere moments at the most. Tracie

Burlingame had somehow spiritually burdened him with her plea for help. It had been laid on his shoulders like heavy cargo.

The preacher lifted his head up. He gazed at the streaks of sunlight streaming through the stained-glass windows of the church. Despair washed him in her streams. He somehow knew it would be a long road for this strange woman, whoever she was.

A flicker of something he had seen in the long-ago past flashed in his memory. It couldn't be. He immediately distanced himself from the thought.

He stared at the flickering light from the candle, trying to empty his mind. There it was again. But there was something more than the volume of words that had crowded into his mind. He shook himself free from the incredible possibility.

When he had bowed his head in prayer, he had seen the vision of the quilt. As she had walked up the aisle of the church, she had been covered in a spiritual patchwork quilt. The hollowed-out patches were raucous with voices of their own. There were multitudes of them. The black patches were seekers, the likes of which the preacher hadn't even heard whispered about since the ancient times of many centuries before. They were the whisperings of myths and folklore, and he had certainly never witnessed it.

The legend of the quilt had been buried much the same as the Egyptians of old had buried their treasures in tombs.

Years and years ago, when he had been a young man studying in the ministry, he had been taught, and he worshipped under the guidance of an old pastor.

He was every bit of a hundred and twenty years old, the oldest living man on earth at the time. There had been much speculation whether he could have really been that old, but the black, leathery parchment of his skin, and the gleaming wisdom that shone from his eyes had indicated that it might be so.

In any case the old man had shared the vision of the legend with him. He had bestowed on him the gift of the ancient, worn trunk with its precious contents. He had instructed the young preacher on its use. He also bade him be silent until the time should come.

He shook his head at the memory. He didn't even know if he had believed in it all until today, until this woman had shown up in the church. In the spiritual draping of the quilt, he had seen the vision.

So it wasn't a myth. It did exist. He sighed. To this end was his calling. And it jolted him to know he had been instructed and taught in this matter long ago. It had lain dormant inside him all this time, until this woman had awakened it.

The preacher retreated from the church. He made his way to his tiny personal chambers. His chambers were sparsely furnished, only functional, really.

He did not require elaborate furnishings or everyday comforts in his personal life. In his chambers were a bed, a desk, and a chair, with a lamp on the desk, on which also lay his Bible and his writing journals. He had a phone. Hanging on the wall there was a crucifix of Jesus Christ. The room contained little else. The chamber was attached to his own personal bath.

The preacher shed his robes, hanging them carefully on a hanger in the closet. The colorful robes stood out against the simple plainness of his chamber.

When he had done this, he took a key from the desk drawer and removed some boxes to reveal a door built into the floor of the closet. He unlocked it and reached inside, hefting out the ancient, worn trunk.

This would be the first time since the old minister had passed this on and instructed him that the trunk had ever been opened.

Unlocking the trunk, he took out the old canvas, tweedlike bundle that was laid neatly inside the trunk. He rolled it out to its full length on the floor.

Next he reached inside for the hermetically sealed jar that was filled with a black substance. He closed and locked the trunk.

When everything was safely in its place, he made a telephone call to one of the other house ministers. When the minister picked up on the other end of the line, he said, "I will be in prayer and supplication for the next three days and nights." He hung up the phone.

The preacher would know he could not be disturbed until this amount of time had passed, as he had indicated.

With that, he shut out all avenues of light to the room. He lay down on the floor, opened the glass jar, and poured the black ashes all over his body, covering himself from head to toe. Then he rolled himself in the sackcloth canvas bag, on the hard floor, and whispered the Our Father prayer.

After that he prayed for forgiveness in the name of Jesus Christ, in His Holiness, for the sins of the royal priesthood of the ministry, of which he was a part, and the Church, as one body, so he could stand in wholesomeness of spirit before the Lord. He prayed for the spiritual washing until tears of exhaustion ran down his face.

He prayed so he could be in favor before the Lord

Jesus Christ. He prayed so that his utterances could enter into the Kingdom, returning tenfold with the power of the Holy Ghost, which would be needed.

With the holiness of his preparation done, he proceeded to pray for the repentance and remission of sins for the strange woman who had asked for his help. And for those before her and for those after her, within her ancestry and among the seeds that had been implanted in her womb.

He now had a singular purpose, and to that end he would remain for three days and three nights. Tracie Burlingame. Her name blew from the mists of the air into his mind. He had not known her name. And as her name blew into the recesses of his consciousness, he knew it was true. That thought he had tried to escape. Tracie Burlingame was a spiritual patchwork quilt. Her very birth had been written.

The prayers rose up from the depths of his throat, from the bowels of his being, aligning his spirit as he prayed against the principalities of darkness in high places, and against the rulers thereof.

The blood of Jesus.

The preacher would pray in the sackcloth and ashes for three days and three nights, for Tracie Burlingame. The spirit would be his only sustenance. The path had been set. It was strewn with the legends of old. When his penance and his prayer were fully realized, the chains that bound Tracie Burlingame would be broken.

In his freshly resting place six feet under the ground, the bones of the old minister, who had taught the one repenting in sackcloth and ashes, turned in the grave of their own accord.

His placement in the course of things had been fulfilled. The old dead minister had never laid eyes on the Ancient Book of Prophecies, nor had he ever been told of its being.

But he had been given knowledge of the trunk in a dream. He was told upon whom the mantle should fall: he should be the one to carry out the sacrificial prayer. Upon whom it would fall: he would be the official intercessor.

When the time had come, the old preacher had passed it on to the younger one, of whom he had received the sign. Now that preacher was repenting in sackcloth and ashes.

It had been prophesied to the old preacher that it would be known when the person requiring the sacrificial prayer should appear. And he who would carry out the sacrificial prayer would know when the person arrived.

And so it had been set in place the moment Tracie Burlingame had stepped foot in the church.

When the old preacher had awakened from the dream, the old, worn trunk and its precious contents were sitting in the middle of his chambers. There was no sign or trace of who had left them there.

That had been one hundred fifty years ago, long before Tracie Burlingame had ever existed.

39

He had arrived in the darkness of the night. He stood in the middle of the exhibition room at The Schomberg Center for Research in Black Culture, on 135th Street and Lenox Avenue.

It was right across the street from where Randi Burlingame had taken his final tumble on the concrete sidewalk in Harlem. He looked on with disgust at the Harlem Renaissance authors whose portraits were proudly displayed on the walls. He snorted, and someone sneezed.

He knew them. Oh, yeah. He had known them all at one time or another. He'd known what their mission was, their slim visions of grandeur in the architecture of words.

But he had made sure, as they had drawn their wordy landscapes over the seasons of time, that not one of them had truly captured or been able to divulge the truth. They had not possessed the underlying foundation that could piece it all together.

Oh, they had tried. Many of them had been extremely gifted, and skilled at their crafts. But the written legacies they had created were missing the essentials. They had not truly understood the full scope of things at all.

Nor would they have believed the sheer incredibleness of the raw truth. He knew that their basic natures would not allow them to accept something that had been staring them in the face since the beginning of time. Not these people. They had been stripped from the first stage play.

But he had to acknowledge that as separate entities they had managed to carve out tidbits. They had strewn them around like pieces of a puzzle, in many cases around the world. And if a person had the vision, the dawning realization could have grave consequences.

That he could not allow. That was why many of their spirits were sequestered, the gifted ones. Yet he was lucky, as there was not one yet who truly knew how to string together the tidbits to make up the whole.

Me scowled with scorn at the small wooden stage platform in the exhibition room. The Harlem Writers' Guild, he knew, took great pride in holding their meetings in this particular room, where they felt that their ancestors and predecessors had laid a foundation of future success for them. They clung to these relics like drowning rats. Me laughed. He loved it when he had time to reflect on the well-placed stumbling blocks that had been placed in front of these people.

He hated these people. He specifically hated writers,

those crafters of words, trying with all their might to be like their maker.

His utter destruction over time, as well as his deep hatred of them and his role in their pain and suffering, should have been enough. But it wasn't. So on that night he decided to leave them something else to remember.

He had already been to the Manuscripts, Archives and Rare Books division in the research center. This precious division held personal papers, records of organizations and institutions, subject or thematic collections, literary and scholarly typescripts and playscripts, sheet music, broadsides, programs and playbills, ephemera, and rare books.

It held the history, literature, politics, and culture of peoples of African descent, or it had before Me's visit tonight. After his visit, it just held many thousands of sheets of paper. Blank paper.

It served them right, Me decided. This center was the pride and joy of Harlem. What a shallow people they were. Me snorted. Tracie Burlingame's future contribution would never be seen here, that was for sure.

As Me looked on with scorn, the rage welling and swelling inside him, Rashod Burlingame stared in rapt fascination and vivid horror as the implications of what this bald bodybuilding monster had been doing began to take shape in his mind.

From his place in Me's biceps Rashod struggled to see through Me's eyes. His gift was becoming stronger. When he had lived in his body on earth, his gifts, he realized, had been limited due to the abuses he heaped on himself on a day in, day out basis.

But having shed the restraints of his body, his spirit

was somehow growing stronger. Along with it, his view and his ability to manuever were somehow gaining strength, credence, and power as well.

Soon he hoped to figure out how to speak to Ms. Virginia. He knew she was here. He had heard the familiar voice not long after his arrival, but he had not known quite how to communicate with her. He'd heard about her death shortly before his own.

The woman had been a mainstay in the Harlem literary scene since before he was born. She had probably educated more black babies than Harlem's entire school system combined. Her store, Visionaries, had been a much beloved home and icon in Harlem. Like a favorite pair of old, comfortable slippers, always there for you.

Although he had never had any aspirations other than getting high and sketching when he was living, Ms. Virginia used to hire him. She'd give him a little change to run errands and move boxes of books and stuff for her. The fact that he was a junkie had never stopped her from doing it when she felt he was in need. Or when she wanted to give him what she called "productive work." She was one of his mother's oldest salon customers.

He needed to talk to her. He just had to concentrate hard and figure out how he could do it. The space in which they were contained was like a vast vacuum with invisible walls. They were invisible but extremely solid.

He wondered briefly if he had enough strength to prevent Me from totally destroying this section of the Schomberg Center, because that was exactly what Me intended to do.

He had run up on the fact that Me's destroying the Schomberg Center was a personal vendetta. In truth it was only a distraction from the true events that would take place.

Rashod was beginning to peer inside—just brief glimpses of pictures, really, were being transmitted to him from Me's mind, and he didn't like the portraits he was seeing. Whether he could do anything about them was a different story. But he would try because he wasn't going to let this bald monster take out his home ground like that. Me was an evil incarnate.

He kept seeing pictures of Tracie. Rashod didn't like it one bit that his mother was residing in this monster's mind. He didn't have the full picture, but he was not going to let this beast hurt his mother if he could help it.

He hoped Michael would gain some understanding from what had happened in his studio. They needed to put a plan in effect to take this bastard down.

But he had a feeling that Michael had fallen for Me's little mind game. Michael actually thought Rashod had been suffocated and swallowed up by the snake and that he couldn't communicate with him anymore.

It wasn't true; all Me had done was put forth a grand illusion before Michael, so that he could back him off and scare him. He'd wanted to create doubt.

But, that was all right, Rashod decided, because what went around came around. He would find a way to defuse this demon.

Me approached his first portrait. He had never before stolen pictures. He did not intend to do so now, so he quickly swallowed the names and dates of birth and death of the immortalized authors. He found this a bit unsatisfying. He needed to defile the faces of his enemies. So he generated a heat that caused the images to melt.

Rashod fought, but he was unable to get the right foothold he needed to defuse Me. Frustrated by his futile attempts, he banged against the invisible walls. They shook and trembled but did not move an inch.

Rashod felt Me turn away from his point of focus as another presence entered the room. Rashod peered through the layers. He spotted the uniformed security guard. Good, maybe he would put a stop to Me. But before the thought could get a purchase in his mind, Rashod already knew he was wrong.

"Who the hell are you?" the security guard spoke menancingly to Me. "There isn't supposed to be anyone on these premises at this time of night."

Me stared. "I am Me."

"Listen, fellow, don't get smart with me. You have no business being in here."

Me's bald head glistened under the hot lights.

The security guard, upon his entrance, had flicked on the overhead lights. They were beaming on Me's bald scalp. Me hated the feeling that was raining down on him from the lights, like hot lava being poured on his head.

"I have business," Me said.

"What business?"

Like a lightning strike, Me struck the security guard with one deft blow. His feet left the floor; his body went airborne. He crashed into the wall outside, beyond the small gallery. The security guard lay with his neck twisted at an odd angle. His chest was still.

Me knelt down, feeling for a pulse, although he

knew there wasn't one. Me stood over him momentarily. He didn't want his spirit—the man had no gift; he was just a plain old human, and Me did not want to taste his spirit on his lips.

"Not for Me," he said as he stared down at the prone, twisted body on the floor.

"You punk!" Rashod shouted out loud enough for Me to hear. Me cringed at the sound of Rashod's voice. The boy's voice grated on his inner nerves. Me looked at his biceps, found Rashod's place, and whacked him back and forth until Rashod's head spun.

But Rashod had discovered a secret. The only thing Me was seeing was his image where he usually resided. Rashod had managed to hide the substance of his spirit and project his image, which was really only a shell.

He had moved back into a corner of the vacuum where Me couldn't see him. When Me grunted in satisfaction after whacking Rashod, his satisfaction was brief, because Rashod loomed up in front of him. His stance was menacing. "Back off, you bastard!" Rashod told him.

Me reached for Rashod, but before Me could grab him, he was back in his corner of the vacuum.

Me let out an animal-like roar in his anger. He reached inside his pant leg and pulled out the large, shiny knife. He then proceeded to slash the walls of the Schomberg Center to smithereens. It was a totally human act, one he did not usually engage in, but he was seeking relief from his anger at Rashod.

The last thing he did before he left was to cut off the head of the bust of Othello that was residing in the lobby of the Schomberg Center. Othello's head crashed to the floor, breaking up into hundreds of tiny pieces.

Me never noticed the tiny black charcoal scroll lying among the ruins of Othello's head, but Rashod did. He scooped it up. Unknowingly, he now held the key to many things.

40

He was absolutely delirious with joy. He was bathing in plasma, blood plasma. His supply would be sufficient for a long time to come. The blood he was bathing in was of a recognized breed. It was high-pedigree. It felt thick, like gooey molasses against his skin.

The bodies that had been emptied of these precious fluids most likely wouldn't be discovered until morning. When they were found, a cry would go out throughout Harlem, such as hadn't been heard since Rachel had cried for the slaughtering of her children during the time of the birth of Jesus Christ.

There would be many Rachels in the morning. He loved it when he pulled the same scam throughout different times in history, and the current generation fell for it as well. He was on a high. In any case, Tracie Burlingame would no longer be a lone ranger. There would be plenty of weeping on the streets of Harlem when the sun came up.

He lifted a plastic cup to his lips and took a long, hearty swallow. The blood dripped along the sides of his mouth. He swiped at it with his back hand and then leaned back in the tub, relaxing. He loved the pungent smell of it in his nostrils.

"It's all in a night's work," he spoke aloud. Soon he would need to talk to Me. But for now he was saturated.

He stretched. He had no idea which gift he would use, or when. He certainly had his choice of them now. During the course of the night, he had gathered unto himself artists, musicians, poets, journalists, athletes, authors—hell, he even acquired a young concert pianist, as well as several brilliant minds that would have grown in the elite worlds of medicine, science, and technology, making new discoveries and casting African-Americans in a new light.

Would have.

Oh, they were just mere seedlings, not developed of their future potential, and that was the point. He had snuffed them out before any of that crap could begin. But there would be great suffering, because all had been aware and had seen the potential of their gifts for the future.

And he had managed to throw a nice curveball to the police by having that sap who was sniffing after Tracie Burlingame murder her sons. The police were fully concentrated on those murders. Then he had switched gears, duplicating the murders at a much deeper level. Fantastic. He was almost in awe of himself, such was the cleverness of his plan. But then, he had created clever.

Hadn't he?

He sighed. Anyway, once the little seedlings he had killed matured, they would have wanted to grow and manifest, planting their brilliant, gifted seeds in the generations to come. Hell, no.

Yeah. On this night he'd left a mark to remember. He climbed out of the tub, not bothering to dry himself off, and walked into the living room, which was covered with sneakers, one of each pair. Pure joy shot through his body.

He got on his knees and crawled over to the sneaker collection. He sniffed the lingering scent left behind by the boy it used to belong to. A bunch of damn fools these kids were. They actually worshipped these damned rubber shoes, and because they did, unknowingly they had turned sneakers into an idol.

It had been so easy. All he'd had to do was have the heads of America's hungering corporations put them in a suitcase, light them from the bottom, tag on the word "air," pump them up with some star athletes, and suddenly there was an entire generation panting for them, robbing for them, and killing for them. And the corporations? Well, they were drowning in the glitz of the almighty dollar, worshipping him, too. Two birds with one stone, so to speak.

These kids were so shallow, he would have felt remorse at the easy pickings if he were capable of it. But he wasn't.

You could find the poorest kid in Harlem wearing a pair of one-hundred-dollar to one-hundred-fifty-dollar sneakers. Their bellies might rumble with hunger;

their pockets might be empty; but shining on their feet were a brand new pair of the latest sneakers.

And he loved it because when they worshipped sneakers or other such material things, they worshipped him. Him and his many faces. This generation was the worst type of idolaters. They were the worst that had been seen in centuries. Every time they knelt before the coveted rubber beings, they knelt at his table.

And, their God was mad. No. Mad was too light a term. He was fuming at their ignorance and lack of respect. Apparently, none of them had read the Book of Jeremiah. He laughed. If only they knew. It was a good thing for him that they didn't.

He was the idol of idols in all his many forms. He preened at the actual brilliance of his idea with mere sneakers. In one smooth stroke, he had reached out and cast his net on those little seedlings, and now, through their yearnings, he had captured them.

Them and their gifts that would have been.

It was too bad he would have to trash this body soon. It had proved to be very useful since as far back as before the thumb-sucking stage, when it had reached out and touched the red, slippery substance.

The child had fragmented and splintered into many emotional pieces upon touching the substance and witnessing the violence of death. That was when he had stepped in to rear the child, raise him in his own right. But soon he would trash him and be done with him.

Who the hell cared anyway?

He sat back as if on his haunches, though in reality he was sitting on human legs, still admiring the sneakers and the brilliant brand of destruction they represented. He could hear their spirits, still crying out after having been body-snatched from the little rubber demons.

Tomorrow. Alas, tomorrow Alexandra Kennedy would be busy with the new shipment of sneakers that had been dispatched to her office that night. She'd be busy with that and with matching up all those boys' bodies to all those missing sneakers. What a chore. The thought bored him.

He headed back to the tub. "It's all in a night's work," he sang.

And a very good night for him it was. It was almost time to put the ultimate plan into effect and pay a visit to Ms. Tracie Burlingame . . . the host mother.

41

It had rained blood in Harlem. Black, male, adolescent blood. Young blood. Virgin blood. Imperial blood. African-American blood.

It had been drained along with the gifts that had been swallowed for an undetermined amount of time. Me had swept through after his master and swallowed the gifts and the spirits whole. It had been quite a night in Harlem. The frolicking of beasts had occurred at the expense of a people who had already paid a huge price.

The rising of the morning sun would bring a wail of pain from Harlem that would reach heaven. Unbeknownst to them, their cries would not fall on deaf ears.

The drops of blood were splattered against a land-scape of a generation untold. And yet there was not a drop to be found on the streets. There certainly wasn't a drop to be found in the bodies that had been strewn about Harlem. But no deed goes unrecorded.

Tracie Burlingame didn't know yet that there were many who had joined her in her grief. All she knew was that she was bone weary tired, and she needed to face Dre and Michael. But they weren't home yet; the house was empty. She also needed to make burial arrangements for her son.

When that was done, she was going to pay a visit to Anita Lily Mae Young. She could still hear the old woman's words: "Don't you be coming back here to me, girl, I mean it."

To Anita Lily Mae Young was exactly where she would go. This woman had seen something, and maybe she could help lead her to finding out who was killing her sons. Tracie intended to find out, that was for sure.

She dropped on the couch in all her bone-weary tiredness. She kicked off her shoes. Unconsciously she went to put her feet up on the table, until she realized it wasn't there anymore. She had smashed it with the fireplace poker.

She tucked her aching feet underneath her instead. She pulled a cushion under her head. Instantly she fell asleep.

She stayed that way until she felt someone standing over her, hovering, the shadow falling over her facial features. Tracie knew she must get up. She struggled to pull herself from the deep, dreamless sleep back to consciousness.

"Tracie," Souljah Boy said. "Take my hand." She did. "Come with me."

Tracie looked at Souljah Boy, wondering what he was doing here. She didn't see Dre. Usually he hung out with Dre. They'd been tight since they were kids. But Dre wasn't in sight.

As they walked, Tracie turned to look at Souljah Boy.

She was visually struck by his appearance. There was a light shining from him. He was illuminated from the inside out.

"Souljah Boy, what . . . ?" Tracie began to ask, but Souljah Boy cut her off.

"Shush," he said.

Together they walked to the front door of the brownstone. Souljah Boy opened the door. He stepped through, still holding Tracie's hand. Tracie gasped. This wasn't her street. They were standing on the edge of a cliff.

Souljah Boy pointed. "Look."

Tracie looked down and saw a black, gaping hole. It was sucking in little black babies. There were so many of them. It was like a huge black vacuum, just sucking them in.

Someone stood at the edge of the hole. Tracie saw the person shoving something. Finally she realized they were shoving what looked like a manhole cover over the black hole. She heard a loud clang; the hole was covered. She couldn't see the babies anymore. They were gone.

Before Tracie could catch her breath or even begin to question Souljah Boy, many little black babies began to fall through the atmosphere. Just as in her dream, some force was grabbing them and wrapping them in a white, silky swaddling. Right there on her doorstep in the middle of Harlem.

She turned to Souljah Boy.

"Have faith. Do not be afraid of your losses, Tracie," he said. "In time all things will be rectified."

Before she could respond, Souljah Boy was gone.

Tracie looked up to find her son Michael staring down at her on the couch.

"Michael?" she asked. "How did you get here?"

"I live here, remember?" Michael said.

"Yeah, I know that, but I mean . . ." Tracie's voice trailed off. She looked around the living room. "Never mind." She struggled to sit up on the couch. "I've got something bad to tell you."

"I already know, Ma. Rashod is dead. We need to talk."

Tracie's eyes filled with newly formed tears. "Where's Dre?"

"I don't know. I haven't seen him yet, but I'm sure he'll be here, Ma. He'll be here."

Tracie nodded past the lump in her throat. "Would you mind terribly if I just laid down in my room for a while? And then we'll talk when I get up. I just need a little time."

Michael looked at Tracie. He reached out and pulled her to him, hugging her tightly. He smoothed her hair down. "Naw, Mommy, that'll be fine."

Michael kissed her tear-stained cheek. He released her and headed for his room. "I'll be here whenever you're ready. I ain't going anywhere."

Tracie nodded her appreciation. Michael had always been the mature one out of all her children. Dre was the one with attitude. Rashod had been the one with anger. Randi had just been the baby. Her boys, her family, all she had in the world, and now two of them were gone.

Her thoughts leaped to Souljah Boy. She could have sworn he was here. It had been so real. He had told her to have faith. Not to be afraid of her losses. This was the boy Tracie used to feed, yell at, and give a good beat-down to along with her own kids.

She shook herself. At the thought of Souljah Boy, goose bumps had broken out on her arm. "Michael?"

Michael stopped and turned around. "Yeah?"

"Did you see Souljah Boy when you came in?"

"Naw. Dre's not here, so he wouldn't be here. Why?"

"Nothing. I was just wondering; that's all."

Michael gave her a queer look, then continued on to his room. He had things of his own that he needed to sort out in his mind before he talked to Tracie anyway. He needed to decide how much she could handle. He would have to tread carefully with her.

Tracie knew she must be bugging. Of course he wouldn't have seen Souljah Boy. Nor would he have seen the steep cliff that was just outside their door, or the many black babies falling through the atmosphere. For some inexplicable reason she knew that.

Tracie got up. She walked to the front door and pulled it open. There was no sign of Souljah Boy, the cliff, or falling black babies. There was only the street, as it had always been. She sighed and went to her room for some much needed rest.

She couldn't explain what she had seen, but one thing she knew for sure: she wasn't going to run from it this time. It had happened. She wasn't crazy. She knew she had seen what she'd seen.

She had stood with Souljah Boy looking out over the cliff, just as sure as she had stood at her front door. Of that there was no doubt.

"Have faith." Tracie embraced the spoken words as they enveloped her in their cloud. She knew she would need it. She could not rely on anyone. She hadn't thought about what it meant to have faith, or what it meant to reach out to the spirit of the Lord, in so long.

All she had relied on was herself. Her own power. Her own capabilities and her money, which she wielded like a sword in front of people. But none of that had prevented her sons from being murdered. Murdered. The word startled Tracie as it entered her mind like a foreign invasion.

She hadn't wanted to admit that to herself, but it was true. Her sons had been murdered, just as Raymond had been murdered long ago. She had fought against it, but now she would have to face it.

Now she knew that she'd require more help than she could give herself. It dawned on her in a sudden realization that someone or something was trying to help her. That must be the reason she'd been having the weird dream.

Or maybe it was just a nightmare. But for some reason she was starting not to think so. Souljah Boy had looked so different to her. Why? What was going on?

Something was trying to reach her. Tracie shook herself. Maybe she was going off the deep end. Maybe she was under too much pressure.

Suddenly, unbidden, she recalled a long-buried incident. There was a woman who used to take her to church when she was a kid. She used to spend the night at the woman's house with her kids. Old Mrs. Peyton. Laura Peyton. She hadn't thought about her in many years.

On this particular night Tracie had leaned back in her chair. The chair slipped, and she fell back, busting her head open on an old radiator. Immediately, blood gushed from the wound.

When Mrs. Peyton had called her mother to tell her

what had happened, her mother had told her to take her immediately to Harlem Hospital.

Instead, Mrs. Peyton had asked her, "Do you believe Jesus Christ can heal you?"

With all the faith and innocence of a child, Tracie had answered, "Yes."

"Then he will," Mrs. Peyton had told her.

She had anointed Tracie's head with oil, told her to get on her knees, and there they had prayed together. Tracie's little heart had reached out and yearned for Christ to heal her, and he had.

The following morning a wound that would have definitely required stitches was completely closed and healed on its own. Tracie had been delighted. "It's healed," she had told Mrs. Peyton. "It's healed."

"I know, child. All you have to do is believe. That's what I told you."

Where had that memory come from? My God, that had been so long ago, she'd forgotten about it. Nothing else like it had ever happened to her.

Suddenly a picture of the old black preacher at the church flashed in her mind. She felt a profound sense of comfort. She could see the Bible with its two flames of fire shooting up on the sides. She could almost reach out and touch it. She wished she had.

On her way to the bathroom the phone rang. She picked it up to hear Whiskey's voice. She arranged for a special courier whom both Whiskey and she trusted to deliver the guns to him from her salon.

She wondered what had made him change his mind and suggest this, but whatever it was, she was grateful. She didn't ask questions. It was too much to deal with all that was happening plus Whiskey and his weapons.

She was beginning to hate him, his dangerous aura,

and his weapons that she had made a mint off of, not to mention his extreme selfishness.

The real deal was, Whiskey had had a momentary change of heart with a little help from outside forces. He had decided that with all her troubles, she didn't have to do it personally, as long as she agreed to the arrangements—which she did.

The truth of it was, Whiskey had decided that Tracie Burlingame was too hot on the streets of Harlem. He quickly wanted to disassociate himself from her after learning that it had rained blood in Harlem, following the same pattern as the deaths of Tracie's sons. The police would be all over her.

Soon. Very soon.

Whiskey, being the shrewd man that he was, simply decided it was time to part company. Time to move his assets straight out of Harlem. Harlem was raining blood. Whiskey didn't want to get splattered with any of it.

Besides, Whiskey would never admit it in a million years, but he was scared, in a major way. Me had stepped to Whiskey on a personal level and simply told him, "I am Me. You will leave Tracie Burlingame alone."

Me had stared at Whiskey.

Something in Whiskey's bowels shook loose. Whiskey nodded without ever saying a word.

"Good," Me said.

He had taken his leave of Whiskey then, but not before Whiskey heard the symphony of voices that swelled in him. Not before someone sneezed, and it wasn't Me.

And not before he witnessed a legion of snakes writhing and slithering inside Me's form, their lizard-like tongues whipping out and swallowing people, actual people, whole. It was all Whiskey could do to keep from fainting like some punk.

Yes, it was raining blood in Harlem, but that was the least of all that was going on. Whiskey hadn't wanted any part of it.

Tracie lay down on her bed after her conversation and arrangements with Whiskey. Then she wondered, where was her son Andre Burlingame?

Tracie Burlingame trembled at the thought.

42

Dre. Andre, actually. Andre Burlingame. He sat in a semi-stupor in Souljah Boy's crowded living room. Souljah Boy had a one-bedroom apartment in the Abraham Lincoln projects, and every room in the house was stacked and littered with books, papers, DVDs, videos, tapes, and recordings of every kind.

There was barely anywhere to sit. Souljah Boy had moved a stack of manuscripts, essays, and papers from a small footstool so Dre could sit down.

Dre had gone to Souljah Boy's apartment in his current state after having been summoned by one of his many confidential contacts to 139th Street and St. Nicholas Avenue the night before to shoot photographs of another murder that had taken place in Harlem.

He had already delivered the ones of Randi to his contact. They were at the *Amsterdam News*. He wasn't going to let them bury his brother's life like so much garbage, so he figured the close-ups would shake somebody into action. He hadn't counted on the second set of photographs he was to take being of his brother Rashod. But they were.

He had arrived to discover that another one of his brothers had been slain. It had shaken him to his very core. He couldn't go home. He couldn't stay on the streets. It looked as though somebody was trying to kill all of them.

So he had gone to Souljah Boy's apartment. He didn't know where his mother was. He didn't know where his now only brother, Michael, was. He'd been calling the house, and no one answered. He'd paged Tracie and gotten no answer, either. He hoped they weren't dead, too.

He had sat on the footstool with Souljah Boy's aging documents and many papers scattered at his feet. He had not moved from that spot since his arrival.

It wasn't helping matters that Souljah Boy was different, too. More reserved—he didn't know—more something, as if he had been dipped in a ray of light or something. His world was being turned upside down.

Souljah Boy's face had a sheen almost like when a person sweated hard and glistened with the moisture of it, except that Souljah Boy's face was dry.

He looked as if he had swallowed the sun and it was shining from inside him. Maybe he was just losing it . . . seeing things that really weren't there.

Finally Dre had voiced his worst fear: "I hope Tracie's not dead."

"She isn't," Souljah Boy replied.

Dre looked over at him from lowered long, silky

lashes inherited from Tracie. "How do you know? Rashod is, you know."

"I know Rashod is. But Tracie isn't."

"Somebody's killing my family, man. Straight up. Maybe we're next. We should have police protection or something."

"You don't need police protection, Dre. Nobody's gonna kill you."

Suddenly something stuck out in Dre's mind. "How did you know Rashod was dead? I just told you."

"I hear things, Dre."

Dre nodded. That was probably true. Souljah Boy was plugged into his own brand of information sources. Dre let it drop. He'd never known Souljah Boy to tell a lie in his life, even when they were kids. Even when Souljah Boy knew that the truth would land them in hot water, especially with Tracie. He would tell it anyway. Then they would all endure Tracie's wrath.

Dre had constantly told him to stop doing that truth crap when they could get in trouble, but Souljah Boy had his own mind.

"The truth will set you free," he had told Dre once when they were in trouble.

"The truth will get our asses kicked," Dre had replied. And sure enough, it had. But that hadn't ever stopped Souljah.

Dre was silent for a time. Souljah Boy just watched him intently.

"How do you know, man, that we won't be next?"

"Because I know."

"How do you know?" Dre repeated, not satisfied with Souljah Boy's answer. Though he would never admit it, he suddenly found himself wanting to hear some of Souljah Boy's religious ramblings. He needed to hear something, anything that was going to make him feel better.

But whereas Souljah Boy usually answered almost any question with some type of spiritual coating, he had not done so, so far.

Souljah Boy sighed.

He knew Dre couldn't handle much, but he was seeking comfort in the spirit. Souljah Boy needed to give him something. Maybe it was time he grew up to the real world anyway.

"Your family is under the protection of Jesus Christ, Dre."

Dre snorted, although subconsciously this had been exactly what he was looking for. "You think so, son? Then why are two of my brothers dead? Some protection."

Souljah Boy was patient. "Sometimes things happen for a reason. They are for a higher purpose. Besides, Dre, just because they're dead doesn't mean they aren't under his protection."

Dre was exasperated. "Stop talking to me in riddles, Souljah. Dead is dead. They're dead." Dre began to wring his hands so Souljah Boy wouldn't see them trembling, but of course, he did.

He had known Dre would tremble before he actually did.

" 'Yea, though I walk through the valley of the shadow of death—' "

Dre cut Souljah Boy off. "Don't start this again, Souljah."

Souljah Boy got up. He went to the bookshelf. He removed a big old black and gold, ancient-looking book. It was so dusty he had to blow dust off the cover. He returned to sit across from Dre.

He opened up the Bible, turning to the Twenty-third Psalm.

"This is exactly where it does start, Dre. Close your eyes and just listen and feel. Don't question. Just listen. Okay?"

Dre nodded, even though he was starting to feel somewhat foolish. He had always told Souljah Boy not to do this, to live in the real world; now he was listening because he suddenly didn't know what was real anymore. His world as he had known it was gone.

So what was there?

He realized he didn't know. Which meant he had nothing to lose by listening. Besides, Dre had always known there was something special about Souljah Boy, that he was different.

He didn't know what it was exactly, but he knew that Souljah Boy was connected in a different way from the rest of them. Maybe whatever looked over Souljah Boy, whatever resided with him, would protect Dre and his family, too.

What was left of it. After all, Souljah Boy, as far back as he could remember, had always been a part of his family.

Definitely there was something that was moving with him. It always had been. Dre had just never accepted it or really looked at it, was all.

"Okay," he agreed, closing his eyes. "Go ahead and read, Souljah."

"'The Lord is my shepherd; I shall not want. He maketh me to lie down in green pastures; he leadeth me beside the still waters. He restoreth my soul; he leadeth me in the paths of righteousness for his name's sake. Yea, though I walk through the valley of the shadow of death, I will fear no evil; for thou art with me; thy rod and thy staff they comfort me. Thou preparest a table before me in the presence of mine enemies; thou anointest my head with oil; my cup runneth over. Surely goodness and mercy shall follow me all the days of my life; and I will dwell in the house of the Lord for ever. Amen.' "

Souljah Boy finished reading the scripture.

As Dre listened to the reading with his eyes shut tight, images had appeared before him. He had heard the words differently. The word "application" had sounded in his mind as though on the wings of the wind. *Application.* He would have to apply those words to what was happening.

He opened his eyes. "I was wrong, wasn't I, Souljah? I said Harlem wasn't the valley of death. I said, 'This is Harlem, not the valley of death.' But I was wrong wasn't I? Harlem *is* the valley of death."

"In Harlem, Dre, is both death and life for us and our people. Believe that."

Dre couldn't stop himself. He was waterlogged. He would have been embarrassed if his life weren't in such tragic condition.

The tears slid from his eyes unabashedly.

And he had been so mean to Rashod the last time he had seen him, while he sat there drawing some stupid sketch—actually maybe not stupid, but definitely weird.

Dre regretted his attitude. He wished he could take it back and do it differently. But now he couldn't. Rashod was dead, too. Rashod was one of the images he had seen while his eyes were closed and Souljah Boy was reading from the Bible.

Souljah Boy rose from his seat. He laid the old Bible on a table. He hugged Dre. In that instant Dre felt the arms of many holding him, although all he saw was Souljah.

Souljah Boy released him and stood back. "Go home to Tracie, Dre. She needs you to come. She's at home now."

Souljah Boy pulled Dre to his feet. Then he issued him a prophecy. "There are many more hurdles to overcome, Dre, but your family will survive. There is one who can save all. Have faith."

With that, Souljah Boy showed Dre the door.

Dre arrived home to find things just as Souljah Boy had said. Both Tracie and Michael were there. However, there had been no time for teary reunions, recriminations, or explanations.

The minute Dre had entered the house, Tracie, having received a phone call from Renee Santiago and having awakened from having exactly the same dream once again, had instantly declared to both Dre and Michael, "Come on. We have to go."

From the tone in her voice and the look in her eyes, they had both known it was no time for questions.

And with that, Tracie Burlingame had fled the brownstone with her two remaining living sons in tow. They had left with nothing but the clothes on their backs.

She had managed to escape only moments before the police arrived.

The number one girlfriend, Renee Santiago, had delivered one high-placed favor. Not only had she put Tracie Burlingame up on what was going on and the fountain of blood that was spraying Harlem, she had also imparted some serious wisdom unto Tracie, which was good, because she would definitely need it.

Her parting words to Tracie were, "Have faith, girl-friend. Have faith."

43

Alexandra had known that was it, the beginning of the end of many things, the instant the mayor of New York crossed the threshold into her office unannounced. It had all exploded right in her face, just as she had feared. She knew it was true as she stared across her desk at the mayor.

She ran a hand through her short blond curls. She resisted the urge to gnaw on the eraser of the pencil that was beckoning to her.

The phones were ringing off the hooks. There were fifty young black male bodies sitting on ice in the morgue. There was no way to tell if there would be more.

The FBI was there; pictures of the dead boys and details of the murders were being downloaded to the top profilers in the country, down in Quantico. Oh, and the Schomberg Center had been defiled.

"Desecration" was the word that kept leaping to her mind, although the Schomberg Center was not a religious organization. She did not dare utter the word "desecration" out loud. In her private thoughts was where that word would have to remain.

If she had said that word aloud, the mayor might have gotten up from his chair and personally strangled her with his bare hands.

The dead body of a security guard had been found at the Schomberg Center, and the pattern of the killing did not match that of the other murders. It was a different style and a different killer, to be sure.

The center had been completely, well, "defiled" was the only word that stayed with her. The walls had been slashed by a sharp knife, cut to ribbons—thousands of shreds of drywall, as though it had been fed through a shredder.

And the head of Othello had been cut off. It lay in thousands of broken pieces, scattered across the floor.

Rare archival manuscripts, books, and historical records were missing. Well, maybe "missing" was not a totally accurate description. The books were there. The papers were there. The recordings were there. But there were no words on any of the pages or in any of the recordings.

Literally thousands of pieces of paper, maybe millions—who knew for sure? Anyway, all the precious, ancient, historical African-American documentation that had resided in the Schomberg Center was missing the words.

All the pages were . . . well, they were blank.

The gallery where the Harlem Writers' Guild usually held its meetings, which boasted the artistic depictions, replicas, pictures, and images of some of the most famous African-American authors in the world, had been defiled as well, their images melted across the canvases in grotesque caricatures.

It was as though a liquid fire had appeared and, not being able to stand the sight of the authors, had simply melted away their images in a flame of fire but had left the backdrop on which the images were placed untouched.

Their birth dates and their dates of death were missing as well, as though someone had attempted to erase their very existence from the earth. It was stranger than hell. So far, the many experts who were currently jamming the Schomberg Center had no reasonable explanation for how this could be.

There was just absolutely no way, they all insisted in unison, that pictures on a canvas could be burned away with such extreme heat without destroying the canvas itself. In fact, from what little they could tell, as far as they were concerned, the entire room should have burned down, and yet it still stood.

The lettering that depicted the names and dates of birth and death had simply disappeared from the canvases. But there was no trace that any lettering had been melted in the fire—the lettering was just simply not there.

It was a good thing the Schomberg Center had had the foresight to keep photographs of the photos in the galley, as well as a lot of the rare archives, manuscripts, and literature on CDs, disks, microfiche, and in hard-copy photographs, tucked away in a vault at Chase Bank; otherwise, it would have been hard to believe they had really been there.

Except, perhaps, by those people who had seen it with their own eyes.

The restoration of these works, although stored on some of the highest technology the country had to offer, would still be an awesome job. And some of the older stuff was still stored on microfiche.

African-American art critics, photographers, historians, researchers, writers, and scholars were flying into Harlem from around the world, from as far away as Israel, at the very minute that Alexandra sat in the hottest pressure cooker of her career, across from the mayor of New York.

The photographs of Randi Burlingame, dead and broken on 135th Street, which had been delivered by a so-called anonymous source, were blown up on the front page of the *Amsterdam News,* and all that Alexandra could not have imagined had come true.

The wire services had instantly picked up on the serial-killing grounds of Harlem. The news was being broadcast to every corner of the world, along with the photographs of Randi Burlingame, to which Rashod Burlingame had now been added.

To make matters worse, if that were possible, the *New York Times,* not to be outdone by some community newspaper, had managed to obtain a picture of Tracie Burlingame.

Its lead story boasted a picture of the sleek, beautiful clotheshorse that was Tracie Burlingame with the incredible flashing eyes, in between her two dead sons. The images vividly showed every detail of Randi and Rashod, frozen in a death mangle.

The headline read: SORROWS FROM A MOTHER'S WOMB. It was horrific beyond measure, horrific beyond human imaginings, yet it was happening.

The bodies of the boys were drained of blood. One of each pair of fifty sneakers had arrived at Alexandra's office. The boy's throats were stuffed with sunflower seeds. Their parents, friends, communities, ministers, teachers, and any bum on the streets had become one collective wail of outrage, fear, and pain as the news had spread out of their control.

It had been reported that fifty dead black boys, all eighteen years of age and under, had been murdered in Harlem in one night. And they all had one thing in common. They had all been highly gifted in one way or another: in the arts, music, writing, sports, science, medicine, or technology, to name a few.

They had been bright and rising stars, with the potential for great futures. There had even been a young and studied concert pianist among them. He had just recently returned from England, where he had played for the queen. Bright and rising little stars, all snuffed out in a night.

Rachel was weeping for her children. So was Tracie Burlingame.

The medical examiner could not begin to handle the massive autopsies that needed to be conducted. As a result, forensic scientists and pathologists were flying in from every corner of the United States.

Although Hubert Noskog could not have physically handled all the autopsies, he certainly knew exactly what they would find. He knew that all of them would be identical to Rashod Burlingame, with pieces of their anatomies missing and pieces of their brains having been absorbed.

He wondered if the others would agree, when they arrived, that this was not something that should be recorded outside the scientific and medical communities. He could not see how his colleagues would not arrive at this wisdom.

But he would have to wait and see. Harlem was a bloodbath, and not just in real blood. It was a political bloodbath and a hotbed the likes of which they had never seen. It was simply a nightmare.

The mayor of New York stared into Alexandra's eyes as though he were a drunken pirate washed from the sea, who had somehow landed on dry, desert land.

"This is impossible," the mayor said.

"Yes, it is," Alexandra automatically replied.

"The governor called this morning."

"What did he say?"

"He said this is impossible." The mayor seemed incapable of evoking the suave display of politics he was usually known for. He sat in shocked surprise, unable to tap into his usual reservoir of resources.

Alexandra sighed. They were getting nowhere fast with this conversation. The National Guard was posted outside the police station to ensure there would be no entry. There were two guards posted outside her own office door to prevent entry.

And all she and the mayor could agree on was that it was an impossible situation, which they already knew.

She had borrowed police recruits from every borough in the city. They were turning Harlem upside down in their quest for answers and were reporting in on the half hour. Extra telephone lines had been added.

They had twenty-four-seven coverage, so that no rock could go unturned. And still there was nothing.

There was not a drop of blood. There was not a fingerprint. There was no saliva. There was not a clothing fiber. There was not even a fiber of hair so far—nothing to link up the killer. There was nothing.

Nothing except swarming, angry parents, their representatives, and all the black constituency of New York City, which was hanging outside on her doorstep, demanding answers that neither she, the police, the police recruits, the mayor, nor the governor of New York had.

In the process she was also being beaten up for not investigating Ms. Virginia's death at Visionaries. Because somehow it had leaked that all the words were missing off the pages in her bookshop as well. There was not a single word, in a single book, in the entire bookstore.

Save one.

Now that story was being linked in connection with the missing words in the Schomberg Center. The media was on a roll.

She had thought it was ridiculous when Maya had first reported it to her. Besides, Ms. Virginia had not been murdered. She had died of a heart attack, a natural cause. There had been no reason for her to investigate. Anyway, she had already had her hands full at the time, even if she had wanted to make a courtesy call.

She had better not find out Maya had leaked it. If she did, she would see to it that Maya never worked again in this lifetime. Maya told her things. She kept her abreast of the situation in Harlem. But Alexandra had always suspected that Maya resented doing it and was just biding her time.

If she had picked this time, her ass would be out on the streets sooner than she could say, "Boo." That was for sure. She would not tolerate a lack of loyalty at this time.

She also wanted to know where the hell Lonzo was.

Monica had delved into Tracie's background and had set up the detail on Tracie Burlingame's house, albeit too late, because by the time they arrived, Tracie was gone. There was no trace of her or her remaining sons.

Given, of course, that they were still remaining.

Who knew?

She didn't think they were in the morgue, but there was no way she could be absolutely certain of that at the moment. Nor could she be certain that they wouldn't arrive there, just as Randi and Rashod had.

All of Tracie's salons were being covered. The employees had all been questioned. There was nary a trace of her or her boys.

Alexandra had had Monica issue an APB for Tracie Burlingame because they needed her desperately. All the murdered boys had been killed in the same way as Tracie's sons.

Maybe she knew something, even if unconsciously. In any case, Alexandra needed to haul her ass down to the precinct station, and she needed to do it fast.

And she couldn't protect those boys or follow them, hoping they might lead them to the murderer, if she couldn't find them.

There was a knock on the door, and the special edition of the newspaper was delivered to Alexandra. Normally there was no special edition, but with all that was going on in Harlem, the newspaper editors had decided to be accomodating. *How very good of them,* Alexandra thought.

The headline read: WHERE IS TRACIE BURLINGAME? the leaks in this case were endless.

Alexandra closed her eyes. She shook her head and reached into her center desk drawer. She had never thought she would do this again, but here she was at the mercy of old King Tobacco once again.

She took her lighter out of the center drawer. She lit the cigarette, inhaling deeply. Ignoring the New York Law against smoking in its public buildings.

The smoke seared her lungs, which had been nicely dumping all the past years of cigarette tar built up in them. Alexandra choked and coughed, her lungs unaccustomed to the live shock of smoke.

The mayor of New York watched her for a time; then he echoed the headlines of the newspaper: "Where is Tracie Burlingame?" he said.

44

Anita Lily Mae Young awoke from the same dream at the same time as Tracie Burlingame, watching the many black babies sailing through the atmosphere.

She had no way of knowing this.

When she did awake, she wasn't sure if she would be better off in this world or the other one. Both of them were treacherously scary.

The television and newspapers were full of nothing but Tracie Burlingame. The details of the deaths, and methods of the killing of her sons, were everywhere. A serial killer was on the loose in Harlem, and the offspring of Tracie Burlingame had been his primary target.

Anita cringed just looking at the woman on the electronic devices. She had seen her on television and on the Internet. Her image dominated the newspapers. The woman made her insides crawl.

Tracie Burlingame had suddenly been stamped all over her private residence. She was in her life. It seemed her image was everywhere she looked. She could not get away from her.

Somehow Tracie Burlingame had managed to invade her space, her thoughts, and profile herself into her very existance.

It was Tracie Burlingame in the dream, from whose womb the many black babies were dropping.

Anita never wanted to see her again. Anita didn't want this particular vision. For the first time in her natural life, she was seriously regretting this sight. It was better sometimes that you didn't see things, that you didn't know nothing.

Right in front of her eyes the patchwork quilt floated, as though a testament to her gift and participation.

"Oh, my," Anita moaned.

She had known that that girl was trouble from the first moment she laid eyes on her. But, the magnitude to which Tracie Burlingame had risen stunned even Anita. And that was only in this world.

There could be no measure for her role in the next. Her picture and those of her sons were everywhere.

Tracie's eyes were like a chameleon. Anita could see their flashing depths, even though she wasn't in front of her, live. Tracie Burlingame didn't have persona—she *was* persona.

She was also the most dangerous black woman alive at this time.

Tracie had absolutely no clue to the truth of this.

Finally the last nail in the coffin was hurled Anita's way. The story came on the news about the Schomberg Center. It was cordoned off, and the newscaster was reciting words that were unbelievable.

"It couldn't be," Anita mumbled as she stroked Pesky's black, silky fur. But it was. The Schomberg Center for Research in Black Culture had been destroyed. Rare archival treasures had been defiled.

Ms. Virginia's store, Visionaries, had also been entered by a thief—a spiritual thief who had stolen all the words from the books. Although the media was only reporting and had no real clue to the meaning of this, Anita did.

They were hyping the stories and creating trails and links, though they could have no idea of the actual impact.

Anita sighed as though in great pain.

Mr. Schomberg, the original founder of the center, had dedicated his life to researching the history of African-Americans the world over after having been told that black people had no history.

His life's work and dedication were all reflected in that center. He had proved that black people had roots, that they came from a powerful history. Now that had been defiled. It was disgraceful, absolutely disgraceful and intolerable.

All Anita could hear was the big bald-headed man stating, "I have come to collect the gifts. I am Me."

"Oh, God. Oh, no. Oh, God, no," Anita whimpered.

Without a doubt she knew that a spiritual prophecy was now alive and manifesting itself in Harlem. She bowed her head at the horror of it. When the big bald-headed man had unblocked her vision, she hadn't wanted to see or believe.

Anita ran to her door. She threw the extra bolt on it. She didn't want any part of what was going on.

Although deep inside, way down on a level she wasn't

dealing with, she knew she was as much a part of this as if she had destroyed the Schomberg Center herself.

There would be no escaping it. Maybe she could reach the Master for guidance, before this went too far. What the hell was she thinking? It had already gone too far.

"It done went too far already," she said to Pesky.

She pulled the rabbit closer to her for physical comfort.

"Oh, no. Oh, no," she continued to moan as she closed all the shades on her windows. She wondered to what avail this would be, but she couldn't stop herself from doing it. She knew there were forces out there that didn't need to enter by the front door.

She also knew that she was one of the conduits that would have to help Tracie Burlingame. And the Me thing would not be happy. But she would have no choice. He would come.

He would come for Tracie Burlingame to destroy her.

No sooner had the words entered Anita's mind than she was snapped into a trance and transported to a different place, where what she needed to know was given to her. The time was near.

Unbeknownst to Anita, mercy and grace had been granted to her for the times she had misused her gift. There had been many misuses and abuses over time by the people with their gifts.

It had not gone unnoticed.

If the abusers had ever known or understood the pain they had inflicted, or the parts they had played in the destruction of many—their respective roles as stumbling blocks for their own people—well, anyone with sense would have gotten down on their knees and never gotten up until forgiveness from above had been restored.

Until mercy and grace had been granted, as with Anita.

Now Anita would come full circle in her repentance and participate for the glory, for the change of things.

While she was there, she repented for the remission of her sins in the name of Jesus Christ. She was baptized and then sanctified with the spirit of the Holy Ghost, cleansing her gift and putting it on solid and holy ground.

She would never again peer through a card or through a crystal ball to see the things she would see. There was one who had never needed a device through which to see. While she was there, she also saw a man in a state of repentance.

"My Lord," she said.

He was repenting in sackcloth and ashes, as though from long ago.

The old black preacher continued to pray in the sackcloth and ashes. His body was drenched in water. His face looked as though it were carved in granite. His startling silvery-gray hair against the tar-black skin had turned pure white.

He prayed in the gift of tongues, totally submerged in the spirit of the Holy Ghost. When he was finished praying, the chains that bound Tracie Burlingame would be broken. And so would the chains that bound the seed. But for now he needed to continue, as Tracie Burlingame journeyed closer to the *Unspoken*.

45

Me had been summoned to hold court with his master, just as before. The time for final judgement had arrived. Me was spiraling again, totally out of control. The wind was whipping with the fierceness of a hurricane. He was twirling, twirling, caught up in the spirit of the storm. There was nothing, as usual, that he could do about it.

He knew it would take him where it would. When the hurricane stopped twirling, he found himself standing on dry desert land under the scorching brightness of the blistering sun.

Legion knew he hated the light, which was precisely why he had brought him to this spot. It was called control. Blisters broke out on Me's bald head and face, such was the heat of the sun.

He couldn't see anything on the vast horizon. The earth had shaken under his feet. The wind roared in his ears like the voice of loud thunder, and then the world around him went pitch-black. It was just as if someone had come into a brightly lit room and turned off the light switch.

Me felt coldness within him—not in his soul, as he didn't possess a soul, but in the inner parts of his being. Once he had possessed a soul, many eons ago; now it was gone. Once he had lived in a beautiful place, but not anymore.

He couldn't allow himself to dwell on what was lost. What was lost was lost. There had always been a payment for all things.

Then he heard it: a sound like a zillion scabs being picked at the same time. It rumbled from the pit of his stomach and exploded inside him.

"Me!" came the rumble from inside him.

It shook his whole body. The blisters opened wide and began to ooze pus.

Me was being pummeled, pummeled with spittle. It rained down on him, turning into baseball-size hail. As soon as the hail hit the ground, it turned into balls of fire that rose up, searing his feet, moving, moving, and scorching his skin along the way, but he did not burn.

He was one livid motion of burning, searing pain. The Quest. It was time. It was time for a visit from he who was above all of them. From he who had created the master plan that had landed them all in this predicament and had made him the leader in the process.

Me could feel his presence in all his power. Suddenly the blackness surrounding him came alive. The air shivered. Standing in his wake was the One.

The Ultimate One.

Me fell to his knees in front of the great power.

Legion took note of Me and his acquiescence, although he was not impressed. He considered people kneeling and bowing before him his just due. It was nothing less than what was expected from his underlings. He had taught them much, given them many powers, and shown them how to use them.

"Tracie Burlingame cannot be allowed. Are you aware of what that means, Me?"

"Yes, Legion."

"A new spirit has been added to the dimension. Are you aware of it?"

"Yes, Legion."

"He is here to aid the girl. He was planted long ago for that purpose. He knows about the Ancient Book of Prophecies. He has felt it."

Me nodded.

"Souljah Boy." Legion spat his name as though the very taste of it were dirt in his mouth.

Me nodded, shivered, trembled and burned, in the flames of fire in his spot of worship on the ground.

"You have the gifts," Legion stated emphatically.

"In you, you carry centuries of evidence. You must use all your powers to ensure that this is where it stops, that there will be no, shall I say, special future generations to carry on. Tracie Burlingame is the host mother. Destroy the coming of things. Destroy what she will bear, in accordance as it is written. You must destroy the seed before its great birth. In order to do that, you must destroy Tracie Burlingame."

Me nodded. He dared not speak.

"Hmmm. One of them is still tied and bound in spirit to her womb. When she dies, he will die; the umbilical cord will be CUT!"

With that, the darkness took on a new intensity, a new depth; it turned blue-black in the course of things.

"Yes," came Me's reply.

The searing flames released him. The blisters stopped their oozing and closed up. The ground opened under his feet and bounced him through the realms, back into the soil that was Harlem.

Legion had been merciful.

He had delivered him in a dark alleyway where there was no light, not even a streetlight, to beam on his head. Me smiled.

He peered through the darkness so he could read the sign on the street. He was just where he should be. Legion was, as always, orderly.

Although this was not where it would take place, it would be interesting to watch his sappy comrade in action. He was as inferior as they came, because he was of the flesh. He thought he was in charge. He thought he could withstand the test of Me. But Me knew better. Me knew that flesh had been born with lots of limitations.

However, Legion wasn't the only one who could be merciful. Me could be merciful, too. As far as he was concerned, he had been. He had done his comrade a kindness. He would have a rare opportunity to tangle with Tracie Burlingame before the final outcome.

Me could have taken this from him, but he had chosen not to. Me had done him a favor. He had brought him out of darkness, to the light. He had shone the light on him so that Tracie Burlingame could see him.

Before Tracie Burlingame had fled her residence, Me had given her the evidence of what she was seeking. She didn't know it was him. Me had his ways. It was easy enough to use the arrogance of one of her sons to reach her. He had put the evidence in her path, where she couldn't ignore it or miss it.

He had also taken care of Whiskey for her.

Then he had built the yellow brick road leading Tracie straight to where she could find her tormentor and the killer of her sons.

He had thrown it right in her lap. Now she knew who had killed her sons. Me smiled as he recalled the stark shock and trembling that had occurred when she learned the identity of the killer. The information had been right there under her nose all the time, while in her mind she flitted back and forth in stark denial.

Being the bold lady she was, there was no doubt: she would be there with revenge and hatred in her heart. She now possessed all the pieces, save one. She now knew who had killed two of her sons.

What she didn't know was who would kill the two who were left. What she didn't know was the real truth of why, and that her own destruction was imminent.

Yes, there was a time for all things. His planning had been perfect. Once Tracie Burlingame played out her little street game tonight, it would be time for him to put things straight with his comrade.

It would then be time for his comrade to take his place. But Me had thrown him a bone that he'd better be grateful for. Me could not kill him, but he would have to move over. He couldn't play with Tracie Burlingame after tonight.

She would be off limits to him.

It was time for Me to step to the plate and complete the culmination of all things.

46

Monica had thoroughly searched Tracie Burlingame's entire residence. The evidence recovered was damning. The killer had decided to preen in his cleverness, and Monica had it all in live Technicolor view.

Had she not reviewed and recovered the evidence from Tracie's brownstone herself, much of it would have been difficult to piece together, much less believe. However, there was no doubt.

Tracie Burlingame was no more than a beautiful shell, one who had become the unwitting pawn of an obsessed madman. The killings had nothing to do personally with her sons at all.

But they had to do with her, and with the professed love of her sons' murderer.

It was one of the most senseless serial killings Monica had ever heard of. And she was smack dead in the middle of it.

She had sat at the white baby grand piano that Tracie loved so much, while pondering exactly how to handle what she had found. Given the circumstances, it would need to be handled as delicately as possible.

She also now knew about Raymond, a depravity that had started and stopped for some fifteen years, only to start all over again.

Monica was in private agony as she thought on the best way to approach this, an ingenious way to present it to Alexandra. She was already picturing Alexandra's reaction. First there would be disbelief, then hysterics, then panic, and last there would be a horrible resolve leading to a final cold calculation of facts.

Alexandra would have no choice in this. One hadn't been left for her.

There was more at stake here than just Tracie's sons.

It was too bad she hadn't moved faster. Too bad the levels of shock and disbelief that held her had slowed the recesses of her mind. It was too bad because by the time she did move and put the process into effect, it was already, once again, too late.

The police were still a day late and a dollar short.

47

The vision insinuated itself in front of Tracie. It wouldn't budge. There was no avoiding it. She saw herself when she was younger, leaning over a man's broken body, one year after the birth of her last son, Randi Burlingame.

Her eyes roamed the man's body. They stopped when they reached his feet. There were no shoes. A scream erupted from her throat as she walked down the distant corridor of the past.

There she had stood in the school corridor with her friends when a boy had approached her. "Tracie, will you go to the dance with me?" he said.

Tracie arrogantly looked him up and down. "I don't think so, Pee Wee. Please, I wouldn't be caught dead."

Shouts of laughter, teasing, and hooting had come from her friends as they laughed Pee Wee to scorn.

Tracie tilted her head, smiled, and started to walk away. Then she turned to look at her friends.

"Does he have a name outside of Pee Wee?"

One of Tracie's girlfriends had keeled over in laughter. "Who the hell knows," she said.

"They call him that cuz his thing is little and he can't get it up. Little Pee Wee. Get it?"

They all howled in laughter.

Tracie walked away. He followed her. He shouldn't have. She turned to mock him. "No, thank you, Pee Wee. I want superior babies one day. You know, the stuff legends are made out of. Doesn't sound to me like you'll be shooting off any legends with that little thing in your pants."

There was more laughter. Pee Wee's humiliation settled over him like a dark cloud. It had taken everything he had to ask Tracie out to the dance. He had been building up to this moment for two years. Now he was the laughingstock of the school, as well as the butt of her jokes.

Tracie looked into his eyes. Pee Wee's despair was cloying. She felt nothing. She was reigning queen, and everybody knew it. She didn't care. She could have any boy she wanted. Pee Wee wasn't it.

"You'll be sorry, Tracie!" Pee Wee shouted, pure anguish lacing his voice.

Tracie tossed her mane of hair.

"One day I'll make you sorry," he said in a much softer tone.

Tracie's eyes flashed once, twice: hazel, cocoa brown, and then a third sledgehammer flash to midnight black. Then she was gone, leaving Pee Wee standing alone.

"No!" Tracie sobbed as she zoomed back to the present.

The past was her haunting. And now she had paid the price for her callous conceit. She had paid for it with her own blood.

There was no denying it, because if it weren't so, she wouldn't be at the Lenox Terrace apartments, where Randi had met his brutal death.

She wouldn't be watching this saddening, sickening tape on this VCR that depicted all the revenge he had inflicted on her. He hadn't wanted her to miss a thing. It was all there, in every murderous, sadistic detail.

Tracie was watching the stalking and brutal murders of her own sons as though their lives and deaths were some movie of the week. Except they weren't. This was her flesh and blood.

Someone had left her the live tape, so she could witness every detail. Along with it an address had been furnished, though once she had watched the tape, finding the address would have been mediocre—child's play, really.

Tracie couldn't bear any more. She needed to finish this so she could pick up Dre and Michael. She had stashed them away after fleeing the brownstone, so that she could exact her own brand of revenge.

When she finished with this monster, there wouldn't be any pieces left for them to autopsy.

She would cut him to shreds.

It never occurred to her that she might not get out alive.

She clicked off the VCR, ejected the tape, and leaned back as dark shadows cast themselves across the room. Tracie lounged in the shadows, welcoming the darkness and anonymity of them.

She didn't know how long she had been sitting

there, but after a time there was a loud click in the total silence of the apartment.

Lonzo walked in. He slammed the door behind him.

His fingers reached for the light switch, but before they could find it, a voice penetrated the darkness. The voice was magnified, coming from an amplifier in the room.

"You've been taking things that don't belong to you, Pee Wee Morgan," Tracie said.

The room flooded with eerie spotlights from overhead. Tracie had to close her eyes momentarily against the horrors and stench of blood coming from the room. She must have been sitting there in a zombielike state, because it was as if she had only just noticed that she was sitting in the middle of hell.

Lonzo jumped, looking startled. He automatically pulled his revolver.

He saw Tracie lounging on the sofa, the microphone lying beside her. She was a vision, sitting in the flesh before the many blown-up photographs and posters of her covering the walls, spanning her life.

It was quite a homage he had paid her.

Some of them had been splattered with blood, but her image was strong, beautiful, sensual, and sure. There was an entire history, dating to back in the day when they were in school. Lonzo had made it his life's mission to follow the trails and scents of her life.

He holstered the revolver. A mixture of emotions crossed his face, from disbelief to pure adoration. He couldn't believe it. Here she was in the flesh. She was so close, he could touch her. He could feel her. He could smell her. He shifted nervously in her presence.

Me enjoyed a grand view from his darkened corner

of the balcony. He didn't move a muscle. The spirits knew to be quiet and still. He observed the scene unfolding in front of him, just as he had known it would. He had laid the ultimate groundwork.

Tracie watched Lonzo steadily. Hatred flashed in her eyes, which were changing colors at a rapid pace. The golden-green hazel of her eyes twinkled at him. There was a flash of cocoa brown, and then they finally settled on midnight black.

"You can run, but you can't hide. Right, Lonzo?"

Tracie shifted, crossing one leg over the other. She looked at Lonzo seductively.

"Come on over and I'll sing you 'Rock-a-bye, Baby.' "

Lonzo stared at her as anger crept into his voice. "Don't play games that you can't win, Li'l Caramel." He walked closer to Tracie. His eyes glazed over, becoming somewhat adrift.

"Who says I can't win?"

Lonzo focused. "I do. I'm writing the rules." He stared down Tracie's blouse. Perspiration appeared on his forehead. His breathing escalated. "It's my game, slut."

Tracie shifted. She popped open a button on her blouse. "Is it? You're on my court. Those were my sons that you murdered."

Lonzo walked to the closet. He opened the door. Hanging by their strings were one of each, a boot and a sneaker, belonging to Tracie's murdered sons: one Karl Kani, Randi Burlingame; and one Air Jordan, Rashod Burlingame.

Tracie's face froze in a sort of ethereal beauty, like a statue frozen in time. She looked at the boot and sneaker of her sons. Lonzo stared at her for a beat. He left the closet door open, then headed for the front door.

He stopped to look back over his shoulder. He stared for a fraction of a second at Tracie's frozen features.

He felt nothing except pure animal lust. A cold satisfaction had begun to crawl through his body. How dare this whore have called him inferior?

How dare she laugh at him with her friends?

He didn't see her friends now. And she didn't seem to be able to find anything to laugh about.

He could recall the words as though they were yesterday. Well, that was yesterday and this was today. And today he was reigning king.

"Checkmate, Li'l Caramel," Lonzo told Tracie.

Tracie dipped into the waist of her skirt.

Lonzo hit the light switch, plunging the room into darkness. She rose in the shadows and fired off a shot. It landed in the door over Lonzo's head.

"Checkmate? Oh, hell, no. Not yet, Pee Wee. Not yet!"

Lonzo burst into insane laughter. The front door banged shut in the darkness. Tracie stood silhouetted in the dark shadows. She dropped to her knees. She wept.

The phone rang. Tracie followed the sound of it, crawling on her hand and knees. She located it and put it to her ear.

Lonzo stood down in the dark alleyway outside, with the phone to his mouth. A streak of light from the streetlight illuminated him.

"Tracie. Tracie. I'm sorry. I love you, baby. All I want to do is to dance with you."

"I'm a slut, Lonzo. How could you love a slut? What makes you wanna dance with a slut?"

"I have a taste for sluts. I have a taste for you." His breathing was loud and harsh.

"My mother was a slut. Just like you, Tracie. I—think she was," he said in confusion.

Pictures flashed before his eyes; pain reached out and held him in her grasp. "I think it was my mother. Maybe it was my daddy."

The past had crippled Lonzo for life. It had splintered him in fractions, leaving him a bewildered, open vessel and doorway. There were blank black spaces throughout his life, where he couldn't remember a thing . . . with the exception of Tracie Burlingame.

He started to cry dry, racking sobs. He leaned his head against the building. He looked up at a brilliantly clear moon hanging suspended like a yellow globe in the sky.

In a flash he was cold and calculating again. The dry, racking sobs had stopped. "Tracie, you and me, we can make new babies. Superior babies. The stuff that legends are made of, just like you wanted."

That was it. He had knocked Tracie over the edge with that simple statement. She hovered just on the edge of reality and insanity. "Your seed is inferior, Pee Wee. You'd be shooting off blanks."

Rage, pure rage, carved itself across Lonzo's features. He closed his eyes and distanced himself. "Meet me, Tracie. Meet me on the roof. I have a surprise for you. Let's dance."

"I'll be there. Count on it."

Tracie had never hated anyone so deeply in her life. She slammed down the phone and headed for the roof.

On the roof of the Lenox Terrace apartments, Tracie clicked the door closed softly behind her. What she saw in her immediate line of vision made her gasp. "Oh, no."

She couldn't believe her eyes. It wasn't possible, but there they were. Tracie had stashed Michael and Dre away while she dealt with Lonzo, but somehow he had found them. She stared at them, tied and bound. She trembled.

"Surprise, Tracie." Lonzo laughed at the incredulous look on her face.

"Do you think you can build legends out of an inferior seed, Tracie? Miss High and Mighty? Raymond was the one who had an inferior seed. Here's the remaining evidence of his inferiority sitting right here."

"He was a punk, too. You should have heard him squealing like a pig. Oh, that was just before I jammed the seeds of his inferiority down his throat."

Lonzo held up a journal before Tracie's startled eyes. Gently he caressed it. "Dreams and secrets, Li'l Caramel." He worked his mouth in a strange and twisting motion.

"So soft and chewy."

Me stood in a dark corner of the roof, observing the continuing drama between Lonzo and Tracie. His comrade was more obsessed with this girl than he had originally thought. He had thought he just wanted to play with her, but his need and desire went much further than that.

He might have to intervene. Lonzo had thrown him a curveball. He had the other two boys. Me had since learned it was not written that he should kill them. Me could not allow that. For the time being he decided to wait and see.

Tracie's voice sailed through the air, breaking into Me's thoughts and hitting Lonzo with precise little darts that found their target. "You don't have a seed. You didn't come from a seed." She laughed. "You're seed-less. Manless. You're demon spawn."

Lonzo threw his bag of sunflower seeds at her. He lost control and roared at her, "I'm your savior, Tracie! A savior is much more than a man!"

He snorted.

Then he whispered menacingly, "A savior is a god. I'm your god, Tracie. Because I HOLD the power of life and death."

Pure insanity stared at her. "You ready to die, Tracie Burlingame?"

Me inched closer. Lonzo was stepping out of bounds.

Tracie answered Lonzo calmly and serenely. "God doesn't play games, does he, Pee Wee? He sent his son into the world to die for their sins. So they could be re-deemed.

"He didn't go around executing people." With that simple statement Tracie Burlingame came into her own. The truth of what she'd spoken washed over her, cleansing her soul and her spirit.

Lonzo flinched.

His eyes glittered dangerously. He cut a nick in Dre's throat, drawing blood while never taking his eyes from hers.

Michael glanced over at Dre to see if he was okay. He waited for his neck to be nicked next. But Lonzo left him alone for the time being. Michael was glad that Tracie was focusing.

Although she hadn't said his name, he knew she was focusing on Jesus. He was glad because he knew this was the man who could help them. He had already helped him once.

Maybe more than once, now that Michael thought about it.

Lonzo yelled out to Tracie, his tone almost musical, "It's time for atonement."

Tracie tilted her head. Her eyes flashed an incredibly haunting gold at Lonzo.

Nastily he said, "You know what atonement is. It's the shedding of blood. It's the payment for sin. But no Savior is going to pay for yours. I'm going to see that you pay for your own.

"You and you alone must atone for what you've done, Tracie. You and nobody else."

Tracie stepped to Lonzo. Sweat dripped down her face. Her eyes were glazed. Her entire posture and demeanor were different. Her sons were staring at a stranger. Tracie was locked in an immortal battle with Lonzo.

Dre struggled against his bonds. Michael started to struggle against his as well, but it was to no avail. Lonzo was an expert. They could not free themselves to help their mother.

Lonzo removed three vials from his inner jacket pocket. Each of them was labeled. There was blood in each of the vials. The names of Tracie's sons and of one other person glistened brightly from the labels. Lonzo lifted one of the stoppers.

It popped loudly. He lifted it to his lips. He had acquired a taste for the red, slippery substance long ago.

Rashod scrambled for a better view through Me's eyes. Me had had a serious clamp on the spirits for all the time they had been here but Rashod finally managed to break through. He had heard his mother's voice.

Like a guiding beacon he had latched on to it, until he could rise to the surface.

The scene that loomed up before him was terrifying. His mother and his brothers were at the mercy of the maniac who had murdered him, and he was stuck in the vacuum of the monster that had swallowed his spirit whole.

All the players were here, or so he thought. There was little he could do, but he tried with all his might. His voice finally reached the recesses of Tracie's mind.

"Fight, Mommy. You can win. Fight."

That was all he could manage. Maybe it would be enough. He had a small victory, though, because for the first time Me had not noticed what he had done. Rashod had passed through him without notice.

Tracie turned around in startled amazement.

She had heard Rashod's voice. She'd actually felt his breath near her ear. "Fight, Mommy. You can win. Fight," he'd said.

Her dead, misunderstood son wanted her to win. He was rising from the grave to help her. Tracie drew strength and comfort from the contact.

Then she had a very crazy thought.

She decided to see if she could talk back to Rashod. "I love you, Ra. I love you," she whispered back through the recesses of her mind, using the nickname she had called him when he was a little boy.

Rashod had heard her. "I love you too, Mommy. I love you, too."

Tracie could have fainted with relief, but now was not the time. It was enough to know he was somehow there in spirit.

Tracie brought her attention back to Lonzo. She bit

her lower lip and found herself hyperventilating. This monster was drinking her son's blood right in front of her eyes. He was disgusting.

Lonzo's eyes glowed like dark coals in the midst of the shadows on the roof.

Dre watched, mesmerized, as blood trickled down his neck. He clung tightly to Souljah Boy's words: *"Your family is under the protection of Jesus Christ, Dre."*

Lonzo took another drink from the vial. He took a long swallow this time. He licked his lips. "Ah. That must be Randi, the Shooter. He made his last shot from this roof. Just like his daddy, Raymond.

"Remember, Tracie?"

Tracie remembered Raymond's broken body. The image of him loomed up large in front of her eyes at Lonzo's words. Lonzo stuck the knife in Dre's neck again, a little bit deeper and longer this time.

Disgusted, he threw the vial at Tracie. "Payment for your sins. All the sins of the world have been paid for with blood. It was the blood of the innocent. You said so yourself."

Tracie flinched. Her breathing slowed. She locked eyes with Dre. Michael was safe for the time being. Lonzo, for some reason, didn't seem to be concentrating too hard on him except to make sure that he stayed bound.

Lonzo tipped the other vial to his mouth. "Hmmm-mmmm, Raymond." He licked his lips after sucking down the fifteen-year-old blood.

"Dark taste. Just like his life. He was an NBA contender, too, wasn't he, Tracie?"

Lonzo was enjoying torturing Tracie. "His rebound

skills were good, Caramel. I threw him a shot. He leaped like a gazelle right off the side over there." Lonzo pointed to one side of the roof.

Tracie had had enough.

Not only had Lonzo killed Raymond, but he was also trying to destroy his memory in front of his remaining sons. Making him out to be some punk.

Tracie lunged. Lonzo plunged the knife deeper in Dre's throat. Dre winced in pain. Tracie landed on her knees, directly in front of Lonzo's feet.

"I wouldn't, slut. We're not done yet."

Lonzo rubbed the knife scar on his neck slowly. "Raymond gave me this scar. Now his son will have one just like it, because of you, Tracie. You and your fantasies and your dreams of legends."

"Please. Stop it."

Lonzo tilted another vial.

He poured the blood on Tracie's hair. "I told you before. I detest whining, Li'l Caramel. Oh, this is Rashod. You know, your son, the crackhead. Some legend. He's not worth drinking," Lonzo said as he continued to pour Rashod's blood over Tracie's head.

Tracie gazed up slowly at him, her son's blood dripping down her face. She had a crazed look on her face. It was one step away from insanity. Livid hatred spewed from her eyes. She licked her lips to taste Rashod's blood.

Souljah Boy, the doppelganger, had arrived. He hovered just above Tracie and Dre.

"My son Rashod was a better man than you'll ever be, Detective. No matter how many of my sons you kill, you'll never taste me, Pee Wee, because you can't."

Lonzo sliced with the knife down Dre's throat, a

seamless stream, leaving a trail of blood. Dre looked ready to faint from the pain.

Lonzo leaned down. He hit a button on the boom box he had saved for just this occasion. Slow music filled the roof of Lenox Terrace.

Lonzo looked at her. He pushed the knife ever deeper in Dre's throat. "How about that dance, now? Did you save the last dance for me, Tracie?"

Tracie glanced at Dre. She saw his incredible pain. She floated to her feet and into Lonzo's arms, even though Dre begged her not to with his eyes. Lonzo took the knife away from Dre's neck as Tracie floated into his arms.

He held her tightly, mesmerized, lovingly, but cautious and at the ready as they danced precariously close to the edge of the roof. Lonzo sniffed, loving the smell of her.

Rashod's blood was dripping down Tracie's neck; the knife was now to her throat, and as Lonzo dipped Tracie low, the street whizzed far below them.

Lonzo whispered in Tracie's ear, "I saved myself for you, Tracie. A virgin. I'm pure. I should do you right here in front of your sons, where there's plenty of blood to purify our union. Don't you think?"

Revulsion rose in Tracie's stomach, but she only smiled. She'd see him in hell first.

Lonzo suddenly released Tracie.

The music came to a halt. All the unseen parties were at a standstill. None of them knew what to expect. Dizzy, Tracie whirled a little distance away from Lonzo. She dropped to her knees.

Something dark and black rose up inside her. She looked up at Lonzo, then hissed at him. She bowed her head for a moment, lifted it, and looked for a long time at her sons. Her gaze lingered on Dre, bleeding and bound. Then her eyes found Lonzo.

Raw hatred welled up inside her as she thought of Randi and Rashod. She bellowed out, "This is the final chapter!"

Lonzo looked confused. He was calling the shots. He hadn't called the final curtain.

"Let me introduce you to 'expired.' Drink this, Pee Wee!" Like a blur her hand dipped to her waist. In slow motion she glided to her feet, smooth as silk, and in one swift, sensual motion, with the blade in her hand, she sliced Lonzo's face, knocking him off balance and over the roof.

Lonzo's surprised screams ripped through the night air. Tracie raced to look over the side as Lonzo hung from the ledge. The traffic lights glittered far below him on 135th Street as he hung over the same deadly grave that had claimed Tracie's son, Randi.

He was barely hanging on. Lonzo began to taunt her. "Come on, Li'l Caramel, finish the job. Push me over like I did your sons. Like I did Raymond. Get some guts. Come on. Finish the job, Tracie."

Lonzo heard Tracie's friends hooting, mocking, and laughing at him all those long years ago.

He screamed at her, "Do it, Tracie Burlingame! Get some guts!" Tracie's knife swung in an arc through the air to deliver the final blow.

Suddenly Souljah Boy loomed in front of her eyes. He was hovering at the edge of the roof. "Tracie. Tracie, don't," he told her calmly.

"The only way you'll win is if you rise above him. To live in the past is to have no future. Have faith,

Tracie. Have faith. You're going to need it now. Redemption must be given if it is ever to be received."

Tracie hesitated.

She tried to blink the black from her eyes. Suddenly she reached down, and with all her might, she grabbed Lonzo and hauled him back onto the roof.

Lonzo stared into Tracie's eyes as he balanced himself on his feet. He took a silver heart locket from his jacket pocket. He threw it to her.

"I left you two sons, Tracie. I could have taken them, too. Checkmate, Li'l Caramel."

Then he jumped from the roof, airborne.

Me still stood in the shadows, observing the strange chain of events. There would be no reason to meet with Lonzo now.

Souljah Boy released the bonds that held Dre and Michael. He put a hand to Dre's throat to stanch the flow of blood. The blood stopped instantly.

Dre stared at him.

Tracie ran to the edge of the roof just as Lonzo's body hit the ground.

Monica and her crew arrived on the street just in time to view the broken body of Alonzo Morgan as he lay twisted on the sidewalk, a silver locket clutched in his hand, broken open, with a picture of Tracie Burlingame inside it.

As Monica looked down, she noticed that Lonzo didn't have any shoes on his feet.

What she didn't notice was Legion dumping Lonzo's body of his spirit, deciding he didn't want to use it anymore.

And what she didn't see was the little boy behind the

broken shell of Lonzo. The little boy with the life story that had been written in pain and heartache since his birth.

The dim streetlights cast shadowy, blurry streaks of light in the small room of the decaying Harlem building. The air was tight, humid, sweltering. It smelled like old mildew mingled with the smell of feces.

A strangled, gurgling sound caused the small child to cover its ears. The sight and smell of death layered itself over the room, a thick coating of it.

The beaten, withered man in the corner coughed. He looked at the child he could not help. He beheld the child for a last time as the light of life drained from his eyes. All over a horse and a dollar bill.

The men who had been sent to administer the beating laughed. They were small-time street hoodlums. The dying man was a notorious gambler who owed and ducked out on one debt too many.

Grayson Mounds who controlled all the gambling activities in Harlem had ordered the hit after discovering he was not to be paid once again.

When he spoke it was word. So Joe had played his last horse. They kicked him a last time for good measure. Briefly, they considered the child. Then they discarded any idea of dealing with the child themselves.

They left the room. There was no threat. The child was too young to tell anybody a thing.

The whimpering child crawled over to the leftover carnage of the human being on the floor. The child put out a small hand to touch Joe's face.

Instantly the small hand was covered in a red, slippery substance. That was when it had happened. It was a tiny rushed explosion of separating microcosm, splitting off into different beings, an open vessel for the domination of spirits.

An open vessel for Legion.

The child could no longer emotionally inhabit this space where it had witnessed a man being beaten to death, tortured, and torn apart. No. It would leave this place for safer ground. Taking flight and journey into a different realm.

It was a realm the average human being would never cross. Along the line it would satisfy its saturation, hunger and lust for the red slippery substance. Blood.

Three days later when the remains of the man and the child who was still alive, were found the child sat happily slurping from a bottle of soured milk.

The child was a true orphan now because its mother had died a while ago from poverty and a broken heart. It was just as well because this child's existence would not be predicated on human emotions.

The scene the child had just experienced would mold and create its future. It was the last nail in a coffin that would cripple, as well as rule what would become a shell of a human being on the outside, and nothing but pure black malevolence salivating on the inside.

In the absence of spirit there would be only darkness.

That child had been Alonzo Morgan.

That man had been his daddy.

In the absence of spirit, there had been only darkness. The name of that darkness was Legion.

* * *

Michael and Dre ran to Tracie as police helicopters, sirens, and a host of riot vehicles descended on the area.

Me waved his hand, putting a block on the helicopters' view of them on the roof, and disappeared.

"Come on, Mommy," Dre told her. "We've got to get out of here."

"Why?" Tracie asked. "It's over."

Souljah Boy stared sadly in her eyes. "No, Tracie. It's only just beginning. Lonzo was only a small piece. Dre and Michael are still in danger. The danger to you and your sons is much greater than Lonzo. You must go."

"Where?"

"Follow me."

Tracie had known deep in her soul that it wasn't done. The dreams and visions would not be vanquished.

Besides, Renee Santiago had fed her an incredible story, one that she couldn't ignore. It had come straight from the day's headlines.

But she had hoped, after confronting Lonzo, that she was wrong . . . that this was it. But it wasn't. It was far from over. And her remaining sons might be in even greater danger than the two who had been killed, as Souljah Boy had said.

Tracie was learning that there were some fates worse than death—such as the pain and affliction of Alonzo Morgan's life.

She now knew she would have to go to war on a different level and on a different ground in order to preserve that which must be preserved.

Unknowingly she'd been preparing ever since she'd seen all those little black babies sailing through the air.

As Tracie Burlingame prepared to leave, the old preacher in sackcloth and ashes continued to pray.

He would soon be coming up on the third day.

48

Rashod had finally broken through the barrier and walls of separation. Although the walls were invisible, the barriers and blockages contained within them were like steel. Breaking through them had been a most difficult task.

Finally he had prevailed and reached Ms. Virginia. He had discovered that many, many others were there, too, contained within the different walls.

Many of the sequestered spirits had names he had read about in history books or had been taught about in schools. Some of the most famous names in African-American history were residing in this spiritual prison.

There were also new spirits that had been recently added. They were in quite a state. There was a lot of crying and wailing and fear among them. They didn't know what was going on. They were scared.

Some of them he recognized, since they were all

from his stomping grounds in Harlem. Rashod wondered why they'd all come from the same place so recently. He knew it was somehow connected with Me's plan. He just needed to understand what that plan was.

If he could understand, then maybe he could defuse the demon. For the time being he focused on Ms. Virginia, because he believed that between the two of them they might find some answers.

Besides, she was a real smart old lady, and Rashod had grown into a new respect for her as he had watched her stroke Me to keep him calm and to keep him from hurting the others. Me had actually come to gain comfort from the old woman.

It was as though he thought a demon could have a grandmother, or something. The big, bald monster was really a complicated piece of work as far as Rashod could tell.

Right now Me was curled up in the dark of the closet, surrounded by raw meat. He was in a state of rest, which worked out just fine for Rashod, because that meant he could talk to Ms. Virginia without interruption. He wouldn't have to be on high alert.

He had finally grown to the level of bypassing Me, but it wasn't easy. It took intense levels of focus and concentration. He had had to learn how to block Me's sensors in order to accomplish the feat.

For right now things were in a relaxed state. He and Ms. Virginia needed to figure out something because time was running out. Me was resting up for the next event. That event included his mother.

Rashod had seen her again in Me's thoughts after the incident on the roof, when she had held her ground with Lonzo and then escaped with Souljah Boy before the police could detain her. He had wanted to reach out to Michael once again, but it was too risky at the time, and besides, they were safe for the moment.

But he didn't know for how long, and he knew for a fact that Lonzo wasn't the only enemy.

Me had been called to some foreign place that Rashod didn't recognize, and he was terrified. He had bowed before the power and trembled in his shoes. That meant big trouble because Rashod knew that this big, bald gobbler was afraid of nothing. He was fear itself, so for something to scare him, it had to be awesome. Rashod needed to know what it was.

Someone sneezed, and Ms. Virginia said, "There, there, child," as she patted the head of Shelly, smoothing the soft, thick black ponytail. Shelly was very young and very vulnerable. She rarely ever spoke, but she sneezed at the oddest times. It was a symptom of her fear and nervousness. Ms. Virginia gave her a comforting stroke, and she settled down.

Shelly was the youngest of the group, seven years old. She had been a child prodigy. At the age of six she could do trigonometry and calculus and work most any scientific formula created by some of the top minds in the country.

Me had wanted her for his very own. He claimed her and swallowed her spirit whole. She was actually from the shores of Jersey. Newark. Her face was still on the cartons of milk for locating missing children.

Ms. Virginia adjusted her bifocals. She peered across at Rashod through the huge vacuum of space. "This is a mighty fine predicament we've got ourselves in, wouldn't you say?"

"Yeah. Check that. We've got to get ourselves out of it, Ms. Virginia."

"How?"

"I don't know yet. But, there's gotta be a way."

"Rashod," Ms. Virginia said.

"Yes, ma'am?" Ms. Virginia was one of the few adults Rashod had always shown respect to.

"We're dead, you know."

"I know. But I have a feeling we're not at our final destinations. It's like we're stuck in the in-between, or something. And since we can talk and see each other as we looked when we were alive, that must mean there's something we can do. I guess . . ." Rashod's voice trailed off.

Ms. Virginia thought for a moment. Rashod had always been a bright boy; he'd just never used it. Maybe it was his time to use it now, in this strange place.

"I reckon you're right, Rashod, so we'd best start figuring it out."

"I've been wondering," said Rashod. "Have you noticed that everyone here had something that was special about him or her? That they're all gifted in some kind of way? Well, except for me."

"You stop that nonsense, boy. Ms. Virginia's not going to listen to that foolishness. You know me better than that. What do you mean, except you? You're just as gifted as the rest of them," Ms. Virginia stated emphatically, hurt by Rashod's lack of self-esteem.

Rashod hung his head in shame. "No, I'm not. I'm just a crackhead. Well, I *was* a crackhead."

"What you were, Rashod, was a brilliant, gifted young man, especially with those sketches, who was a bit misguided. Or maybe you just couldn't handle what you knew. Some of the most talented people I've ever known or heard of were drug-addicted. Sometimes I just think they're scared of those gifts and the things they know, so they run, and they run hard. You sure figured out how to break through these barriers. As far as I can see, you were the first one who did."

A smile lit up Rashod's face.

It reached his eyes. Ms. Virginia was the first person he'd known who understood. He was scared. He'd been scared of what he'd seen in people, scared of what he might achieve and how he might be perceived. Scared of competing with his brothers and their talents, so instead he had run away.

Hearing it put so plainly restored something to him that he had been missing for a long time.

Unwilling to let Rashod ruminate too long, Ms. Virginia said, "So what's your question? I know you've got some—I can feel it—and we'd best be moving 'fore Me wakes up."

Rashod cleared his throat. "Well, it's like I was saying, Ms. Virginia; all the people here, well, all of us seem to have some special quality that attracted Me. When he killed the guard at the Schomberg Center, he didn't swallow his spirit.

"When he went to visit Whiskey, he didn't kill him or swallow his spirit, either. You remember Whiskey, right?"

"Uh-huh," Ms. Virginia said without further comment.

"Ms. Virginia, what I'm trying to say is, all the spirits that Me possesses are of an elite class of African-Americans. The man has swallowed our gifts and our histories."

With those words Rashod triggered the unholy sight of Me, swallowing the words from all the books in Ms. Virginia's store, save one. Why hadn't she noticed that before? Save one?

Ms. Virginia leaned forward, her scholarly mind working overtime and her presence suddenly rejuvenated with an excitement beyond measure. "That's it, Rashod."

"What's it?" Rashod asked, puzzled.

"That's the answer. Oh, my God."

"What's the answer, Ms. Virginia?"

Ms. Virginia had turned inward almost as though Rashod weren't there. He practically had to pull her back to their realm.

She started and then shared with Rashod what she was thinking. "Me swallowed all the words from all the books in my store. He swallowed every word in every book, save one. All that was left were pictures or illustrations, nothing else."

"The only book he couldn't touch was the Bible. It was the only book left in the store that wasn't defiled."

The implication and dawning reality of what she had witnessed stunned Ms. Virginia. Me and whoever else he's involved with is trying to cover a secret, a trail."

Ms. Virginia wasn't as strong in the spirit as Rashod, so she had not witnessed all that Me had done, as Rashod had. So she asked, "Did you say he did the same thing at the Schomberg Center?"

"He did that and more. He swallowed all the words on all the rare manuscripts, documents, and histories. All the rare archives, Ms. Virginia. And there was another thing he did."

"What?"

He melted the pictures of all the authors that were hanging on the walls. He hated them, Ms. Virginia. His hatred was so strong, it rocked this vacuum. You must have felt it. He melted their images right off the canvases. Then he swallowed their names, dates of birth, and deaths, as though he wanted to erase them from history."

Ms. Virginia let out a shocked gasp.

"That's it, Rashod. Don't you see? Throughout time each of those authors and those books must have been exposing him in some way—bits and pieces, maybe, about his identity."

Ms. Virginia took a long breath before continuing, "Some of those books are biographies, about great people who have been assassinated in our time. Who would want to assassinate or kill people who were bringing the truth? In the beginning was the word, and the word was God. Words are a powerful thing. The authors—he must equate them as having some kind of power over him."

She paused.

"The power to reveal his identity. Maybe in a way that people would really understand. Maybe there's *one* who has the power to reveal his plan and pull the covers off his actions. Maybe they have the power to give the people recognition to see him. To see him when they didn't know that they were."

Ms. Virginia halted to think. Rashod didn't move. For a time it was silent. Rashod knew she was onto something. He waited patiently.

It was all coming together for Ms. Virginia. "He's been swallowing the gifts because the generations have been failing to honor God with their gifts, which left him an open door to go after them."

"What do you mean, Ms. Virginia?" Rashod said.

"When the people misuse their gifts, Rashod, they're in danger of losing the blessing that goes along with them. God is deserving of honor and glory. He hates sin. Now, I know you're young, but you see and hear the movies, the stories, and the music.

"Some of it is the narrow road to destruction, particularly for our people. We all haven't been honoring God with our gifts. In many ways we've been glorifying Satan. Worshiping the material things of this world, not respecting things of the spirit. We only respect what we can see, feel, and touch."

Rashod's eyes grew as big as saucers, for he had many a memory of what Ms. Virginia had just said, and he was only nineteen years old.

"And so," Rashod picked up where Ms. Virginia left off, "the only book he hasn't been able to touch is the one that's holy. The Bible. It's the only book that was written and inspired by holiness itself. Jack, Ms. Virginia. So, if the writers throughout time have been revealing bits and pieces of him, but we are a people out of grace, then that means . . . Ms. Virginia, if he's able to do this, then he must be . . . he must be . . ." Rashod's voice trailed off.

"He's the beast, Rashod, under direct orders from Satan. That means if we're here, we're in big trouble." Ms. Virginia's bifocals misted over.

Rashod put a hand over hers. "Maybe not, Ms. Virginia. I ain't no religious student or nothing. But I know that time after time throughout the history of the Bible, God has always come back again and again to save his people, no matter how many times they've fallen out of grace. Right?"

Ms. Virginia sniffed. "Yes, that's right, son."

"Jesus Christ was descended from the house of David. Ain't that right, Ms. Virginia? And he was the savior."

"Yes, that's right." Even through her fear Ms. Virginia was proud of Rashod. She'd always known there was something special and smart about him. Now she was discovering he was brave, too.

"Maybe there's another plan in effect. Maybe we don't know all the pieces yet. Satan doesn't have the power to totally destroy the Lord's people," Rashod said with hot conviction.

"Perhaps Jesus will save us from this place. Look."

Rashod pulled out the tiny black charcoal scroll he had scooped up from the broken head of Othello in the Schomberg Center. The paper was old, crackled, and parched. Slowly he rolled it open.

Engraved inside was a miniature cross. It was stained with what looked like dark blackish-red blood that was centuries old.

"I found this in Othello's head, when Me cut it off in the Schomberg Center. Me never even saw it, Ms. Virginia."

"My Lord Jesus," was all Ms. Virginia could utter.

Suddenly Rashod was glad for Rozzie. Everybody thought she was a crazy woman. She was a bag lady—wore winter clothes on ninety-degree days, and things like that. She walked around Harlem picking up things off the ground and putting them in her bag—invisible things that no one but her could see.

That woman shot more heroin than any three men put together. Her arms were covered with scabs and sores.

Rashod had had the pleasure of witnessing this once when she was looking for a place to hit. There wasn't a clear spot on her arms. The tracks trailed every inch of her flesh.

She was the one who had taught Rashod about the Bible. She had even dragged him to a small out-of-the-way church one Sunday, where, in a lucid, moving moment, he had gotten baptized and accepted Jesus Christ as his Lord and Savior.

He had figured he didn't have anybody else, so what did it matter? Roz had also taught him about Jesus being descended from the house of David. She knew all about the houses of Abraham, Isaac, and Jacob, too.

Roz had loved Jesus with all her heart. Without a doubt she was one of the most hard-core junkies Rashod had ever met. But she had been absolutely convinced when it came to Jesus Christ.

Rashod had felt sorry for her.

She had deserted and abandoned her daughter for old King Heroin. She hadn't seen her daughter for many years. She spent almost every waking moment of her life trying to forget about her child by shooting heroin—that and picking up invisible things from the ground.

One day when they were getting high, Rashod had finally asked her the question: "Roz?"

"Yeah?"

"What is it that you're always picking up from the streets of Harlem and putting in your bag?"

Her runny eyes had cleared for a moment. She had stared at Rashod directly. "Why, I'm collecting the souls, Rashod. I'm collecting the souls for my brother, Jesus. Satan is trying to hide them. But he can't hide them from my brother, Jesus."

49

Tracie had been taken to a safe house. The church. She was stunned when she realized that arrangements had been made for her to stay at the Pentecostal House of Prayer. It was the same church she had visited, with the two flames of fire burning beside the Bible.

She was given a small private bedroom and connected bath on a separate floor from the church. Her boys were given equal accommodations, except they were sharing a room.

It appeared they had been expected, and they were welcomed warmly. What in heaven's name had brought her back to this same church, seeking refuge? She didn't know, but she was grateful. It was a strange set of circumstances, to be sure.

After seeing that Dre and Michael were settled in, she went to her own room. She was still ruminating over the fact that Souljah Boy had merely touched the cut Pee Wee Morgan had made in Dre's neck, and the flow of blood had been instantly stanched. The scar itself had healed.

It brought back memories from long ago.

What was happening to her life? She didn't know. Or maybe the question should be, what was happening to the life she used to have? In any case, she was too exhausted to ponder so many questions to which she had no answers at the time.

And it was a good thing she didn't know that in another part of the brownstone, not so far away, there was a man praying for her in sackcloth and ashes, and he was coming up on the third day—because that bit of information would surely have freaked her out.

There was a quiet knock at the door. "Yes?" Tracie called out.

"It's Reverend King," a quiet voice answered.

It was the pastor with whom the arrangements had been made for her and her sons to stay the night.

"Coming," Tracie had said.

She pulled open the door to find the Reverend King standing with a Bible, two candles, two candlestick holders, and a lighter in his hands.

"I thought you might enjoy having these. If you light the two candles on either side of the Bible, it can produce salve for the weary soul."

The Reverend King smiled and handed her everything he had in his hands. He pointed to a table that was situated under a crucifix.

"There's a good spot for it. Good night."

"Thank you. Thank you very much," Tracie said, touched by his generosity of spirit and not believing her good fortune in receiving the Bible and candles when she had been yearning to go sit in the church and just look at it. But she hadn't wanted to ask.

"Good night, Reverend."

"Good night, child. Sleep tight," the pastor said, and then turned away to descend the stairs. Tracie would never know that he had watched her the day she entered the church, while she stared at the Bible and its leaping flames of fire. He'd known that she would return.

Tracie smiled. It had been a long time since anyone had called her "child" or bidden her to sleep tight. But his words were exactly the medicine she needed after her ordeal. She would need a good night's sleep because the next day she needed to visit the old woman.

She also needed to find out why, at the last count, fifty young black boys had been slain in Harlem in the same manner as her sons.

In a single night.

Had Pee Wee killed all those boys? If so, why? She knew why he had killed Randi and Rashod. But why would he kill all those other boys? And how could one person massacre fifty young males in a night?

Some of them, it was reported had been taken out of their beds from their homes in the middle of the night. Slaughtered before sunup. This was a nightmare.

Tracie couldn't remember ever hearing of such an odd atrocity. The police had an APB out on her, thinking that because of the nature of her own sons' murders, she might be able to shed some light on this insane situation. Now that Pee Wee was dead, they would certainly step up the pace.

Thus, she had needed to seek shelter in the church. Somewhere that no one she knew would ever think to look for her. The refuge at the church was courtesy of

Souljah Boy, though what would make him pick this one out, she didn't know.

Then there was Ms. Virginia's store and the Schomberg Center. All the words were missing from the rare manuscripts there, just as Renee had reported happening at Ms. Virginia's store, Visionaries. Tracie had thought that Renee was losing it at the time.

Apparently she hadn't been.

Now Renee had added something new to her story. Apparently it had recently been discovered that the only book in Visionaries that didn't have the words missing was the Holy Bible. It was intact. Every letter, every word, and every page of the Bible was exactly as it had been.

Tracie knew that Renee had played her part; now it was up to her. Renee had given her valuable information; there was nothing more that she could do. Renee was the number one girlfriend, without a doubt a valuable ally.

Tracie's head had begun to ache from the constant flow of questions. She was confused, and she didn't understand any of it. But she knew that the matter wasn't closed with her discovering her sons' killer. And Pee Wee Morgan's death was not bringing closure to the entire situation.

In fact, if anything, it had created more of a puzzle.

Now she needed to know if her sons were part of a bigger picture. Was Pee Wee playing her to hide the massacre he had planned to inflict on Harlem?

If so, he had played her right up until the end, just like a fiddle. Were her sons' deaths just a cover for what was to come?

She had to talk to that old woman. She had seen something connected to her. Tracie needed to know what it was—soon. It was the only possibility she could think of, and she wasn't going to take no for an answer.

Anita Lily Mae Young would talk to her if it was the last thing she did. She just needed to know why. That was all. Why? Why were her sons really dead? And why were fifty other boys just like them dead as well?

"Stop it. Just stop it," she told herself aloud.

Tracie went over to the table. She set up her Bible and lit the two candles. Suddenly there was a warm feeling of serene peace that came over the room as she stared at her own personal copy of the Bible and the two burning flames of fire.

What a treasure.

She stared at the picture of holiness. Her eyes grew heavy with sleep. Tracie sat down on the edge of the bed and continued to stare at the gilded words that read: HOLY BIBLE.

The leaping flames cast shadows on the wall.

Before she knew what had hit her, Tracie was lulled into a deep unconscious state, where she stood before the *Unspoken*.

50

Dre and Michael couldn't sleep. It was no wonder. Michael dropped across one of the twin beds while Dre paced the room like a caged tiger. He couldn't get the image of Souljah Boy out of his mind.

Neither could he forget about his healing.

Michael, for his part, was boiling over like a pot that was on high heat and full of steam. He had thought about things and thought about them. There was only so much thinking he could do. Michael got up and opened the small window in the room, welcoming the gentle evening breeze.

He flopped back down on the bed and put his hands behind his head. He watched Dre pacing. He tried to keep his nerves under control because Dre's pacing was making him want to scream.

Instead he said, "Dre, I used to be a masochist."

He felt like a man in a confessional. Relief swept through his body.at the release of the words.

Dre stopped pacing. He leaned his lanky frame against the wall. He stared at the crucifix hanging on the wall. Then he turned to Michael. "Yeah, I know that. Are you looking for absa . . . absa . . . what's that word?"

His voice trailed off for a minute while he thought about it. "Are you looking for absolution?"

Michael smiled. "Naw, man, I already received it. It sort of rained down on me."

Michael glanced at the crucifix and saw the image of a tortured man, hanging in agony, but through it all he felt the man's honor, bravery, and something else. He tried to think what it was that he was feeling.

Humility. Christ had been a humble man.

And through his pain and agony he had shown great power. This man had shown him his power. He just hadn't known what he was seeing at the time. And if that was the case, it had to mean that despite how it looked, everything was going to be all right.

"How did you know? Michael said.

Now it was Dre's turn to smile. "Let's just say I lived with you, son. It don't make no difference what you was, Rebound. It's what you are now and maybe what you will be that's the sum of the total, brother. You know what I mean?"

Michael looked at him. "Thanks for the love, Dre."

"No doubt it's your props. You're not the only one who's not what they appear to be." Dre didn't elaborate, and Michael didn't push it.

"I saw Rashod," Michael said, changing the subject.

"You went to the morgue?"

"Yeah, I saw him there, too."

Dre gave Michael one of his what-the-hell-are-you-talking-about looks. He sat down on the bed across from him. Michael rose from his bed. "Do you mind if I light one of these candles?"

"Naw."

Michael lit the candle and returned to sit across from Dre. "Rashod's body is in the morgue, but his spirit isn't."

"You'd better put a spin on this, Rebound, cuz I ain't feeling you."

Michael sighed. "His spirit ain't at peace, Dre, because he needs our help, and this ain't done."

"The hell it ain't," Dre said. Then he clamped a hand to his mouth, remembering where he was. "Sorry, I ain't mean to say that, but you know what I mean."

Michael nodded.

"It's over. That punk cop Lonzo is down for the count. That's all there is to it."

Michael smiled. "Is that so? Then why are we here?"

Dre clamped both hands to his head and shook it, as though he could free himself. "Lay it out, man. Straight up. After all, we've got all night. Souljah Boy showed up on the roof of the Lenox Terrace apartments as a spirit, not a man, and he's as real as I know, so just break it down, brother. It looks like I ain't going nowhere."

Michael untied his sneakers. "You heard about the other fifty boys that were murdered?"

"Who hasn't? Man, you think the toy cop did them, too?"

Before Michael could answer, a distinct voice called out both their names. "Rebound? Dre?" The voice belonged to Rashod. They had both heard him.

They turned in the direction of the door, where the

voice had come from. They saw Rashod, hovering and flickering just like the lit candle.

"We ain't got time to be tripping, so listen up. The toy cop ain't all there is, Dre. There's more. We gone have to get ready to hold court in the streets, cuz there's a new kid on the block, and a few Glocks and Uzis ain't going to kill him."

Dre rose from the bed. He stared at the image of his dead brother.

Rashod stared back. "Are you feeling me, Dre?"

51

"Tracie." He had called her name, the calling of which sounded like it was blowing on the wings of the wind. Tracie felt her name rising, billowing up from the inside of her. She felt it rather than heard it.

Gone were the Bible and the flaming candles blazing staunchly beside it. For some reason Tracie thought of the flaming sword with the guardian angel the Lord God had put outside the Garden of Eden upon Adam and Eve's banishment from the garden.

Tracie frowned. Now, where had that come from? And how had she gotten on her knees? She didn't know, but she was on them.

All around her was a bright blue sky and clouds. Just miles and miles of endless blue sky, and clouds that were fluffy white, like big feathered pillows. It was as though she were kneeling in the middle of the atmosphere. The whole idea of gravity was not a factor in this place. She was like a balloon that was at one with the air.

Up in front of her, someone was walking toward her. Tracie squinted, trying to get a better look at the person who was venturing closer to where she was kneeling. Laura. It was Laura Peyton. Tracie hadn't seen her since she was a child. What was she doing here? Where was here? Tracie wondered.

Tracie tried to remember. Yes, she had been looking at the Holy Bible and the flaming candles casting dancing shadows on the wall, and then . . . and then she was here.

Laura Peyton looked radiant, serene.

Tracie thought she looked like an angel. The spirit of her had always been so, but her physical demeanor was different. She was Laura, that was for sure. She looked like Laura, and yet there was a totally different quality about her, as though Tracie were seeing a dimension of her she had never noticed before.

Laura stopped in front of Tracie. She reached out a hand to smooth her black, silky locks of hair. "Remember the healing, Tracie?"

"Yes. Yes, I do." For no reason at all, tears sprang to Tracie's eyes.

Laura shook her head at Tracie's tears. "It is a time for joy, child, not sorrow. Real joy. Just remember that the path to most things that are holy is fraught with many stumbling blocks along the way. Only you can know when you've reached holiness, Tracie. You know that by your belief."

Tracie blinked back the tears. And the reservoir that had been stored inside her long ago, the one she had tapped into when she was a child, the reservoir of innocence and childlike faith from which she had received the healing, rose up inside her like a spring day.

Her body suddenly felt light, as if the strain of it were no longer there. As though she had laid her burdens down.

Old Laura Peyton smiled and nodded. She was the same woman who, in life, had imparted faith to Tracie when she had hit her head on the radiator. "Have faith, Tracie, and believe all that you will see here, because there is no untruth in this place. When you return, you will know all that you need to know. But you will win by belief."

"Win what? Tracie asked.

Laura only smiled serenely at her, which brought Tracie to another question. "Are you dead, Laura?"

Laura made the sign of the cross on Tracie's forehead, and then she outright laughed at her question. "Child, I have never been so alive." And with that, Laura was gone.

"Wait!" Tracie screamed out to her. "Someone called my name."

"I called your name, Tracie." Again the voice rose as if on the wings of the wind. It was felt more than heard by Tracie. And, now in Laura's place, there was a book lying in front of her.

She read the cover. "The Ancient Book of Prophecies," Tracie whispered the title out loud.

As soon as she had the book open, the pages beckoned to her. *Come.* Tracie reached out a hand, and then she turned to look behind her.

The Holy Bible was directly behind her. The cover had opened, and the pages began to flap rapidly as though a great wind were flipping them. The Bible closed when each page had been turned.

She felt her name again. "I called your name, Tracie." Tracie had been touched by the *Unspoken*.

She turned back to the book in front of her, and as her hand touched it, she was pulled through to begin her journey. There she beheld many things, and many things beheld her.

Graced. That's what she was, purely graced.

Tracie was walking to the beat of a different drummer. It was to a tune no one heard but her. But that was okay, because she was like two going on ninety.

She had always walked as though she knew a secret nobody else did, and now it was true. Her stroll through the streets this time would be much different.

Tracie Burlingame ran in the spirit just as she had run on the streets of Harlem, as though she had a victory to reclaim.

And she did.

Before she left the path, she threw her head back, threw her arms out spread-eagled in the air, and said the two words that left her spiritually on holy ground.

The mere utterance of those two words left her standing in the spirit. "I believe!" she shouted to the *Unspoken*, "I believe!" With that, it began to rain on Tracie, a baptismal flood. "Thank you, Jesus."

At the very moment that Tracie Burlingame shouted, "I believe!" the old black preacher, praying in the sackcloth and ashes, said, "Amen," ending his three days of repentance for Tracie Burlingame. And then he closed his eyes in eternal peace.

52

The fruition of many things before, about, and surrounding Tracie Burlingame had come to a turning point. It was time for the branches to bear fruit. And, as in any vineyard, the weeds had to be cast out. They had to be thrown into the fire so that good fruit could come to bear.

And so they would be, because Tracie's branch, of which she was not in full understanding, was attached to the true vine. In that vine was great power.

Tracie found herself standing at the front door of Anita Lily Mae Young's apartment. Although she had some answers concerning the deaths of her own sons, she was compelled to understand what had happened to the other young boys in Harlem.

Without a doubt, Anita Lily Mae Young knew something; she had always known something. Tracie had just been too arrogant and self-important. She had been too much of a diva to read the handwriting that had been on the wall.

She had had literally no preparation for things she could not see. So therefore, she had no basis by which to judge.

There was no way she could have imagined that she would go from where she was in her life on the day she had decided to toy with Anita Lily Mae Young to this day that stood before her.

And yet that day had been an omen for her. She had laughed to herself, thinking this old woman a fool. She had been bored. She had simply wanted to amuse herself with one of Anita's readings that day.

The events that had been set off in her life were catastrophic concerning that one sunny, sweltering day on the streets of Harlem. No, she had not been prepared. How could anyone be?

Tracie pulled herself back to the present. She was not at all at ease with the killings of her sons. The answers that she had diligently thought would bring her some semblance of peace had not. Pee Wee Morgan's death had left an open gap rather than a closed chapter.

Having run parallel to the street and criminal underground pipeline for a good portion of her life in Harlem, Tracie understood that she had been set up.

She had been manipulated and led to sources and information that were not all that they seemed to be. And she knew that this meant she was in trouble, because she had been lured into a trap not of her own making. On the streets the fittest of the fit survived. Those with the knowledge and power ruled the course of events.

Tracie thought about all she had seen. She diligently hoped that she was standing on the right side. Deep inside she knew she was.

When Anita beheld Tracie standing at the door, she just pulled it open wide and let her in. No words passed between them. The path had already been established.

It was a different Tracie that Anita looked at. Gone was the cover-girl makeup covering her exquisite features and accenting the high cheekbones. The flashing eyes now held depth, inquisitiveness even, and light.

Her eyes shone like rays of sun shining through crystal. Tracie looked at Anita through naturally long lashes without the aid of cosmetics, and Anita realized that she was a stunning woman—even more than Anita had noticed before, because a sort of natural glow was lighting her from the inside out.

Tracie's hair was swept back from her forehead and hung in a black, sheetlike sheen straight back from her face and down to her shoulders. She was unadorned in any way, yet she was adorned. Anita was astonished by the change in her, although she didn't dare say so.

Tracie made her feel as though she were standing in front of a black princess, descended from royalty, with the spirit and meekness of an angel. One who knew her true power. One who had come to give, not to receive.

"Come on in, Tracie. Tracie Burlingame, isn't it?" Anita said.

Tracie smiled. "Yes."

"I've been expecting you."

"Yes, I know you have," Tracie replied meekly.

Tracie stepped into the small foyer. Anita led her into one of the most uniquely decorated rooms Tracie had ever laid eyes on. Yards of fabric covered the sofas and walls.

Pictures upon pictures of so many of the famous hung in gilded frames from the walls. The room was an array of antiques and splashes of vivid colors and silks.

Tracie noticed the mannequins draped in different designs and decided that Anita was also a woman of great class and style.

Old Louisiana style was what she possessed. Tracie smiled. Those were deep roots with a tinge of class about them.

There was also something different about her since Tracie had last seen her on the streets. It was as if a harsh covering had been peeled away, revealing a pearl underneath the layers.

Anita had not failed to notice that Tracie didn't carry herself with the same arrogance that had struck her originally. She could sense the strength in Tracie, but it felt as if it was contained.

She actually *walked* toward the sofa, as opposed to her original "look at me" strut that captured the eye of almost any person the instant she entered a room.

Tracie sat down demurely on the couch. She crossed her legs at the ankles. Anita shook her head to clear it just a bit. Then she took a real look at Tracie Burlingame.

She peered though the layers, looking for the spiritual patchwork quilt that she knew Tracie was.

It was not as immediately apparent to her as it had been on that first day, out on the streets, when she had seen it on Tracie. That quilt had been her haunting, and now the woman who represented it was sitting in her living room as though it were the most natural place in the world for her to be.

As Anita reflected on what had been revealed to her, she decided that perhaps it was in relation to the path of things.

There was nothing she could do to alter the time or events. It had been written, and so it would be. She had sworn she would have nothing to do with Tracie

Burlingame. She had, in fact, become a recluse in her own apartment and shut down a lucrative source of income because of what she had seen on this woman sitting across from her.

Yet here they both were, entwined in a path not of their making, and yet bound by the sacraments of the spirit.

Incredible. She would have to have lived it, seen it, and been given it to believe it, and so she had. As Anita's second sight came into focus, she saw that the spiritual patchwork quilt had in fact become more vivid.

The voices were raucous, shouting. But there was a different tone to them this time. The hollowed-out patches had become hallowed in their being. Anita gasped, sensing a different spirit on the horizon.

The black patches that were seekers had been alive with movement before, but now they were still. There was no movement in them. That was because two of Tracie Burlingame's sons were dead. The hunter had captured them.

And then the sharp, lizardlike tongue whipped out. It lashed and thrashed around, looking to swallow and devour. Anita had seen enough.

She shut off the sight because she was allowed to.

She sat back in her place on the sofa. The entire quilt was now bathed in an extra, invisible layer, but it was there.

Tracie settled herself and looked over at Anita. She had known that Anita was observing her, weighing and calculating the costs and risks. But, Tracie had come into some understanding of her own, so she said, "Ms. Young, the quilting is the laurel of my being, of my wind. It is my eternal wind."

Tracie was silent for a minute. "I guess you can call it my essence, so to speak. It represents the fruit, which in turn are the generations—the seeds, in a manner of speaking. It also represents past, present, and future."

"So it does," Anita said without elaboration.

"I know that's what you saw on the street that day."

"So it was."

Tracie looked down beside her to see an antique trash pail filled with an array of crystal balls. The trash was overflowing with them. Their colors glistened; they had come from almost every corner of the globe.

Why were they in the trash?

Tracie gave Anita a questioning look. Before she could form the question, Anita said, "I won't be needing those anymore."

"Why?" Tracie inquired, although she thought she might know the reason.

Oddly enough, the old woman took Tracie's hand in hers and said, "Because I've been given real sight . . . just as you have."

Anita lapsed into her southern twang without even realizing it. "And I ain't no longer got to rely on false symbols or trickery, Tracie. There ain't no falseness in the eternal living God; everything about him is real, and so I ain't got no need of those things anymore."

Tracie nodded, thinking about the cards Anita used on the streets of Harlem.

"I ain't got no more use of the cards, either," Anita said. "None of that. What I got myself is a pure sight now, and forgiveness by the Lord Jesus Christ. I'll see what he gives me to see and I ain't gone be peering through little glass balls or cards to do so anymore.

"I found out those things ain't of him, and they stirs up the wrong spirits, girl. I had a real gift all along, and

I ain't never needed them there things. I just didn't know it. If the Lord wasn't merciful, I coulda lost what gift I been given."

Me suddenly surfaced in Anita's mind. She heard him say, "I have come to collect the gifts."

Anita shivered.

So, the pearl was shining through the peeling, Tracie noted. Tracie covered Anita's hand with her own and smiled. But as she did, Anita drew back as a sense of impending doom swamped her being. When she looked down, she was no longer holding Tracie's hand but instead she was holding a piece of fabric, a piece of the patchwork quilt, a black patch—and it was alive with movement.

Anita raised her head.

Tracie Burlingame was staring at her with eyes that had become as wide as Frisbees. The whites of her eyes glowed pure in their color. Her pupils flashed hazel-green with golden specks. She said not a word.

But she was gripping Anita's hand to the point that her nails, which were buffed and manicured but not colored, were slicing into Anita's flesh.

Sensing a presence, Tracie looked over at a beautiful French covered chair to see two things. Anita's black, silky-looking rabbit Pesky was the only rabbit in sight. He had taken refuge under an old wooden desk. The hairs on his back were standing straight up like the hairs of a cat.

The second thing she noticed was her dead husband, Raymond, sitting in the chair, looking at her. He had a look of such profound longing in his eyes that it knocked the wind out of Tracie.

Her body became one tight spasm of pain.

Tracie loosened the grip on Anita's hand at the sight of him.

"Raymond?"

Raymond crossed his legs. He sat back in the chair. He had always been a sharp dresser, and today was no different. He was Saks Fifth Avenue from head to toe. His trousers had a razor sharp crease that matched the grin that he gave Tracie.

"I've missed you, Tracie."

Tracie was stunned. She couldn't believe Raymond was sitting in front of her. She ignored the part of her brain that was trying mightily to yank her back to her senses.

"Raymond, I . . . I've missed you, too." Tears sprang to Tracie's eyes but did not fall.

"Come to me, baby." Raymond sat forward in the chair. Tracie rose from her seat.

"No," Anita said.

Tracie halted.

She looked at Anita as though she were in a trance. "Ms. Young, this is my husband, Raymond. He's my children's daddy."

Tracie's voice dropped to a pained whisper. "I'm so glad to see him. I'm glad he came to visit. I haven't seen him in such a long time. You of all people should know this is possible."

"It ain't so, Tracie." Anita grabbed her arm, but Tracie pulled loose from her grip.

Raymond stood up. He looked at Tracie endearingly. No more words were needed. He held his arms out to her. Tracie's heart soared. She took a step toward him.

Anita was bugging. She was willing Raymond's presence to leave the room, but she discovered she had no power here to do so. The only person who could do that was Tracie.

Tracie halted once again.

She tilted her head. When she did, the shining sheet of black hair fell over her shoulder, creating a cloud of illuminating beauty.

"Mommy . . ." The voice sounded as though it was far away, as though it were coming through a tunnel. She recognized it instantly as Rashod's.

"Fight, Tracie. Fight."

Why was Rashod saying that? Where was he? Tracie looked around like a person who had been stranded on a desert island, who was seeking help.

"Look at him, Mommy. Please, Mommy. Just really look at him," Rashod said.

Tracie did.

She recoiled at once at what she saw. "No . . ." She backed away. There was nothing but the couch behind her. She backed into it with such force that she fell down on the couch, still staring across at what she thought might be Raymond.

But there was a problem.

It was a very serious problem. Underneath the savvy Saks Fifth Avenue gear, underneath the slick silk of the suit and the veneer of Raymond's smile, was something else. And it was a crawling and slithering mass.

Tracie closed her eyes. "No," she whispered again. It seemed to be the only word she was capable of speaking, as though the entire English language had been stolen from her vocabulary.

Tracie's backing away and refusal to step into Raymond's arms had set off a collision course of things. And with her reluctance came great pain.

Raymond's body was broken up in front of her eyes.

He was dismembered piece by piece. Then the pieces of him were strewn across the beauty of Anita's Persian rug.

There was no blood; there were only body pieces. He looked the same way he had looked some fifteen years before, lying broken on the concrete of the streets of Harlem.

Tracie couldn't bear it. A scream rose from the depths of her throat, but the only thing that left her mouth was silence. Her mouth gaped open, but no sound came out.

What left Tracie's mouth instead of sound was a stream of alphabets . . . alphabets that made up words . . . words that made up a single sentence.

The words rolled out and hung in the air, one passage written in the Ancient Book of Prophesies: IT IS TIME.

Total silence gripped the room. Even Anita's worn air conditioner ceased its humming. It was silence of a depth that rarely reached human ears. The summons had been issued. The air in the room shivered with unseen life.

Me stood in Anita's foyer like a huge mountain that had appeared out of nowhere, raised out of the bowels of the earth. Tracie lay on Anita's Persian rug, retching over the pieces of Raymond's body.

Someone sneezed.

"What a mess," Me said.

He stuck out his hand. Raymond's parts were sucked into a funnel, then sucked out through a vent. All that was left was mist.

"What do you want?" Anita asked, knowing the answer all along.

"I have come to collect the host . . . and that which is contained within."

Anita ran over to Tracie. She knelt next to her, putting a protective arm over her shoulders.

"No," she said.

Me smiled. He advanced slowly into the living room. He glared at Anita. Her body rose in the air. It slammed against the wall like a rag doll. Then Me shook her while she hung in the air, suspended as though from unseen ropes.

Blood flew out of her mouth. The old woman gagged.

Tracie was having a hard time gathering herself, but the sound of Anita's body rattling in the air, the sight of blood streaming from her mouth, commanded her attention.

Slowly she glanced up at Me. She rose to her feet. She looked at the old woman being shaken and rattled so hard that her teeth were clattering.

Tracie dug deep.

She stretched forth her arm and slowly moved it downward. As she did so, Anita descended toward the floor. Tracie extended her hand in front of her. Slowly she turned her hand palm up. The blood stopped streaming from Anita's mouth; she ceased shaking. She landed on her feet softly on the carpet.

"Leave her," Tracie said to the bald mountain.

Anita wiped the bloodied spittle from her mouth with a silk handkerchief she took from her dress pocket. Me stared at Tracie in stunned disbelief.

He was under the impression that he had come simply to take what was needed from the street diva. He had known that Tracie was a fighter. He had observed her on the roof with Lonzo.

However, he had thought that was only in the physical realm. He had not known that she possessed spiritual capabilities as well. That information had been hidden from him.

He decided just to disarm her quickly. He would get it over with. He would not play with her. All he needed was one thing: that should be a simple matter. That was all it would take to alter the future.

So Me looked into Tracie's eyes with the intention of stripping her. He peered through her and reached in to get what he wanted.

Tracie matched his look. A simmering glow climbed from the irises of her eyes, blocking Me from seeing anything but the physicality of her.

An echo sounded in the room, like the collective wailing from some African ritual. It rose in volume. Anita crossed herself.

Me was pissed. He exhaled. The windows in the room blew out with the force of an explosion. And then a gentle calm swept through the air.

Tracie stood her ground until the soothing touch of motherhood smoothed a hand through her hair. She turned, noticing as she looked down, that she was standing on rose petals.

"Tracie," her mother said as she planted a warm kiss on Tracie's forehead. She took Tracie's hand in hers.

"Mommy."

"Aw, Tracie, it's been a long time."

Her mother took a long look at her, as though she wanted the memory of Tracie to remain her possession forever.

"Sit down." She pulled Tracie down next to her on the sofa. "Tracie, why didn't you listen to me long ago?"

Tracie tried to run from the memory, but there was

no escaping it. She could almost feel the chastity belt cutting into her flesh even now.

Her mother had come from an old, old school of thought. When so many of the teenage girls in Harlem were turning up pregnant, Tracie's mother had gone away for a short time and had returned with the dreaded belt. The belt that would protect her daughter's virtue—or so she thought. Tracie had caused her a lot of pain.

Tracie Burlingame had been a beautiful, vain, and arrogant young girl with the spirited actions of a newborn calf. Sandra Gaines regretted the day she had been born. She had known that a barren womb, for a black woman, was a blessing in disguise. But she had not been blessed with such. Tracie was her cross to bear.

However, there was nothing that said she couldn't intervene and ensure that Tracie didn't birth what could be nothing more than seeds of pain and hardship.

Tracie had rebelled. She hated the projects. She secretly hated her mother and all that she stood for. More than that, she hated the chastity belt—with a passion. She decided she would have none of it.

She wanted to love and be free.

With Raymond's help she had gotten rid of the belt. She had obtained her freedom and married him, without ever looking back at her mother and her timeworn beliefs. And the babies had come freely and abundantly, one right after the other.

After the birth of Rashod, Tracie had secretly gone to visit her mother, thinking that this sweet bundle of a bouncing baby boy would soften her heart. That she would realize that she was wrong. She didn't. Her actions had left Tracie harboring a secret that had never been revealed until this moment, when her mother appeared in Anita Lily Mae Young's apartment.

Sandra Gaines had taken one look at the glowing, fat cherub of a baby that Rashod Burlingame was, one spirited look into his eyes. Her eyes had met Tracie's with a fear that Tracie had long ago buried deep inside herself.

"He is a sacrifice," she had said to Tracie. "What have you done?" And with that, she had been stricken. She dropped dead of a major stroke at Tracie's feet.

Now she glanced into Tracie's eyes. "Why did you kill me, Tracie?"

"I didn't." Tracie wrenched her hand away in horror as all the horrible old feelings of guilt began to invade her being.

She had always felt that in some way she was responsible for Sandra's death, just as surely as if she had put a gun to her mother's head and pulled the trigger point-blank.

With the little bit of money her mother had left her, Tracie had tried building a legacy to her through her salons. But even that gesture, a legacy to a poor black woman who died in the projects, hadn't absolved her. It had only made her more driven.

And it hadn't stopped the constant nightmares that woke her up in the middle of the night, sweating. She would see a vast ocean of water. Sandra was trying to swim to shore, but Tracie would grab her ankles from underneath the water, pulling her under and drowning her in the process.

It was the same old dream, all the time. That was until she began to receive the one about the black babies falling through the atmosphere. That dream had taken precedence and erased the nightmare that was Sandra.

Now Sandra peered at her and asked her again, "Why did you kill me, Tracie?"

Tracie began to sob. "I'm sorry. Oh, God, I'm so sorry, Mommy. I didn't mean it." Tracie collapsed in tears. Sandra took her in her arms.

"Just give him what he wants, Tracie. It's the only way. You never should have carried the eggs anyway. I warned you, but you didn't listen. Now look what you've done. You've stepped on the wrong toes. If you'd never been a carrier, if only you'd never produced these babies or allowed your womb to be fertilized, this never would have happened."

Sandra paused, holding Tracie at arm's length so she could look into her eyes. "If you'd never opened your legs in the first place, heifer, this wouldn't have happened." She whipped back her hand with the speed of light. She slapped Tracie Burlingame soundly across the face. The sharpness of the slap crackled through the air like a gunshot.

Anita lunged toward Sandra Gaines, trying to protect Tracie. Sandra gave her a read-the-hand motion that stopped her dead in her tracks. She had no feeling in her legs; she was paralyzed in her spot.

The slap had awakened Tracie as though from a long slumber. She saw the many black babies sailing through the atmosphere. And suddenly she knew it was her job to protect them. That was why she was here.

The future of that generation was in her hands. Sitting before her was nothing more than a mirage of evil. A mirage of evil that had put its hand on her, even long ago.

Tracie rose up from her place on the couch. She

stormed over to stand in front of Me. When she reached him, she turned her back on him.

"Oh, God," Rashod shouted out involuntarily. He was scared. His mother had turned her back on the demon.

But Tracie was not afraid. She hit the reservoir and came up with strength. "It's time you left, Sandra."

The whites of Tracie's eyes shone as she spoke the final words, "In the name of the Almighty Savior Jesus Christ, be gone!"

Sandra turned to ash.

Tracie saw her hourglass sitting in the destroyed window. She wondered how it had gotten there. When she saw the ash being swept into the hourglass, and it turned upside down as the ashes slowly sifted through, Tracie knew it would be a time for new beginnings.

And Anita knew that Tracie Burlingame had come into her own.

Tracie looked at Anita. Life returned to her paralyzed legs. Anita smiled.

Yes, Tracie Burlingame was a princess—a black princess warrior.

She had been chosen long ago.

53

Tracie turned her attention to Me. She was standing so close to him that she could feel the rumblings of the spirits he held inside him. She also saw something else.

The spirit of her son, Rashod, was hovering in back of Me.

So that was where her son's voice had been coming from. He had her son. Rashod put a finger to his lips to warn Tracie not to tip off the bald demon mountain to what she was seeing, but she knew better anyway.

Tracie blinked.

Me's innards opened up to her like petals on a flower. Tracie could not stifle the gasp that rose up and tumbled out of her mouth. In him were housed many spirits. Some of them were famous legends that were hanging in portraits on Anita's very walls—some old, some young, some in between, but they were all there.

And now Tracie knew what had happened to the fifty slain boys in Harlem. Then Tracie saw a face she recognized. It was Ms. Virginia.

"Oh, my God," Tracie echoed Rashod's earlier words. She looked at Me.

Me was disturbed because he could not get access to her thoughts. It was as though he was experiencing a power failure. The generator was not kicking it. Me looked into Tracie Burlingame's eyes. For the first time, he felt real fear.

There was something behind the surface, and it was strong. It wasn't vulnerable. Vulnerability was what he had plied his trade on over the centuries.

He poked and probed, but he could find no weakness in her. Tracie decided to take another look. Something was disturbing her, something she needed to see but had missed. Looking again, she saw them. The murdered boys—their spirits were being housed in a secluded section.

They were scared and confused.

When they saw Tracie looking, they stretched out their arms to her in unison; they spoke in one voice: "Release Us!"

Tracie shook her head at the impact of what she had seen. She turned to Me and said, "There is forgiveness in the holiness of the imperial blood. The gifts will be restored. The future generation will learn how to use them to glorify the Almighty."

Me stared at her. "I have come to collect the gifts."

Tracie stared right back. "So you have. And I have come so they might be reclaimed by the one to whom they really belong."

Tracie thought for a minute. "Me, isn't it?"

Me took a step back. How had she known his name?

Tracie didn't keep him in suspense. "I know all about you, Me. You've been . . . shall we say . . . jacked, haven't you? Jacked, played, and used by your master. I know there's someone else, cuz you don't have what it takes."

Me was angry now.

"I swallowed the gifts. Just like I will swallow your egg. Just like I will leave you dead in this house. This is your final resting place, Tracie Burlingame." Me's tone had turned into a growl of blackness.

Tracie turned to Anita. She was tiring of the game. No, actually she was becoming bored with this beast and the games being played. "Enlighten us, Anita. Enlighten the bald mountain here, who obviously hasn't been told all by his leader."

Anita came over to stand next to Tracie. The old woman stood beside her, with her shoulder touching Tracie's. A great pride rose up inside her. She, too, had been deceived, had been made to use her gift falsely. Now she had an opportunity to atone for that.

"Me, today you ain't gone leave her with nothing."

Me gave her a look that normally would have shriveled her. But the image of Christ Jesus and his grace kept her standing.

The thought of possible deceit kept Me listening.

"Tracie Burlingame here and I have been dreaming the same dream. In that dream there are many li'l black babies sailing through the atmosphere. Droppin' like sweet tomatoes from a branch, from between a woman's legs," Anita spoke softly and with total conviction.

Tracie looked over at Anita. She gave her a warm smile. Never in Tracie's life had she felt as she did at that moment, when she was being bathed in the light of Christ and his awesome magnificence.

She shivered at the raw power of his being.

She had known that this woman had the answers, and so she had spoken to her, to reveal them. By her faith and belief, and by the power of the spirit of the Holy Ghost, Tracie knew that it would be.

"There's a force, Me, that's been sweeping some of them there babies away. I think you know who that is. But there's also a force that's been wrappin' them little old black babies in pure white swaddling. Hmmph, now, I'm sure that wouldn'a been you."

Anita made a sound that was somewhere between a laugh and great distress.

"Yes, Me. You've been so busy just swallowing up the gifts. You could never had done that if our people hadn't misunderstood, thinkin' that all they had, all their talents, was of they own doing and came from them, while they was wrecking destruction among our own people.

"If they had any inkling of how to tap into their true power, you wouldn'a been able to touch them. Just like you can't touch Tracie Burlingame and me right now. Can you, Me?"

"Me can do all things."

Anita couldn't help it. She laughed. "You can do only those things that you are given the power to do. I'm an old woman, Me. I told you before, don't play with me. I done figured it out, Me.

"Throughout the centuries some of our people have been trying to tell on you. In bits and pieces they've been sorta revealing you over time. You were afraid that one day somebody'd come along and piece together all the broken pieces.

"That's why you stole the words from the books in Ms. Virginia's bookshop and in the Schomberg Center.

Explains why you desecrated the authors' pictures in Schomberg, too. They each tried to warn the people, here and there.

"I guess what you ain't counted on was one thing: all things come to an end, sooner or later. There's a beginning and there's an end. The woman in the dream from whose legs those li'l black babies is falling is standing in front of you, Me."

In Me's eyes devastation flickered.

He hadn't been aware of that. She was just the host from whom he needed the egg—the one he needed to destroy. But the implications of the old woman's words began to loom large in his mind.

He felt the very earth shake under his feet. He knew that soon there would be a shift in things.

Anita ignored his reflections and continued. "Those li'l black babies that are being caught in the pure white swaddling represent a new generation, Me. A generation that will be born with understanding. A generation who will honor the Lord God Almighty and his Son, Christ Jesus!

"Which means that your trickery and treachery will no longer destroy our people so easily as you and those of your pattern have done in the past. John the Baptist spoke once and said God is able to raise up these grains of sand to worship him.

"I know you is familiar with them there words, Me, cuz that's the only book you could never swallow the words in. You ain't swallowed those words, cuz you can't hold that which is holy. Cuz you are the unholy. Spawn from the enemy of God. Spawn from darkness."

* * *

Roz's words sounded off in Rashod's head. "Why I been gathering the souls for my brother Jesus. He can't hide them from Jesus." Rashod suddenly knew. His eyes opened as the scales fell from his sight.

He looked at Tracie. He projected the vision of Dre and Michael kneeling in prayer in the church, before the altar with the Bible on it. Both flames of fire were flickering beside it.

Rashod had given them understanding. He had taught them how to fight—not with the weapons of street warfare, but in the spirit. As the two live boys who remained to Tracie Burlingame, it had been imperative that they become of one accord while this battle took place.

It had been imperative because there could be no link through which Satan could move or which he could use to disconnect Tracie Burlingame.

Jesus had promised he would not forsake his people. If they believed, he would be there.

Through his faith and belief, Rashod had been able to assist in bringing his brothers through that fold. Michael had already been somewhat prepared, and so had Dre, through his dealings with Souljah Boy.

They had decided to become true warriors and to learn what being tough and not being a punk was *really* all about. The preacher had been on standby. He had baptized them immediately after they accepted the Lord Jesus Christ. They had risen up from the holy water, in one accord with the spirit. It had been a sight to see.

That was shortly after the Reverend King had found the old preacher dead, lying in the sackcloth and ashes after his three days of repentance for Tracie Burlingame and her seed.

The spirit had spoken unto him, "Baptize the boys, and leave the body be."

So he had left the old minister where he was and had gone to do as he had been instructed. Now he knelt beside them in a vigil of prayer, as the war that had been thus declared before any of their times raged on.

He hadn't gone back to the old preacher's room since the spirit had thus spoken to him. So he had no way of knowing that the body of the old man was no longer there. Neither were the sackcloth and ashes, nor the ancient trunk.

54

Legion did not like the script that was being played out in front of him. Me was a damned imbecile. That was why he had only used him in a limited capacity. He would destroy this fool. A mere woman was taking him down.

Didn't this fool know that he had used a woman to cause the original destruction that had set the tides a-turning?

Before Me stood a hood rat. Nothing else. Some little black girl, all grown up from the hood, who thought that because she fell on her knees in an unknown spot, that gave her power.

He would show her what real power was.

Legion shook the very ground that Harlem was sitting on. Anita's apartment tilted. It rocked from side to side, like a sheet blowing in the wind. The three of them were toppled from their feet.

They fell on the floor as everything in the room became unhinged and fell in ruins all around them. Anita's rabbits became one ball of fur that tunneled through the room and straight out the broken windows.

Anita screamed out, "Pesky!"

But Pesky was blown away in the wind. The walls began to tear away from their joints. The room descended in pitch-black darkness.

A voice funneled through their sphere.

"Tracie Burlingame! I am Legion!" The voice had an eerie commanding quality to it. The gravelly, authoritative tone made the hairs on Tracie's neck stand up.

"You have something that belongs to me. I want it now." A force that felt like many hands grabbed at Tracie. They were all over her. She felt them trying to crawl underneath her skin.

Trying to get inside her.

While the hands continued to try to invade her being, Tracie looked up to see a creature swathed from head to toe in black. What she saw was not human. He had more eyes than she could count. He had a multitude of noses. His mouth was lizardlike. A long, slimy-looking tongue protruded and swiped itself across her face.

Tracie almost fainted from the shock of it. Suddenly the hands stopped pulling at her, because they had another mission. They had been instructed to bury her alive. She was dropped into a black coffin, covered in black silk. As she screamed, the cover on the coffin slammed shut. It was dropped into the bowels of the earth. Mounds of heavy earthly dirt descended on top of the coffin.

Tracie beat her hands against the coffin as the air was sucked out of it, until they were red and bleeding. All the sound had been sucked out. So there was nothing but the hollowness of her screams. Her screams were completely muffled.

The dull thudding of her knocking against the top of the coffin was in vain. And she was running out of oxygen fast.

"Keep your egg, Tracie. It will never be fertilized anyway. I didn't need to steal it. All I needed to do was bury it, along with you."

Laughter resounded through the air.

The coffin flipped bottom side up. The mounds of dirt continued to rain down on it, pushing it farther and farther, deeper into the earth. Tracie's coffin was some four hundred feet below sea level.

The preacher and Tracie's sons kept praying.

Anita had screamed out at the sight of Tracie being dropped into the coffin, "Jesus! Oh, Jesus! God! Help us!" And then she had proceeded to bellow and cry from the depths of her belly; the sweat rolled down the old woman's face in rivulets as she called on the only word that she could get out of her mouth, "Jesus!"

Satan was clever. He hadn't come the way they had thought he might. He had simply decided to snuff out the host mother and what she carried in her womb. It would be buried forever. It would be buried in the dungeons of his creations, along with the carcass that was Tracie Burlingame.

Why should he exert himself playing grandstand games? He had it like that. It was over. Tracie Burlingame was over. It was the end.

As he listened, he heard Tracie take her last earthly

breath. It was done. For good measure he plunged the coffin another six hundred feet beneath the earth, never to be seen or heard from again.

He put his hooves together, and he applauded a job well done. Me smiled at him. He fell down on his knees in worship, secretly hoping that Legion wouldn't destroy him. That he would be so happy with his victory and with the job he had done, he would spare Me his wrath.

And actually Legion was feeling quite pleased with himself. Even though Me had been stupid, there was no reason to act hastily. He could always continue to use him for the small things, the light work that he himself had no time for. Anyway, Me was an official extension of him, which meant that he would be killing off a part of himself if he got rid of Me.

There was no need to dilute his power in this way. So instead he looked at Me and told him, "Stay on your knees until I tell you to get up."

Me was grateful for the reprieve, so he just nodded his head, not even wanting the sound of his voice to trigger anything.

There was one partying host of demons as they realized what Satan had accomplished. They could continue their reign of destruction among this people. They could continue to deceive them and lead them astray from the truth. Now they would never have to worry about a generation that might fight back as a whole, one that might know better. No.

The two fools Tracie had left behind were no threat—Satan and his demons knew that. Legion was a longtime student of the spirit. The sons would falter without their anchor that was Tracie Burlingame. It had not been given to either of them anyway.

Tracie Burlingame's living sons were nothing more than mere shells of her womb. Tracie was thirty-eight years old when Legion buried her alive. In her future had been a new marriage, but more than that, in her future there had been a new birth. It had been written that on her fiftieth birthday she would have given birth to her last male child.

That child would carry the seed from which the future generations would have been raised up to know the Lord Jesus Christ. They would have learned to respect their gifts and talents. They would have learned to worship the eternal living God and his Son, Jesus Christ, with honor and respect.

There would have been a new vineyard that was planted. A vineyard that was in direct connection with the true vine and with his Father, the husbandman. The real Holy Father who had originally given his all, by sacrificing his only living Son for the sins of the world.

Yes, he had given all that could be given.

In exchange, all he had ever really wanted was to be in one accord with his people, that they should seek his face and turn from their wicked ways.

Also, Tracie Burlingame had been the intended future scribe, the one who would pen her memoirs through her journey in the spirit, leaving a legacy of hope for her people.

The one who would string together the bits and pieces that the authors, over a term of many centuries, had been laying the groundwork for.

Legion had thrown another stumbling block in front of them. He rejoiced as his liquid blackness shook like a bowl of Jell-O. One more was down in the course of things. He had buried the host mother alive. He threw open his dungeons to the festivities. Then he retired to his private quarters to enjoy another victory.

Tracie Burlingame . . . the spiritual patchwork quilt. The voices had been silenced and could no longer reach her. At one time they had been raucous. Those were the spirits that Me had swallowed, being reflected back in her being, seeking her help.

The black patches had represented her sons—her dead sons, as death was coming upon them—as well as Raymond, who had already been killed. And the other sequestered spirits that had died including the fifty black boys murdered in Harlem.

The hollowed-out patches she had lived in her journey through the spirit.

The lizardlike tongue had swallowed what it wanted whole. Now it salivated in its victory. It was the representative of Satan, devouring the African-American people through their sins.

It had also swallowed the whole of Tracie's quilt in the ritual of the burial. Her quilt was no longer alive. She was no longer a patchwork quilt with the prophecies alive in her being. She wasn't anything at all.

Legion laughed.

She was just no more. Victory. The taste of it was sweet on his lips.

He closed his eyes so he could relive the sweetness of it from the beginning.

Besides, it had all been recorded.

55

While Tracie Burlingame had been expiring, the police and all their experts were left with no real answers to the multitudes of bodies that occupied the morgue. The people had to be given some answers.

A private meeting had convened. It would mark the first time all the leaders had pulled together and decided on one course of action, which none of them would ever speak differently about again once the news release had been revealed to the public.

They had all taken one sacred vow. It was called CYA—"Cover your ass."

Alonzo Morgan had provided them with a convenient alibi, although not one of them—Alexandra, the mayor, Monica, or any of the community leaders and experts who attended the meeting—believed it.

They had nevertheless agreed that Alonzo Morgan

would become the foundation on which the official story would be built.

He was something they could actually point to.

Alonzo Morgan would be charged with fifty-two counts of murder, although he was dead. Two charges for Tracie Burlingame's sons, Rashod Burlingame and Randi Burlingame. He was charged with the other fifty on the basis of his obsession with Tracie Burlingame and because the murders all had an identical MO. The killing off of Tracie's sons was only a cover for a sick mind to commit a mass murder.

Alonzo Morgan was a psychotic serial killer. He had infiltrated the police force; therefore, he had access to considerable power. None of the department's psychiatric evaluations, medical exams, or testing had indicated anything out of the ordinary with Alonzo.

He was a cross-sociopath. Scientific evidence pointed to the fact that his type could seep right into mainstream society and appear as normal as the next person.

The police were not fortune-tellers. They did the best they could, but they did not have the ability to peer into another person's mind. There had been no indications. Alonzo Morgan had graduated in the top five of his class in the police academy. They had evidence of having done all the appropriate checks.

It was an unfortunate incident, to say the least. In response to it, a more rigorous background check would be instituted in the future.

Neither Alexandra nor the mayor of New York ever mentioned that they had discovered that he was also responsible for the murder of one Raymond Burlingame, Tracie Burlingame's husband, some fifteen years before.

Because they could not explain how Alonzo had

managed to kill so many boys in the course of a single night, they connected him to a nationwide cult.

They lied, saying they had corroborating testimony from protected sources, who placed themselves in imminent danger by linking others to the crimes—shadowy characters who had flown in, helped to commit the murders, and then disappeared.

Because there was no blood found in the bodies, they concocted a story of a secret web of psychopaths that had a passion for drinking blood. They were modern-day vampires; that was why they had killed the boys.

At the time of the publishing of the press release, Harlem Homicide, along with the FBI and CIA, had issued an international police warrant through Interpol for those persons who had participated in the murders that night.

It was believed that some of the participants might have been from other countries. "It is believed," they reported, "that some of them came from as far away as Africa."

Black male serial killers were a rarity, and a foundation for these needed to be established.

They were piecing together fragmented descriptions from the few witnesses they had.

The police had lied, big-time. No human being would ever be charged in connection with those murders, except for Alonzo Morgan, for whom they had a real dead body to point to.

The story was nothing more than a scam to buy time and let the uproar die down. Every parent of every one of those children had been bought into silence—except one, who was never heard from or seen again.

Eventually, The Schomberg Center for Black Culture

and Research was restored, from a construction standpoint at any rate. The documents were restored from the backups that had been held in vaults in Chase Bank. The reams and reams of blank pages were burned.

The room with all the portraits of the authors hanging in it, where the Harlem Writers' Guild held their meetings, was restored to some semblance of what it looked like before Me's destruction.

People could not handle what they had seen. They were not prepared to delve any further.

The story went away on the surface, though it had never gone away in people's minds.

But just as they had been trained and conditioned to do, people believed what was convenient. They believed what they were told, what they saw and heard in the press, simply because that was the way it was.

That was the way it was in Harlem after fifty gifted and talented young black boys had been slain in a night, their blood drained from their bodies, their bodies broken up on the streets of Harlem, sunflower seeds stuffed in their throats, and the coveted sneakers removed from their feet.

That was just the way it was. The story, just like those boys, in time had expired—expired on the surface, anyway.

But it could never be extinguished from people's souls.

56

When Tracie Burlingame had fallen, she had not fallen alone. With her the many little black babies had fallen, too. The family had been ready.

Leading the pack was Souljah Boy.

A council had been pulled together. It was made up of the ones to whom the existence of the Ancient Book of Prophecies had been whispered.

They had been summoned in the spirit to Anita Lily Mae Young's apartment. They had witnessed the events that had taken place. They had been summoned for just that reason, just as it had been written.

When Tracie Burlingame descended through the layers of darkness, so had they, following her descent through layers upon layers of the earth. They were in a tight-knit circle.

They all held hands.

On the wings of eagles they followed the coffin that held Tracie trapped.

Just as Tracie was one step away from running out of oxygen, she heard the whispered words of Laura Peyton: *"Just remember that the path to most things that are holy is fraught with many stumbling blocks along the way. Only you can know when you've reached holiness, Tracie, and you know that by your belief. Have faith."*

A tidal wave rose up in Tracie at the whispered words. She closed her eyes as calmness swept over her. She saw a part of her journey where she had been walking near a pool of crystal-clear water.

She had stood and watched as it dribbled through rocks that looked older than anything she had seen in her life. As she had watched, the water had turned into black, slimy mud. She had reached her hand down into the creek because she couldn't believe that the crystal water had turned to mud.

When she stuck her hand in it and brought it before her face for inspection, she discovered a clear, crystal stream flowing through her fingers.

There was a reason she had seen that.

Her faith had almost faltered from fear. That fear had almost killed her—almost, but not quite.

Tracie realized that her dilemma was nothing more than an illusion, a mind game. There was no way she could be descending that far down into the earth, because that would mean she was descending into hell.

And there was only one man in the history of the world who had ever gone there and come back out alive, with the keys to heaven and hell.

There was also no way Jesus would let Satan bury her alive.

He only appeared to be getting away with it, because in her fear she believed he was doing it. So that meant that the demon bastard was still in Anita's living room.

Tracie prayed, "Lord, give me the strength I need. I know that by the power of your holy blood I will complete what I was sent here to do."

With those words, the family descended on the coffin. Souljah Boy unlatched the lock to the coffin. Tracie rose up and out. The coffin fell away. His was the first face she saw. He was smiling at her.

"Have faith, Tracie Burlingame. Have faith."

Tracie gulped the newly found air. She touched his cheek as she momentarily glanced around at all the other council members. Souljah Boy was the youngest one in the group. He was the only one she recognized from the time they lived in. Praise Jesus for him!

Tracie threw her head back in the air. She closed her eyes. Then she tapped deep into the reservoir. She found herself standing in front of Me. He looked up from where he had been kneeling, in complete shock. Something was wrong.

"You're dead," he said.

"Only to the likes of you, Me," Tracie told him.

Anita burst out in song.

She started singing, "Hallelujah, Hallelujah, Hallelujah!" She sang those same words over and over again.

Tracie looked inside Me and cried out in a loud voice, "In the name of the Lord Jesus Christ, I command you to RELEASE them." She stated this with extreme authority. Her voice never wavered.

And release them she did, through the almighty power of the Holy Ghost. She released them in the name of the Lord and Savior Jesus Christ.

They were released through the blood that had already been shed, and the price that had already been paid on a cross, long ago, on Calvary.

Last but certainly not least, through her faith, Tracie Burlingame unleashed the spirits that Me had been swallowing.

They began to break free and rise.

A stream of golden light lit their way. It streaked like a rainbow toward the sky. One by one they rose out of the shell of him; he could no longer contain them.

Me rolled around, agonized. He screeched. He howled. But it was to no avail. They were free. They were going home to their true resting spots, until the time should come.

Tracie looked at the rising souls. She saw Rashod. She didn't see Randi, because Me had never swallowed his spirit. But she knew he was safe because she had seen him on her journey.

She had been allowed to see him through grace.

Rashod hesitated before her. A solitary tear slid down her face. She knew that he had to go. He would be released with the others.

Her throat tightened for a moment with tears, but finally she spoke, "Good-bye for now, Rashod."

Rashod looked into her eyes. He blew her a kiss. And then he bowed low before her. "My mother, a princess in the spirit. Imagine that. You fought the good fight, Mommy. You fought the real destroyer, and you won. Not just for you but for all of us. I'm proud of you."

It was all Tracie could do not to break down and cry. He smiled. Before Tracie could react, she received a gift in all its pureness.

Through Rashod's faith he had made one request. That request was that he wanted to touch his mother—

so she could feel him, feel his flesh, just one last time. And she had.

When Rashod threw his arms around Tracie, she felt him in the physical and spiritual, for one brief moment. She hugged him back tightly, loving the feel of him.

And then he pulled back from her grasp, knowing he must go with the others. He began to float upward, returning to his former state.

"Thank you, Jesus," Rashod whispered. "Thank you."

He grabbed Ms. Virginia's hand, and they ascended together. Tracie waved to Ms. Virginia. Ms. Virginia waved back.

"See," Rashod said, "I told you, Ms. Virginia, we didn't know everything."

Ms. Virginia smiled. "And you were right, child. You were just so right."

Hand in hand together, they made the journey as Tracie watched so many more go behind them, along with the little girl from Jersey, who gave Tracie a bright smile just before she sneezed. But she was no longer afraid. The child could feel the goodness of the Good Shepherd. He was there in the air.

When all the spirits that Me held had been released, a strong ray of light beamed down on the top of his bald head. His destruction was not a pretty sight to behold. He shriveled up into a mass of writhing worms under the heat of the light. Then the worms were drawn down into the bowels of the earth.

From Satan's seat in hell he looked up. He beheld the light that was Jesus Christ, the Son of the living, eternal God. On sight of him, he knew that another of his victories had been short-circuited.

He disappeared because he could not stand before

the sight of one so holy. And he trembled every step of the way as he took his leave. He could not stop Tracie Burlingame. She would live out her works, according to the magnificence of HIS HOLY WILL.

Tracie looked around and found that Anita's apartment had been completely restored. If she had blinked, it could have just been a bad dream, but it wasn't.

Just as Dre, Michael, and the presiding minister rose from their knees in the church, Tracie Burlingame rose from Anita's couch. She walked toward the front door.

She was bathed in a stream of light.

She turned to look at Anita. Light shone from her eyes with great power and radiance.

"Changed. A new spirit I hold," she said to Anita.

Anita couldn't help it. She hugged her.

"Yes, child, I know. You sho do. Me, too."

As Tracie turned to walk out the door, Anita said, "Tracie, you saw them fifty boys that was slain rise, too. Didn't you?"

Tracie was touched in her spirit. Anita had known that Tracie hadn't understood whether her sons were caught up in a mass murder, or whether the mass-murdered were caught up in the murders of her sons.

In the end they had all risen together, just as in life they had been caught up together. It no longer mattered in the scheme of things.

Tracie looked deep into Anita's eyes.

As she did, her eyes flashed dark brown, hazel green, and finally settled on a bright, golden brown. Anita could see the rays of the sunrise in them.

"Yes, Ms. Young, I did. I saw them rise. Today I witnessed the mercy, grace, and glory of the Lord Jesus Christ!"

Anita nodded.

She watched as Tracie walked out the door. She noticed that the patchwork quilt was completely changed. It was just a silvery white, blowing in the wind, for all things had been fulfilled.

Something caught Anita's eye, and she looked up to see that the invisible covering, which she had noticed on the quilt when Tracie had entered her apartment, was floating upward, heading toward the sun.

"What a mighty God we serve," Anita said.

"Jesus Christ is Lord," Tracie Burlingame replied as she passed through the door.

And as she walked the streets of Harlem, a different person, she let that simple fact be known, as people wondered and pondered about what had happened to her upon her sons' murders.

By the time Tracie had resurfaced on the streets of Harlem, the police had not touched or questioned her. They didn't want any part of her. Their stories had been decided; Tracie Burlingame could only muddy the waters.

As far as they were concerned, her sons were dead. They had the killer, albeit a dead killer. But still, they had him. End of story.

Tracie had witnessed and been a part of quite a different ending from the one they reported.

Twelve years later, Tracie Burlingame gave birth, at the age of fifty, to one healthy and bouncing baby boy, the child within whom the promise of a different generation would come forth.

During that time Tracie had also written a great many pages. She had written a legacy really: memoirs of hope, faith, and jubilance in the spirit.

But not one of those pages contained any writings regarding the Ancient Book of Prophecies.

The Ancient Book of Prophecies contained the secrets of many blacks and their roots the world over. It was the book from which the secret of Me, and how to destroy him, had been revealed to her—the book in which both Me and his leader, as well as the end of all things, had been summed up.

Nor had Tracie revealed that on the day the pages of the Holy Bible had flapped and turned of their own accord, for an instant in time she had been caught up in those pages. And she had felt the pain and persecution contained in them. She had also felt the holiness.

It was a love more powerful than she could ever have imagined on her own.

The Almighty, eternal living God and his Son Jesus Christ were love. They were love, pure and simple. The profoundness of it was something one did not experience in the natural world. You had to let go of the things that bound you in life. You had to be able to feel with your spirit, to feel with the very essence of yourself to connect to that knowledge.

You had to tap into your spiritual heart. There were two of them: the heart in the physical, the one that pumped blood; then the heart in the spiritual, the one that encased your soul.

Their glory was greater than mankind knew.

No, the Ancient Book of Prophecies she had not written about, because after all, the Ancient Book of Prophecies had not even been whispered about except among select, chosen people, let alone seen.

And as long as she lived, Tracie would always see the Holy Bible with its two burning flames shooting up

staunchly on either side of it. At times she stopped by
the House of Pentecost just so she could sit in the pew,
watching the flames burn on the side of holiness.

She remembered the first time she had seen it and
the old black minister whom she had asked, "Does
your God dwell here?" He had told her that his God
dwelled in many places. Tracie had discovered it to be
true.

He had dwelled in some places where she had never
expected to find him, yet there he was. He dwelled in
the streets, in the projects, in the crack houses, in the
prisons, in the homeless shelters, even in a mother's
womb.

His spirit had dwelled in her son Rashod when she
had thought he was just another junkie. But Jesus had
used him in a powerful way. While Rashod was getting
high on the very drugs he craved, Jesus had held his
hand.

He had imparted knowledge to him. He had sent
him another junkie in the borough of Harlem, named
Rozzie, to share some things with him, things that he
would use to help clear a pathway for a new generation.

My Lord! Yes, he dwelled in many places.

Jesus had used Rashod to help her. He had given that
boy strength and power. Jesus had not read Rashod's
outer condition. He had read the condition of his heart.
Then he had stepped into the middle of what was evil
and had used him to erect what was right and true.

Yes, the Lord Jesus Christ dwelled in many places.
Some of them were not exactly where people expected
to find him.

Tracie smiled to herself. He had shown up in a lot of

her street stories, where there was complete chaos, desolation, and lack of hope. Yet he had shown up. He had been there.

If only people knew.

She could only hope to impart his presence to people so they could feel him. They would probably be surprised to know that she didn't just deliberately place him there, as a writer. He just showed up. He dwelled in many places.

Later Tracie had discovered that the old black minister with the tar-black skin and silvery hair at the House of Pentecost had passed on during the time of her conversion.

Bless his soul, Lord.

The image of the Bible and its two burning flames had always burned brightly in Tracie's mind as she wrote stories, poetry, inspirational books, and songs that were published and made their way around the country and to other countries, to plant a seed of thought or a seedling of hope.

Stories that always expressed a road map to faith after people traveled down the many different roads that led them away most of the time. But in the end there was salvation for those who wanted it.

There was salvation for those who reached out to touch a single branch of it. If they touched a branch of it, they could connect to the true vine that was Jesus Christ.

Yes, Tracie Burlingame, unlike some who had gone before her, had learned how to use her gift. She wrote diligently as the spirit gave her guidance, to magnify the Almighty Lord, Jesus Christ.

She wanted people to know what he could do for them, just as he had done it for her. Before her experience she had never once touched pen to paper to write anything, except in her ledgers where she recorded her money.

One thing she knew for certain was that Jesus Christ could save anybody.

And he frequently did.

Tracie named her last-born son David Burlingame. The name David was in honor of the House of David, from which Christ had been born fifty-two generations after David's existence.

When the child was a year old, Tracie, her new husband, Dre, Michael, Renee, Souljah Boy, and Anita all attended a small christening at the church, the House of Pentecost, for baby David.

Souljah Boy, or Daniel Thomas Caldwell as he had asked to be called at the christening, had been named the child's godfather.

The boy was just adored by all.

When the preacher had sprinkled the holy water on little David Burlingame, the boy had opened his eyes. Reflected in them were two flames of fire. The preacher had drawn back in surprise, and yet they had all witnessed it.

Renee Santiago had been so touched by the event, she'd told Tracie she was taking a hiatus so she could experience life on a deeper level, hopefully one day to incorporate it into her own writing. She confessed to being tired of the commercial treadmill.

Tracie was both happy and deeply touched that her experiences and those of her family had affected Renee so much. Tracie smiled, thinking briefly of Whiskey. It might actually come to pass that some things would change with him as well.

He had contacted her after all the madness died

down, and there were two things about him that astonished her: he had quit drinking, and he professed to be
looking for a legitimate business to buy, to get out of
the gun trade.

He hadn't elaborated on the details, but he'd told her
he had come across something that made him want to
reevaluate a few things. Then he'd done a strange thing,
asking her to marry him, to which she'd heartily said,
"No."

But she'd kissed him on the cheek, wishing him
well, knowing that what was meant for her would come
along one day, and it had, in the form of little David's
father.

Monica Rhodes, Alonzo Morgan's partner, had briefly
stopped by David's christening to hand Tracie a present
for the baby. She'd realized along the way that she had
severely misjudged Tracie Burlingame, and they grew to
be friends.

Surprisingly enough, she made a little cross on David's
forehead, whispering a prayer for him. She hugged Tracie
tightly before leaving, telling her she was retiring from
police work.

Over the years, she'd had a hard time accepting the
fact that Lonzo had possessed so many faces, all of
them the faces of evil. She'd decided she didn't want to
be that close anymore, so she was getting out.

Besides, she never had been at all comfortable with
the end result of the investigation into the deaths of
Tracie's sons and the murdered boys in Harlem, so she
decided she'd do best just to distance herself, divorcing
her mind of it and trying to cleanse her soul.

She was glad she had stopped by David Burlingame's
christening, because it gave her a feeling of repentant

cleanliness. It also instilled hope in her for a brand-new start.

They had all left little David Burlingame's christening, marked by the experience, as well as marked by the prior events in one way or another. Life was funny that way sometimes.

The night after little David's christening, Tracie Burlingame died peacefully in her sleep at the age of fifty-one years. She died with a smile on her face.

Anita Lily Mae Young had looked out her window on the night Tracie Burlingame died, to see two pieces of the patchwork quilt merging together: the invisible covering she had seen rising toward the sun that day, and the silvery white that was still part of Tracie's essence until her spirit left Harlem. The old woman had muttered under her breath, "Well done, child. You done did well, Tracie Burlingame."

They had said that Tracie Burlingame's eyes were like a chameleon. But really they were more than that, much, much more.

Tracie Burlingame was what she was, and to that end she would be.

The Lord Jesus Christ is what he is, and he dwells in many places. For a time, he dwelled in Harlem. He still does.

One never knows where one might find him.

The following is a sample chapter from
Evie Rhodes' upcoming novel
CRISS CROSS
which will be available in February 2006
wherever books are sold.

Chapter 1

1967
Newark, New Jersey

"Now and forever, Evelyn," Quentin's words were spoken hauntingly, softly into her ear. "Do you know what those two words mean?"

Hungrily and with total authority he pulled her closer to him.

"Umm." Evelyn moaned as she molded her body closer, tighter against his firm masculinity. She loved the absolute feel of him.

"They mean exactly what they say, now and forever. For you specifically they mean you will never escape."

Never escape? The words hung in the air menacingly. *Something was very wrong.*

The rain splashed over them. The wind blew her hair. It was the most sensual moment of her life, until the whispered words of a madman sounded in her ear.

Their vibe and meaning slowly seeped through to her brain.

The night was soft, black and velvety. A torrential downpour soaked the streets of Newark, New Jersey, cleansing the gutters of the city's core. Ridding it of some of the trash but not all.

The street was deserted. Quentin and Evelyn stood in the park, in romantic isolation, a block away from Evelyn's house.

They had taken a walk after a great dinner. Suddenly the sky had let loose with a fury and so had Quentin. Evelyn was totally confused.

She had been enjoying his company. He had elegant manners as well as sophistication. She thought she might come to care deeply for him. She had spent some deeply moving time with him. Then he flipped on her. Like a light switch that someone had flicked off.

She stood on tiptoe in her bare feet. She had removed her sandals in the heat of the smoldering rainy sexuality that had her body awash. As she pressed her body against Quentin's, a subtle change took place without a hint of warning.

Quentin was crazy. He was threatening her. What did he mean she was never going to escape? Warning signals ignited in her head. A cold fear seized her body clashing with the hot, sexy heat rising from her womanhood.

Her thoughts rippled, like pebbles skipping across the water. Her brain was suddenly in total chaos. She tried to order her thoughts into something that made sense. It was no use. Her thoughts were running rampant.

One thing she did know. She couldn't have anything

more to do with him. Something was wrong with him. He was like Dr. Jekyll and Mr. Hyde.

Evelyn pulled back. She stared at Quentin Curry as though he'd lost his mind. "Let go of me." A clammy foreboding crawled up and down her skin. She shivered. Goose bumps began to sprout on her arms.

Quentin gripped her tighter. The force of his fingers left imprints in her skin. "Can't do that, Evelyn. Didn't you hear me? I said now and forever." He laughed at the bewildermeant and utter lack of comprehension that flashed across her face.

A sense of unreality dug its clutches into Evelyn. Quentin's once expressive eyes were now only twin holes of, black nothingness. Gone were any traces of the warmth and compassion that had embraced her earlier.

"You're crazy," she stuttered. "I want you out of my life. Let go of me."

Quentin shook his head. "What you want and what you get are two different things, Evelyn. You're never going to leave me. And I'm never going to leave you. Don't you get it? I said there will never be an escape for you. I always say what I mean. And, I always, *always*, mean what I say."

"No. You're a maniac. Let go of me!" she screamed. Her words blew away on the fury of the winds of the rain, as though a great sea was carrying them away.

Looking into his face, a wave of senselessness rushed over her. She spat a rush of words in his face. "I changed my mind about being with you. You're not who I thought you were."

"You changed your mind?"

Quentin looked up at the stormy skies. "Did you say

you changed your mind? You don't change your mind Evelyn, unless I change it for you understood?" Quentin words were cold and precise. His voice never raised by a note.

Now, Evelyn knew two things: real fear and the fact that she needed to get away from him.

A surge of strength rose up in her. It was a strength born out of desperation. She wrenched her body free from Quentin's hold and ran wildly down the street. Her legs and feet were bare. Her sandals were long forgotten. Long wet strands of hair clung to her head and face.

The echo of her bare feet striking the wet pavement provided her with the rhythmic chaos that spurred her on. Evelyn blew the hair out of her eyes. She willed her legs to pump harder, faster as a numbness clawed at her body.

No way could she stop.

She looked briefly behind her. She panted as she picked up her pace, sprinting toward safety, which loomed not far in the distance.

Quentin Curry was a powerful, arrogant, and magnetic man. He was at the height of his physicality. His limbs were long and lithe. His carriage was tall and erect. He possessed a demeanor that indicated fierce pride.

He watched Evelyn run down the street. He was not at all concerned about her temporary escape. In fact, he wasn't the least bit perturbed.

Quentin was a man of many layers with a sadistic streak a mile long. His extreme confidence bordered on a God-like level. He was a man who knew his own power and one who had come into power by refusing to obey any boundaries but his own. Accustomed to getting his own way, he knew he had time.

Lazily, a sardonic smile crept across his face. His was a face that could have been sculpted by one of the masters. His face was masterful in the pure architecture of it, in the chiseled lines that outlined his features. It was a face with many textures and layers that he used at will.

Quentin wondered why people didn't realize they couldn't run from their fate?

He studied the picture that was Evelyn. He knew he had chosen carefully, oh, ever so carefully. Evelyn was the only child of deceased parents who left her with enough money that she would never have to worry about it in her lifetime.

She was a loner. Very isolated for one so young, always preferring her own company to that of others. She spent most of her time rummaging in bookstores and in the dusty corners of various libraries. The single link that connected her to the world was her writing.

Ah yes her writing, perhaps a most useful tool.

She didn't have any real friends. All of her friends, imaginary to be sure, and relationships resided between the pages of books. Her friends were in the notes of the music she loved so much. That was the extent of it.

Evelyn stumbled in the wet street. She threw her hands out in front of her body to regain her balance. Her legs ached, throbbed actually with pain.

Or was it with fear?

She didn't know. "Legs, please don't fail me now," she whispered desperately. She had never been so scared in her life.

A stray cat ran out from its shelter into the rain. He caused Evelyn to practically jump out of her skin. She turned to look behind her, finding no sign of Quentin. She took a deep breath to quell her quivering body and kept running. She looked around the deserted street. There was no sign of life on the street, just her. "Somebody help," she whispered. "Somebody. Please help." There was no one to hear her.

Quentin lounged in the park contemplating his plan. He knew Evelyn thought he was behind her, chasing her. That was enough to keep her where he wanted her. He was a chaser, though not in the way she would expect. He could chase her without moving a muscle, just as effectively, more in fact, as if he had run after her.

Anyway he knew there would be no prying into the changes she was about to undergo. He thought about the Reverend Erwin Jackson, but quickly dismissed the thought as being of little consequence.

Reverend Erwin Jackson was Evelyn's minister. His was the one relationship she seemed to foster. The reverend's presence might lend a bit of an edge to the game.

Breeding was important and Evelyn's lineage showed good breeding. He'd done his checklist centuries in advance. He'd been waiting for her, for her arrival, for her birth. Now it was time. He'd been watching. Watching was what he did. Watching and observing were part of his highly honed and sharpened skills.

He knew her womb was young and untouched. She

was pure. This was very necessary to his plan. He could not funnel through tainted goods.

He smiled. He was satisfied with the wisdom of his choice. One had to create his own opportunities. And he had certainly created his. In his supreme arrogance, he settled on a single thought: "The girl is in for the treat of her life and she's running from me." Quentin shook his head in amazement.

He dropped his cigarette lighter. He reached to pick it up. Tattooed on the back of his right hand was an "X." He lit a cigarette as the mist of the rainy night shrouded him.

The predator in him inched its way to the forefront. The pull of it tingled through his body. The sleek black panther of spirit he possessed was now on the prowl. It was lurking just beneath the surface.

Evelyn heaved air in great gulps as she raced up the steps of the Victorian house she had inherited from her parents. It was one of the last of its kind left in the Newark neighborhood.

The house carried a certain presence. It had an ominous, yet old elegant air about it. It was wrapped in an air of quiet dignity. In the dark of this night, it was possessed with a spirit of stillness.

Evelyn fumbled with her keys looking wildly behind her. She tried to jam the key in the lock. She fumbled again. The wet keys slipped from her shaking fingers and dropped to the porch floor. She picked them up. She worked at steadying herself. She tried again. The lock clicked. She bolted through the front door. She slammed it shut and locked it behind her.

Evelyn raced into the solarium. She locked that door

too. She stood trembling as little pools of water formed
on the floor from her bare wet feet.

She was completely unaware of the youth, sensual
beauty and vitality that radiated from her. Evelyn was a
petite young woman with several feet of dark, thick
black locks of hair. She had beautiful translucent brown
eyes. And, flawless coffee-colored skin with dimpled
cheeks. She ran her hands up and down her arms, grap-
pling with a terror the likes of which she had never
known.

Quentin lay splayed on the glass roof of the solarium. His gaze was hypnotic as it devoured the sensual
Evelyn Jordan-Wells. He reveled in her image, enjoying the feel of the hunt.

His loins ached with the thought of having her, pos-
sessing her. A groan of pleasure escaped his lips.
Evelyn's fear was a tangible thing to him. He breathed
it in.

Quentin's eyes were liquid pools of midnight black
as he stared through the glass at Evelyn.

Evelyn, sensing his presence, looked up. Her gaze
riveted on Quentin. She shook like a leaf on a tree.

Abruptly, torrential rain, wind and shattering glass
engulfed her as Quentin crashed through into the solarium.

Evelyn hyperventilated in her fear. But Quentin's
hypnotic stare changed the very rhythm of her breathing. Slowly her labored breathing broke into an even
pattern.

Seductively sweet and with a hint of red-hot passion, Quentin touched Evelyn, ever so lightly. "Evelyn

Jordan-Wells," he said. Her name rolled off his tongue like sweet licorice candy.

"Hide and seek. You think you can hide from me? Umm, a game. I like games, Evelyn. I created them you know." Evelyn shrank back from him. Quentin allowed it for the time being.

He continued speaking as though there had been no physical interruption. "I especially like games that change the course of history. Games that upset the balance of power. Sensual, sexual and exquisite games, Evelyn. You and I will play. You do want to play with me. Don't you?" His voice had a languid purr to it. It held the promise of a lullaby.

He grabbed her, pulling her to him. He put his lips close to her ear. A deep rage settled over him. He turned his head. It twisted around like rubber. His eyes produced a laser glow that destroyed everything in its path.

"Come on, dance with me, Evelyn," Quentin purred.

The beautiful greenery and antiques that endowed the solarium room ripped right out of the floor at the force of Quentin's gaze.

His gaze swept around the room. The walls exploded. The windows blew out. Evelyn broke loose. She backed away from Quentin. A scream erupted from her throat as if a volcano had burst forth.

She crouched and cowered in the face of an evil that was so tangible she could reach out and touch it. Nothing in her sheltered life had prepared her for the darkness that had breached her world. In its face, she was completely helpless.

Evelyn briefly looked up. She stared at Quentin as though she had never seen him before. In truth she hadn't. Shock contorted every limb in her body.

The monster in Quentin had unleashed before her eyes. It had replaced the man that she thought she might love. Standing in front of her was a total stranger. It was a stranger who was in possession of a dark and lethal power. He was not of this world. Evelyn recoiled in shock.

Searing, white-hot, glittering flashes of light exploded in her brain. She searched the crevices of her mind desperately for a place to hide. There was no refuge. There was nothing for her to cling to.

A chord of deep fear struck within her. She babbled out loud, "Jesus Lord, Jesus Lord, Jesus Lord."

The sound of her babbling added fuel to Quentin's fire. He burned a flaming "X" into the wall. "I AM THE LORD! I am your Lord, Evelyn!" Softly switching gears he said, "Though my name is not Jesus."

His eyes burned a hole through her shirt. It sizzled but didn't burn her skin.

Returning to his former state he said, "Don't you ever forget that I AM THE LORD! I am Lord over both life and death. I will not be forgotten. Do you hear me? No one will ever forget me. Everyone will know I was here." Quentin fixed his twin holes of blackness on Evelyn.

Evelyn sobbed. She gulped air. Raw fear held her in its grip. Astonishment was her new companion. She could feel Quentin crawling around in her mind, poking, feeling. He found it all. Every secret. Her mind lay spread-eagle naked before him.

His presence was a live wire as he insinuated himself into her thoughts. "My Lord." The words rushed from her lips as if they belonged to someone else. She was barely aware of speaking them.

Quentin laughed. "You're coming along, Evelyn.

You're coming along nicely. It pleases me when people use my title."

Evelyn went mute. She was struck dumb by the supreme arrogance emanating from this creature.

"I am a Prince, Evelyn. The Prince. You've heard of me. You've read about me. Yet you don't believe in me. Few people do. It's what makes me powerful. You're a perfect specimen of the stupidest species to inhabit earth. I know animals smarter than you."

Quentin threw his head back and roared, "I am what I am! Can't you see me?! You don't believe your own eyes?! Well, here I am! In the flesh! I am my own MAKER!"

He paused. "I am also YOURS!"

He pointed to the masterpiece he had seared into the wall. The flaming "X" glowed with a light of its own.

"This is my legacy, Evelyn. It is my mark. It will travel through the generations of my seed to come. It is a life force. It is what makes me eternal. Didn't they teach you all about that in Sunday school?"

He stooped down so he could be at eye level with Evelyn. "Take a look around, because you will spend a great deal of time on these very premises, Evelyn. You will never leave this house again. Oh, no. You will not ever leave. Because if you do . . ." He reached for a handful of her wet hair. He forced her face up to his.

His gaze bore into her. "If you ever try to leave you will die! You will die a death more vicious than the wildest imagination can conjure up. Painfully and slowly, I will release life from your body. Until you beg for death. Until you seek its face. I will kill you and anything you love. Understood? Look at the mark."

His voice now held the musical tempo of soothing waters. "Look at it I said."

Evelyn struggled to rip her gaze from him. She looked at the flaming, spirited "X" seared into the wall. The mark swam like a watery illusion before her eyes.

"You've been chosen to be the carrier of my legend. In your womb the seed of the "X" will be implanted for generations to come. You, Evelyn, will raise a warrior. Remember the number six. Don't forget it because it's a very important part of your future." His words echoed through the chambers of her being.

Venom rose from the depths of her belly. Hatred swelled inside her. Refusal bubbled from the depths of her soul at the despicable evil. It spewed forth from her lips. She warred with him in a single word. "No!" She pushed him so hard he stumbled backward.

The tail of a reptile leaped from his eyes. It lashed around her neck choking her. It left a trailing red welt on her skin. As quickly as it emerged, it withdrew. Evelyn gagged. She wet herself.

Quentin was unperturbed. He got up and in her face just a little bit closer. Calmly he told her, "Yes."

He turned his attention to the "X." It burned brighter under the heat of his satanic gaze. Light streamed from his eyes.

He looked at her. Hot sensuality replaced the light streaming from his eyes, an animal scent of musk rose from the heat of his body.

Quentin slowly licked the outer parameters of Evelyn's lips. He was all lithe sensuality as he gently stroked her wet hair. He kissed the tears from her cheeks.

Evelyn rebuffed his very touch. Her skin crawled from the touch of the beast. Her insides heaved. Then something inside her cracked. It broke down. It disconnected. She lost the last of the tentative hold. She couldn't handle it.

Once again she reached out seeking solace in a corner of her mind she never knew was there. This time the corner embraced her with warm and welcoming arms. It was a place of peace, quietness and refuge.

She floated away as the beast mauled and devoured her body.